"For fans of the serial killer genre, RED TIDE is an engaging, well plotted story with characters you won't forget." — L.J. Sellers, author of the bestselling Detective Jackson series

"This book will go a long way in introducing Brantley to readers as a force to be reckoned with in the thriller/mystery niche." — The Dirty Lowdown, Blogcritics.org

THE MISSINGS

"A top-velocity cliff-hanger, and a thriller with heart. Brantley is the real thing."
— Timothy Hallinan, Edgar-nominated author of the Poke Rafferty and Junior Bender series

"A compelling, complex and emotionally connected story. The tension kept building and I couldn't stop reading. Well done!"
— L.J. Sellers, author of the bestselling Detective Jackson series

THE SACRIFICE

"Peg Brantley's latest, THE SACRIFICE, accomplishes that rare feat of being both heartfelt and suspenseful. A gripping tale of murder and revenge, it ultimately becomes something much, much more." — Dennis Palumbo, author of the Daniel Rinaldi mystery series

"Peg Brantley has done it again. Her third book (after THE MISSINGS and RED TIDE) is another thrill ride, a hyperventilation-inducing thriller about evil and power and

endangered innocence. And MAYBE a new (and very interesting) sustaining female character. Mex Anderson may have companionship in the next book or two."
—Timothy Hallinan, Edgar-nominated author of the Poke Rafferty and Junior Bender series

THE SACRIFICE

THE SACRIFICE

PEG BRANTLEY

BARK PUBLISHING LLC

2013

Thank you for your support of the author's rights.

The characters and events in this book are fictitious. Any similarity to real persons, living or dead, is coincidental and not intended by the author.

Copyright ©2013 by Peg Brantley
Cover design by Patty G. Henderson at Boulevard Photografica,
http://www.boulevardphotografica.blogspot.com
Edited by Peggy Hageman
Formatted by LiberWriter and Patty G. Henderson

All rights reserved. In accordance with the U.S. Copyright Act of 1976, the scanning, uploading, and electronic sharing of any part of this book without the express permission of the author constitutes unlawful piracy and theft of the author's intellectual property. If you would like to use material from the book (other than for review purposes), prior written permission must be obtained by contacting the author through her website, http://www.pegbrantley.com

ISBN (electronic version): 978-0-9853638-4-0
ISBN (trade paperback): 978-0-9853638-5-7

Books by Peg Brantley

Red Tide

The Missings

*This novel is for everyone associated with
The Shaka Franklin Foundation
and the University of Colorado Depression Center.
You make a difference.*

And as always, for George.

Cast of Characters

Anderson, Mex : A former lawman in Mexico, Mex is now trying to make a life for himself in Aspen Falls, Colorado in spite of a devastating loss.

Anderson, Sedona: Mex's sister. The only survivor of a mass-murder meant to send a message to her brother. She's financially dependent on him.

Arroyo, Dia Vicente: The young daughter of Victor Vicente who is searching for a place to belong after the death of her mother.

Johnson, Darius: Mex's journalist friend who knows how to find information. And who is married to Pamela, a pregnant wife trying to hold her family together.

LeBlanc, Cade (Arcadia): The exit counselor in New Orleans who knows how to extract people from cults.

Vicente, Victor: The head of the Senora Ciento drug cartel. Someone in the cartel ordered the murders of Mex's family.

Vicente, Victor Jr. (VV): The son of the drug cartel leader. He has elected not to retain his mother's name and takes steps to procure the safety of his sister, Dia.

CHAPTER ONE

He shouldn't be here, he thought. Not tonight. A bad idea all around.

Mex Anderson watched the young couple argue from his booth, deep in the shadows of the bar. He settled himself further into the corner, the plastic seat cracking when he moved. Juan bent over the table, one dishtowel tied to his belt and another tossed over his shoulder. "Don't you think you should do something?" The bar owner pretended to wipe up some crumbs while he nervously kept an eye on the vocal twosome just inside the entrance.

"They know where to find me if they can't work it out between themselves." Mex reached for a handful of peanuts.

"I don't want any trouble." Juan sniffed and brushed his hand against his thighs, dislodging whatever he had picked up from the table to the floor. Mex caught a whiff of bar soap. Juan's Place was like a second home. "I just got the repairs done from when Chico's woman showed up and found him here with her cousin."

Mex popped a couple of peanuts in his mouth. "Take it easy, amigo. If they start breaking up the place I'll stop them. They're just pushing each other's buttons. If you're lucky, they'll make up and leave before other buttons get pushed." He winked.

Juan huffed and moved back to his customary place behind the old wooden bar. The wood and brass structure wasn't old enough to have antique value. It probably never would. It would just get older. Juan's Place was a neighborhood hangout for the Hispanic community in Aspen Falls. A place out of which Mex liked to work. Clean and convenient. One of those establishments where no one asked too many questions. People who came here knew how to keep to themselves. They valued privacy as much as they valued family. As much as they valued freedom.

Most folks assumed a thing or two about the Mexican with the gray-blue eyes, and that suited Mex just fine. Because they figured he was like them, they trusted him. He needed to make a difference, and the anonymity of a bar on the wrong side of town was as good a place to work from as any. If people knew all there was to know about him he'd lose his edge. They would no longer come to him.

The rapid-fire exchange, punctuated with arm gestures and Spanish words even Mex couldn't be sure he'd ever heard, reminded him of some of the passion he and his wife had expressed on more than one occasion. In another lifetime. Another world.

He watched the woman. Dark. Vibrant. She created sparks while her male counterpart seemed to create moss-laden bricks. Fire and water. But neither had eyes for anyone or anything else. At a moment in time when they seemed to be about to settle and agree, one or the other would find something else to wail about and they would warm once again to the argument. An argument which, Mex thought, must by this time be about at least four different things. *To have a relationship where these things mattered...*

The door opened and the heat flamed by the lovers fled as if it had never existed. Silence loaded with the icy cold of fear took its place in an instant. Two figures stood in the main room.

Masked. Armed. Their own desperate fear charged the suddenly vacuous air.

Mex observed them from his secreted post. Young. Male. Their skinny and unformed frames shouted physical immaturity. They moved with the awkwardness of adolescent boys who weren't quite comfortable with their bodies. He guessed they weren't local—at least they weren't kids who lived in the neighborhood. First of all, they would have known about him. That he kept hours in Juan's Place. Maybe not regular hours, but potentially obstructive ones at the very least. Especially to punks thinking about robbing the place. Second, well... second was probably him as well.

The two young men approached Juan at the bar. One of them pulled his weapon up and his voice down as deep and strong as he could. "Empty your cash register. On the counter. Do it now."

Mex waited while the young couple slipped out the door. The gunmen didn't seem to notice. Inexperienced on top of everything else. This might not end well, he thought.

Juan put his hands in the air, stalling. To his credit the bar owner didn't even look in Mex's direction.

The robbers seemed to gain some footing. Some bravado. After all, they were in control. Macho men with guns.

"Now, spic. Not next week. *Comprendo?*"

Juan moved toward the cash register. He pushed the keys to open it. When the drawer slid out the robbers eyes were both focused on the cash. There wasn't much, but they probably knew they weren't robbing the St. Regis in Aspen.

Mex stepped out of the shadows, gun drawn. "I know you figured this was a cheap little bar and it would have cheap little security. You were half-right."

When the two would-be robbers saw Mex emerge from the dark background of the bar, one of them dropped his weapon immediately and put his hands in the air. The other one puffed up his chest and trained his gun on Mex.

"You don't want to do that, son. Take a minute to think."

"What about?"

"Your future."

The kid blinked and looked around. His gun wavered and like lightning Mex moved in with a roundhouse kick and knocked it out of his hand. The young hoodlum gawked at Mex with surprise then grabbed his wounded hand. "You hurt me!"

"Ah, but you still have a future. It might not be bright but it wasn't headed in a sunny direction anyway."

Mex instructed Juan to tie up the two young men, then call Detective Waters at the Aspen Falls Police Department. He gave Juan the number. He trusted Chase Waters but wasn't so sure about any of the rest of them.

His weapon trained on the two scared kids, one of whom had pissed his pants, Mex felt the familiar heavy darkness that had been lurking in the corners of his mind begin to descend. It didn't surprise him. In fact, he almost welcomed it as he would a friend.

After Juan made the call he turned off the neon lights, then turned to Mex and shrugged. "Might as well not waste the money. Cops leave soon enough and I'll turn 'em back on. Otherwise, I'm closed for the night."

One of the kids, the one with the dry pants, glanced from Mex to Juan. "Look, we didn't hurt anyone. Didn't take anything. No harm no foul, huh? Maybe we can—"

"Shut up," Mex said.

The kid kept looking at Juan. "I'm just saying that if you let us—"

"I told you to shut up. I don't want to hear another word out of your mouth." Depression was pulling him under. Mex was inches away from ending everything for all of them. He hadn't killed a man in a very long time but that didn't mean he hadn't wanted to.

The door swung open and Chase Waters entered with a uniformed officer. It was textbook. Chase swept the room high from left to right and the uniform stayed low, flushing right to left. It took less than two seconds. Chase handed the uniform his set of cuffs and kept his gun leveled at the would-be robbers. "Secure them, then get the owner's statement."

Once the threat was dealt with, Chase looked at Mex. "You look like hell."

"Thanks. Good to see you too."

Chase's face tightened with realization. "Oh, man. I'm sorry. I forgot."

"No reason you should have remembered." *It was my family who was murdered.*

"You gonna be okay?"

"I need to get out of here. Can I come down tomorrow and give my statement?"

"Sure, that'll work."

Mex walked up to the bar to pay Juan for his drinks. Juan shoved the cash back at him. "You're kidding, right? Get out of here."

Ten minutes later, when Mex walked into the drugstore, the pharmacist took one look at him and went to the prescription queue to dig out a package.

Mex paid for the drugs. "Thanks, Carl."

"No problem. But your doc's gotta call in a refill for the next time."

Mex didn't turn around as he walked out of the store. "Call him for me, would you?"

The darkness lured Mex, almost like a siren's song. By the time he turned into his drive the anger and bitterness he lived with every day were a memory. All he wanted was to be left alone. Then he saw the lime green Volkswagen. *Sedona. Like clockwork.*

He turned off the engine.

Six years and one month ago he had a family. Parents. A wife. A three-year old son, a two year-old daughter, and a new baby on the way. He'd had a sister about to bring her first child into the world. Six years and one month ago he had a future.

And he'd sacrificed all of them—everything—for his honor.

***

Mex tore open the package from the drugstore and twisted the cap off the bottle of pills. He dry-swallowed two of them. Should have taken them earlier. He felt the darkness slowly cover him. Tie him off.

Comfort him.

Cold air. A familiar voice. Pulling him up. He fought the desire to rise. *Leave me alone.*

"Come on, Teo. You have to help me. I can't get you in the house by myself."

Sedona. His sister had been named after the place where she was conceived, long before it became popular. She always used her favorite of his names. Mex, the nickname he'd gotten while attending San Diego State University, had been christened Carlos Alberto Basilio Teodoro Duque Estrada de Anderson, and while everyone currently alive—other than Sedona—called him Mex, she preferred Teo. The Anderson came from his father. A tall American from California who fell in love with a Mexican beauty and never looked back.

Had he been away two minutes? Two hours? Two days?

He owed her. He forced himself to open his eyes; to shift his legs when she pulled on them. Carry his weight.

He had sacrificed everyone he loved for his damned honor. Sedona was all that remained of the life he'd left. The life he'd lost. Now she sacrificed her life for his. Sedona also lost family that day. She was the only one they'd left alive for him to find.

To remind him of what he still had to lose.

He got out of the car and shrugged her arms away. "Leave me alone. I can walk."

"Fine. So walk."

He and Sedona spoke mostly English—they'd both spent years in the states—but occasionally they lapsed into Spanglish, a unique blend of both languages. Rather than search for a word in one language, they easily substituted a word in the other.

All color had leached out of the home and landscape that usually brought him incredible pleasure. Now it was flat and gray. Empty. Like his heart. The waterfall sounded distant and filtered. Lighting that normally glowed with warmth and lifted his heart now brutalized his eyes. He craved darkness and lifted his hands as shields.

Sedona ran ahead to mute the lights for her brother. He thought about thanking her but couldn't find the energy.

Somewhere, deep inside, he knew this wouldn't last, that the medication would help him pull through, but right now all he wanted to do was tell the world and everything in it to fuck off. If he cared enough he'd cry.

He remembered Maria's perfume. He'd given her a bottle of Shalimar for their first Christmas. She wore it whenever she wanted to please him, which happened almost every single day of their years together. They had a special morning routine they shared even when it was disrupted by the needs of their children. She would meet him in one particular place in their home and they would share a kiss. A moment. Just the two of them. Sometimes he had other things on his mind, sometimes she did. Sometimes one of their babies would make whatever was on their minds known—loudly. But they still had their moment. Their kiss. When their souls touched. And then the day could continue.

He remembered his son. His huge eyes filled with light and laughter and intelligence. The way he tried to imitate the most important man in his life. Mex had held such hopes for that little boy. He'd felt such pride.

Mex also remembered his daughter. The little girl who was somehow different from other little girls her age. Who they knew was special. A gift from God. A gift that would let them know exactly what love meant. What power and potential were really all about. A gift their peers might never understand—might never benefit from experiencing. A gift he was only beginning to respond to and accept. She had Down syndrome. His perfect baby girl. His sweet, always innocent, always easy and always difficult baby girl. He'd felt pride in her too, and he'd finally come to believe that yes, she was truly perfect in every sense of the word.

The darkness became a part of his skin. His bones. His soul. He followed it—led it—to the place where nothing mattered anymore. He couldn't bring himself to even think about the lost life in his wife's womb. The tiny being who would never see the world. Who they loved without knowing. The child he'd never hold. To have the time to make sure his love landed into another life and made a difference. To validate his own soul. To connect with through eternity.

He crawled fully clothed onto his bed.

Fuck eternity.

CHAPTER TWO

Mex threw off the duvet and sat on the edge of his bed. Sedona must have been in at some point to cover him. He felt smothered. Moonlight gray-scaled his room and he welcomed the diluted sense of place.

He tried to block out his memories—his hate. The two things that had kept him alive that first year. Kept him going. Memories and hate.

Usually when depression hit, all he wanted to do was sleep. The meds he'd taken earlier must be kicking in. He'd taken them so often, off and on, he no longer needed to wait a few weeks for them to begin to work. Timing was everything and this time it sucked. He rolled back onto his bed, closed his eyes, and tried to think about something else. Or nothing. The *"weltschmerz",* his first doctor called this deep sadness. Only bigger.

He heard the doorbell and squinted at his bedside clock. Two a.m. Mex didn't care who had come to his home at this hour or why. He only wanted to be left alone. Sedona would take care of the interloper and send them on their way.

A tapping at his door, then it opened, a slice of subdued light dumping color into his space.

He cleared his throat. "What do you want?"

Sedona slipped into the room and closed the door. She walked over and stood at the side of his bed a moment before she sat. Her back was cast stiff and straight but the rest of her trembled like aspen leaves in the wind.

Mex pulled himself up, physically and emotionally. "What's wrong?" He worked to focus on his sister as he crawled up from the abyss.

Sedona didn't answer him.

"Sedona, who was at the door?"

He watched as his sister squeezed her eyes tight, a single tear escaping down her flawless cheek. When it hung a moment on her jaw line then fell onto her lap, he blinked. Something broke open inside of him at the same time that tear spilled and split.

He pulled the duvet up and covered Sedona's shoulders. "Talk to me."

"You're sick. I shouldn't have come. I should have—"

"Tell me."

He watched the only family member left in his world draw a deep breath. The fluttering of her hands subsided. Still, her skin felt cold to his touch.

"He's waiting for you."

"Who?"

"In your own home, he's waiting to ask you for help. I should have closed the door. Sent him away."

"Sedona, who is here?" But even as he asked the question, the answer began to form.

"I'm so sorry."

"Tell me now."

Sedona spilled in his arms. He pulled her close. Waited for her to compose herself.

"You will hate this, *mi hermano*."

Mex thought about those words. He knew hate. He thought he'd let it go. He couldn't imagine hating anything or anyone as much ever again. "Do not worry about my hatred."

Sedona's body shuddered. He could feel her shrink beside him. "Someone from our past wants to speak with you."

He experienced a scent memory. It flattened his heart and almost sent him back into his bed. He and Maria had finished a picnic of bread, cheese, grapes, and wine. Afterward, their lovemaking had been both gentle and hungry. The scent of what he thought of as an exotic bloom ribboned over him and settled. He never knew what caused that scent, he only knew it had grounded him for years in a field of love.

He had pulled his sister too tight. Sedona's hand pressed against him, pushing him away. He both heard and felt her take a deep breath.

"Who, Sedona?"

Whatever elements in her body that had softened and relaxed pulled taut again.

He reached for her arm and began to massage it. "Tell me."

"It's Vega."

Mex had an immediate reaction to the name. Visceral. Unchallenged. An icy coldness poured itself into his veins. *No.*

"Vicente Vega wants to speak with you."

***

Vicente Vega. The cartel. The reason his family was dead. Why in the world was Vicente Vega in Aspen Falls to see a man who wanted anyone associated with the cartel dead? Fed to the vultures, but only after being tortured for hours, just as he had been tortured over the last six years. Vega may not have been involved personally—he'd run a completely different arm of the organization—but it was... still personal.

Mex fought to suck in some air. "Vega is here? In my home?"

"He was in your foyer. I could not invite him in further."

"Did he say why he was here? Why he wants my help?"

Sedona shook her head. "I didn't ask him. I didn't want to know."

Mex considered all of the possible reasons for Vega's appearance. None of them good. None of them anything he could ignore. "Tell him I'll be out shortly."

"Are you sure?"

"Just tell him."

Sedona rose to leave, head low and shoulders pulled toward the earth like some kind of fallen angel.

"Sedona?"

"Yes?"

"Don't worry."

"No killing? No vengeance?"

"Not tonight."

Mex sat in the quiet room. He needed to find strength. To prepare himself to face this man and listen to whatever he had come here to say. He closed his eyes and centered himself. Said the private words that led him to his core. When he opened them again the gray-scale shifted into a silvery luminescence. He drew on the solace. The power. The optimism the incandescence held out for the taking.

Mex rose from the bed and ran his hands through his hair. It was time to get this over with.

He moved through his house, not in any particular hurry to meet with the man who worked for the organization that had his family murdered. The man might wield power over Sedona, but he had none over Mex. As far as Mex was concerned, Vicente Vega could rot in hell. But he was curious why Vega had come. Why he thought Mex might help him.

At the front entry he stopped and looked around. His sister stood with her back against the wall, her face blank. "Sedona?" He sharpened his tone to get her attention. "Sedona."

She shook her head and he watched as her eyes slowly focused on him.

"You said he *was* in my foyer. Where's Vega now?"

She nodded toward the door. "I made him wait outside."

***

Mex opened the massive wide-planked door. The man who looked him in the eye was at once familiar and a stranger. Vicente Vega had aged. And not well.

Neither man spoke and neither man extended his hand. Mex turned and walked toward his study, leaving the door open. Vicente Vega followed. If Vega looked around at his home, Mex didn't know. He didn't care.

Once inside the den, Mex turned on a couple of lights and closed the door. He motioned for his visitor to take a seat, then backed up to his desk and leaned against the edge. He waited for the man to say something.

"I need your help."

Mex arched an eyebrow but said nothing.

"I want to hire you."

Mex lurched from the desk and moved to open the door. This meeting was over. He still hadn't spoken and now there would be no need.

"My daughter is missing."

Mex stopped on his way to the door. He walked behind his desk and sat, but didn't pick up a pen or give any other sign he might be interested.

Vega took a quick breath and began speaking. "Dia has been gone for two days. I know that does not seem like very long but in my business... " He cleared his throat. "Her nanny is missing as well."

Nanny? The Vegas never used nannies. Guadalupe Vega raised her children on her own. Everyone in the cartel and in law enforcement knew that was a matter of pride and pleasure which set the Vega family apart from other powerful cartel families. They had servants and staff, but never a nanny.

"I have not received any demands and cannot go to the authorities. I fear she has been taken by the *La Familia* cartel.

If I am correct, I will not receive any demand. They will torture her and then find a way to prominently display her body."

Mex spoke for the first time. "Could she have just run away?"

"With the nanny?"

Good point. "Tell me why you have a nanny."

"My Guadalupe died eighteen months ago. My son I know what to do with. My daughter needs a hand. Pilar Villanueva is the fifth one who has worked for us. She is the only one Dia has approved of. She is younger than the others and perhaps my daughter was ready for a friend."

Maybe she did run away with the nanny, Mex thought. "Why me?"

"You know I personally had nothing to do with the deaths of your family."

"If I thought you had, you wouldn't be sitting here now."

Vega bowed his head in acknowledgement. "You hunted the men who killed your family through at least two countries for two years."

"Three countries."

"You know how to track people who do not want to be tracked."

"I never found them."

"My business partners know how to make problem people disappear. It does not matter whether they are our enemies or our employees."

Mex figured that was the case.

"Why should I help you?"

"Aside from the fact that my daughter is an innocent, I will pay you one million dollars to find her. Three million if you bring her back to me alive."

"Look around you, Vega. I don't need your money."

The man sighed and closed his eyes. "I thought as much."

Mex remembered the moment his wife told him they were going to have another child. His beautiful, sweet wife would want him to find this young girl who was in trouble. "Finding your daughter is the only element that intrigues me. Nothing else does. And frankly, you have enough manpower that you could bring almost any government to its knees if that's what you wanted. Let alone a bullshit kidnapper. They may not be able to get you the results I could, but then... their history with you isn't the same as mine."

"Exactly."

"Exactly?"

"I have more to offer you."

Mex sucked in some air. Vegas's tone suggested things he didn't have the luxury of considering. Did he want to go down this road? With *this* man?

Vega leaned forward in his chair. "I can—"

"Stop." If Vicente Vega suggested what Mex thought he might suggest, there would be no going back. Mex would be dragged back in to living his days because of the cartel's influence on his life.

And nothing the *Senora-Ciento* cartel had ever brought into his life had been good. It had only brought devastation and evil.

There could only be one thing Vicente Vega would have to entice Mex into a working partnership.

"If you do this, in addition to the money, I will give you some new information related to people within the Senora-Ciento cartel who were directly involved in the decision and directives to sacrifice your family."

"Sacrifice? I don't believe you. *Sacrifice?* For what? To send a message to other lawmen?"

"It was for the good of the organization. More precisely, for those on top of the organization."

"You're on top, Vega—at least near it. How do I know you weren't responsible for the order to have my family brutally murdered?"

"You don't. Not for sure. But I believe you also understand my code. It is older and less convenient than the code of those who are in charge today. I can look at you and I can look at God and swear I had nothing to do with the killing of the people you loved. On my honor."

Mex considered the man's offer. He thought of the missing girl. Antonio would be about her age if he hadn't been killed. Mex had seen Dia one time with her older brother and mother. They were in a park, laughing and singing. "What kind of information?"

"The best I could give you would be names and last known locations. The rest would be up to you."

"These would be the names of men who were connected how again?"

"I will provide you with the name and location of the man who ordered the murders, as well as the men under him who carried them out. These are men whose names you did not find in your hunt. They are protected."

He lusted for more names of those responsible for the horror in his life.

He hadn't made up his mind, but Mex took out a legal pad and reached for his pen.

CHAPTER THREE

Dia Vega Arroyo flung her arms above her head and spun in a circle, threatening to topple a bowl of freshly picked green beans to the floor of the tiny kitchen. "*Adaché,* of my own free will! I'm so glad to be away from him!" She looked at Pilar and grinned. "I'm so glad you were my nanny. Now you're my friend."

Pilar smiled from her place in front of the stove. Steam billowed into the fragrant air. "As your friend, I could use some help with dinner."

Dia reached for the beans and began to trim them by pinching the ends with her fingers. "I mean, seriously. I'm proud of my Arroyo name. My mother's family name. When Mamá died, his true colors came out. He only loves my brother. Me, he just wants to order around—if he talks to me at all."

"He doesn't know what to do with you."

"Tell me about it." Dia continued to pop the ends of the beans, placing the fresh, usable bits into another bowl and piling the ends on the scarred wooden table. She paused. "He will be angry with us both if he ever catches us, you know."

"Between you and me, your father seems perpetually angry."

Dia laughed. "You are so right. And now his fierceness is no longer in our lives. Thanks to you and *Obatala* we can build our future the way we want." Dia had loved learning about Obatala,

King of the White Cloth. The oldest of the *orishas,* or deities, of Santeria, Obatala was responsible for crafting human bodies. She thought it sort of sad and sort of funny that he got into trouble by creating some deformed bodies one day after drinking too much palm wine.

Pilar's smile dimmed. "I've told you to be careful about revealing to others that you are a *santeros*. Santeria has many influences, and outside of those who share our belief the influence is rarely good. When you speak of an orisha, speak silently—to yourself."

"But it's just you and me, Pilar. And we're not in my father's house."

"Humor me. Only when we're in a ritual do I want to hear so much open talk about Santeria from you."

Dia felt her elation ebb for a moment, but then she considered who was talking to her. Pilar was just being extra cautious. The beautiful young woman who had come into her life when she most needed a mentor and friend would never try to dominate her the way her father had. Pilar exposed her to a world where she felt loved and appreciated.

Santeria gave Dia the feeling of having a real family for the first time since her mother had died a year and a half ago. Everyone in Pilar's group had accepted her from the first minutes they'd met. Not like those terrible nannies her father had forced on her because he didn't want to deal with a daughter.

I miss my mamá. She thought about when her mother was alive. Regardless of Father's wealth and position, when *Madre* was alive, there were no nannies. She made every day fun. Dia and VV never wondered if they were loved. They were a family, even though they seldom saw Vicente Vega. She and VV Jr. went to a private school accompanied by bodyguards. They didn't realize how unlike other kids they were until Mamá died.

Dia gazed out the kitchen window. There wasn't much of a yard, but nearby a stream meandered lazily through the property. On either side, large trees cast their shadows into the water, regardless of the time of day. Puffy white clouds sat like game pieces on a brilliant blue sky.

She looked at Pilar. "Can we stay here? I like this place."

Pilar shook her head. "Luis told me we need to leave tonight. Hector is already packing up supplies."

Dia swiped her forearm across the table and ends of green beans flew into the air. "We're always leaving! For no good reason we leave one place and then we leave the next! I'm tired of it! Tired! Are you listening?"

Dia reached for the bowl on the table, already feeling the satisfaction hurling it would give her. Hot tears filled her eyes and she pulled in a breath. Her fingers curled over the rim and began to pull it toward her when a strong hand grasped her arm and held it tight. She looked up into the flat, unexpressive face of Luis. His dark eyes gave nothing away.

Pilar ran over and touched the arms of both Dia and Luis. "Please. Luis, she is young and passionate and understandably upset," Pilar pleaded with him. Luis relaxed his grip and Dia yanked her arm to her side.

Then Luis grabbed Pilar and pulled her out of the room. Dia could hear his low urgent tone and Pilar's mumbled agreement. Dia again considered throwing the bowl but thought better of it. She'd wait until Luis wasn't so close.

Pilar returned, a wan smile on her face, moved back to the stove and began stirring the liquid in the pot.

Dia squared her stance. "This isn't my fault. I want to stay here. With you. Let Luis and Hector keep moving."

Pilar shook her head. "You know very well *amiga*, it is because of you we must leave this place. Your father is very powerful and his reach is long. We leave these places to keep you safe."

Dia's shoulders sagged and she walked to the stove. Pilar laid the spoon down and gave her a hug. "Will we ever be able to stay in one place, Pilar?"

"I hope so, *niña*. I hope so."

***

Vicente Vegas's son looked at the two men who stood in front of him. The cold interior of the empty warehouse made him want to hug his coat tighter, but no one else indicated any discomfort. He eyed them carefully, gauging their response to his instructions. It didn't matter that they were older than him. It didn't matter that they were bigger than him. He was Vicente Vega, Jr., and he could make their lives heaven or he could make them wish they were in hell.

He took a toke on his cigarette then threw the butt to the ground. Part of him hated the habit he had picked up during his European education. Another part loved that the addiction afforded him physical ways to express himself. "You will get her. You will hold her. She is the key to getting my sister back."

Intelligent eyes met his. "Your father is aware of this operation?"

VV pulled another cigarette from his gold case and turned his back on the man who dared challenge him. "Just do it." He turned around and eyed the man. "Never question me again. Never." His lighter flared to life and he cupped his hand unnecessarily before once again turning away.

His father had become weak. Power was theirs for a reason—to use. And VV knew how to use it, something his father had apparently forgotten.

The older Vega had run to Colorado to get help from a lawman who had virtually laughed in their faces. Even though they'd used him to make a statement to other officials, Mex Anderson now led his perfect little life in Colorado. Untouchable. Or so he thought.

The half-gringo had one weakness left. If the Mexi-Melt wouldn't come to their aid willingly—for a significant amount of money—maybe he would see things their way if the life of his sister was in the balance. VV's father wanted to achieve things one way. The old way. By agreement. But times had changed and at the very least they needed some insurance. Controlling the life of Sedona Anderson was the best kind of insurance they could buy.

He remembered Sedona from years ago. He hoped he wouldn't need to have her killed. She'd been kind to him.

VV called out to the men as they walked toward the exit. "Let me know when you have her."

When he was alone in the metal building, except for the two bodyguards who were his silent shadows, he considered his position. The prudent thing would be to call his father. Explain his actions. Get Vicente Vega to accept and support the decision he'd made. But the prudent thing was also the weak thing. This was the time for him to break loose and spread his wings. This was the time to prove to his father he was ready.

For a moment, thoughts of his mother filled his head. He could smell her perfume—a curious mixture of lavender and something spicy. Her hair was what he imagined sunlight would smell like. She was the only person in his life who had ever loved him unconditionally. Except for Dia.

He shrugged. Even if his mother had lived, VV would be moving away from her protection and closer to his father's world. That was the way things were done.

As Dia's older brother, it was up to him to protect her, especially from herself. Dia's nanny, Pilar, had gone missing at the same time making it unlikely it was a kidnapping. Unless Pilar was the kidnapper. However, the family had received no ransom demands, and the Senora-Ciento cartel was too formidable. It would be suicide to take the daughter of a man as high up in the organization as Vicente Vega.

Carlos, the bodyguard who had been assigned to VV for the last ten years, opened the door at the rear of the warehouse. VV hung back, waiting for the signal that it was safe to leave the building. He touched the gun in his shoulder-holster like a talisman.

VV got the sign and moved quickly to the open car door, looking dead ahead, without checking the surroundings. He slipped into the back seat of his city car while his other guard slammed the door and jogged around to enter from the other side. The car started moving immediately. His guys were good.

Aspen Falls was a beautiful place. He understood why the Mexi-Melt chose to live here. Even though VV preferred the action in the three cities where his father had homes, there was something nice about all of this space and fresh air.

He lowered the privacy shield between the front and back seats. "Do you have that card the woman gave me last night at the bar in Aspen?"

Carlos's expression did not change. He reached into his jacket pocket and passed VV the card.

He thumbed the card and remembered the suggestive looks the woman had thrown him. The redhead had written her cell phone number on the back. VV punched it into his phone. Five minutes later, he sat back with a smile. Looked like he had drummed up a bit of his own action in the Colorado mountains.

CHAPTER FOUR

Mex sat in his kitchen, the empty coffee cup in front of him long-cooled. Sedona cleaned up their breakfast dishes while he gazed out on the scene that filled the space. The view both calmed and troubled him.

His kitchen was more then the perfect place to cook and eat. His kitchen was the view. The windows were floor to ceiling, wall to wall, on three sides. What appeared to be a seamless piece of glass actually had some kind of mitered corner that was almost as clear and transparent as the glass it supported. Cobalt Mountain was the most prominent focal point but at the right angle, Mex could see part of Burnt Mountain near Snowmass. And below those timeless mountains of stone, almost breathing with life, Mex could see the valley with a river flowing not far away.

Calmed and troubled.

Two deer ambled into view. Peaceful but wary. He watched as they munched on their favorite greenery he made sure to have in abundance, then move to the stream that cut through his land. And here he sat, thinking about a missing girl. Her family. The possibilities.

Calmed and troubled.

He remembered the reason he'd built this house in the first place. He'd been lost. His family murdered. Executed. He'd been rendered ineffective at finding...screw that...he'd *failed* at finding their killers. And then he'd stumbled upon the plans for the home he and Maria had drawn up together with an architect right after his investments hit pay dirt. They hadn't known where they'd build it, but they planned every inch of their home.

After two years of searching all over the world for the men directly responsible for the deaths of the people he loved, the trail stopped dead. The men he sought had been killed by their own cartel members in Honduras. Mex booked a flight back to Mexico, but found he could no longer stand to live there. Ghosts haunted him at every turn.

Depressed and disillusioned, he threw a few things in a backpack, grabbed his passport and cash, and literally walked across the U.S. border. While he sat in a rundown bar in some dusty Arizona town he couldn't remember the name of, a couple of tourists walked in. *Lost*, he thought. They looked too happy to be in this hole on purpose.

The couple asked to use the phone, and offered money to the bartender. Their cell had died and they needed to call home.

"Where's home? If it's India or Germany or someplace like that, you don't have enough cash on you."

"Our home is in Colorado. Aspen Falls."

Mex spoke up. "Let 'em use the phone. I'm betting you have free long-distance so just let 'em use the phone. Hell, I'll match what they've already given you."

That's how Mex heard about Aspen Falls, a vibrant-sounding Colorado college town between Aspen and Snowmass. The next day he bought a used SUV and hit the road.

When he first drove into the town, he knew he was in a place that could heal him, and felt guilty. He pushed those feelings down and arranged to have his belongings shipped.

While he waited, he discovered Juan's Place. Juan offered to let him stay in a back room for as long as he wanted. Mex rented a storage unit and as his things were delivered, he hauled them into the space.

That's when he found the house plans. Getting involved in the creation of the dream he'd shared with Maria allowed him to focus on something other than his loss. Building this house had saved him.

He watched the deer.

Calmed and troubled.

Sedona called out to him. "Will you be okay if I go home for a while?"

He turned to her. "What have I done to deserve you?" He watched his sister blush. "Go. I'm fine. I've taken my meds. The darkness is lifting. You go home and don't worry about me."

Sedona looked at him. "I would say I'm only a phone call away, but we both know you won't call."

She came and sat down next to him. "Have you decided what you're going to do about Vega?"

"His daughter is about the same age Antonio would be if he'd lived." He would give anything to have his son at his side. Maybe saving this little girl would somehow help him miss Antonio less.

"She is the daughter of a murderer, *mi hermano*."

"And what kind of a brother would I be to you if I didn't care about other people? Should this little girl be made to pay for her father's distorted heart? Maybe she ran away to a better place and I'll be able to tell Vega that he lost."

"What if the cartel is involved?"

Mex closed his eyes. When he opened them he looked directly into eyes that mirrored his own. He'd made up his mind. "Maybe I can stop yet another sacrifice in the name of the drug cartel—if it's involved. I can make a difference."

"There's more isn't there?" She folded her hands in her lap.

"He promised me additional information on the murders."

Sedona blanched. "The murders?"

"My family, Sedona. Your family."

"I don't think it's a good idea for you to—"

"I've made up my mind. Perhaps I can live to have a little retribution—an element of justice."

Sedona shook her head. "This feels wrong."

Mex reached for his sister's hands, still folded in her lap. "I've decided. And with the information I get from Vega I'll be able to stop worrying about losing you too."

"Me?"

"We both know why they left you alive. They spared your life so I'd always be aware I had something else to lose."

***

After Sedona left, Mex put on a jacket and went for a walk. He saw a herd of deer on a neighboring property, a few of their heads held high for threats. Brilliant mountain wildflowers were in high bloom and he marveled at God's creations. How he would have loved to share these sights with Maria.

Mex thought he remembered the sound of his children's laughter, but he wasn't sure. That bothered him. He could hear the sound of Maria's low voice when they lay in bed at night. He could feel her snuggle close to him when she was cold. He could smell her. But his children's laughter was beginning to sound like any children's laughter.

When he got home, he put on another pot of coffee and went to his study. Sedona had laid a fire but left it unlit. It would be warm today, but even in June the nights in the high country could be chilly. He sat at his desk and pulled the notepad in front of him, picked up the phone and called Vicente Vega on his private line.

It was picked up almost immediately. "Vega."

"It's me."

An extra moment of silence underscored the man's anxiety. "Yeah?"

"My conditions are simple." He heard a sigh and deep breath from the other end of the line.

"What are they?"

"First, a million dollars will be deposited into my account upfront, not on completion of the job. You either trust me or you don't."

A small hesitation. "Fine."

"And the information relative to the murders of my family is to be placed in a lockbox at my local bank, the key and access information for which are to be held by a friend of mine in the event of my death."

"Wait a minute, Anderson. You want me to give you everything upfront. How do I—"

"Take it or leave it, Vega. You won't hear from me again unless you do as I ask."

Mex waited until he heard the dial tone, then slowly lowered his phone to the desk.

He could hear children laughing.

Mex shook out a couple of pills, swallowed them, and decided a short nap might help. He stretched out on the sofa in his family room. When he woke up four hours later the room was in darkness and the image of Dia haunted his thoughts.

He walked to his liquor cabinet and considered his choices. *People. I need to be around people.* He grabbed a jacket and his car keys. He needed to get his mind off the girl who would not be spending the night with her family. The girl who might never go to a prom or walk down the aisle or hold her own baby in her arms.

Get his mind off a boy who would be nine, his sweet girl, and the baby his wife carried who he would never hold. Try to smell something other than memories.

***

The dark bar welcomed Mex. Funny how the darkness helped him forget. Usually.

"*Hola*, Mex. You look better tonight."

"And aren't you just a little ray of sunshine?" Mex sauntered back toward his booth. "Mexican coffee sounds good, Juan."

"Coming up."

Two minutes later, the mingled aromas of chocolate, cinnamon, and vanilla filled his head, further pushing away the sense of loss. Juan splashed just enough kahlua in the coffee to make it even warmer as it went down.

He sat down across from Mex. "Thanks for your help last night. It could've gone pretty bad."

"I doubt those kids would have hurt anyone. This was probably the first time they'd tried anything like that. Hopefully, it'll be their last."

"Of course they would need to pick my place." Juan heaved a sigh and gave a resigned tug to his earlobe. "I'm just glad you were here."

"Me too."

A deep voice broke through the darkness. "Is this a private party or is anybody welcome?"

Mex smiled and winked at the newcomer. "What do you think, Juan? Should we let this gentleman of the press join us, or should we call him a hack and bar the doors?"

Juan shoved out of the booth. "As long as he keeps Juan's Place out of his stories, he's welcome here." He wiped his hands on the ever-present dishtowel slung over his shoulder and stuck out his hand. "Good to see you again. It's been awhile."

"Good to see you too. The road ain't all it's cracked up to be. Especially when I've got a pregnant wife at home alone with two young kids to keep track of. Not a minute of peace even when I wasn't talking to her."

Juan nodded and moved back to his place at the bar. "You want the same as Mex or your usual?" He called over his shoulder.

The newcomer took a look at what Mex was drinking. "Usual."

The barman nodded. "Ask Mex about what happened here last night."

Darius Johnson, tall, muscular, and with skin the color of rich burnished oak, slid into the seat vacated by Juan. Mex saw him take a quick glance at his watch but didn't think much of the gesture. Darius was always glancing at his watch.

Darius's eyebrows formed a question mark. "Last night?"

Mex shrugged. "A couple of young kids decided Juan's would be an easy hit."

"Armed?"

"They may have been young and stupid, but they weren't that stupid. They had guns but no ammo. No one was hurt. Chase Waters took them into custody. End of story."

"Wish it was more of a story. I could use one."

"I thought you were chasing the next great true crime novel. What happened?"

"I was set up. There was nothing there. Four leads aiming in the same direction and every one of them a dead end. Can I tell you how much I hate social networks?"

"Sorry, man. You should know better by now."

Darius flipped him the middle finger.

"Well, I know Pamela is glad to have you home. So that begs the question... why are you here?"

Mex watched as Darius reached into his pocket and pulled out an object. He fingered it for a moment then tossed it on the table. "What the hell is this about?"

Mex looked at the safe deposit key Darius had thrown on the table.

Shit.

CHAPTER FIVE

Mex pulled out his cell phone and entered a number. Then he punched in a few more numbers and waited.

Darius, who had been sitting quietly watching Mex's response, leaned forward. He tapped a long, elegant finger on the key. "What is going on, Mex? What the hell is this key for?"

Mex looked up from his phone. "How did you get it? How was the key delivered?"

Darius reached back into his pocket and pulled out an envelope. "It was under my windshield wiper. My car, man. *My car*. At Sardy. How the hell did someone find *my* car at the Aspen-Pitkin County airport?"

Mex took the envelope. A regular letter-sized envelope with hand-written block letters on the front.

MEX ANDERSON

Juan brought Darius his beer and left. Darius took a healthy swallow.

"Nothing else?" Mex asked Darius. He slid the envelope back across the table.

"Nope. Probably figured he didn't need to give any more detail."

Mex's phone gave a beep and he took a look at the screen. *Damn.* The money was in his account. All of it. He pressed the off button and shook his head.

Darius leaned forward. "I hope that means you're about to tell me what this is all about."

Mex took a sip of his coffee. "We're gonna need another round."

He signaled Juan and considered his words. "You and I have been friends now for a few years."

Darius nodded. "I met you the day you came to town, what? About four years ago. We got drunk."

"You asked about my family and I told you they were killed in Mexico, but I didn't want to talk about it. Right?"

"That's right. And I never asked you again."

It was Mex's turn to nod, the thanks for honoring his request unspoken.

"I was in law enforcement." Mex looked at his friend for a reaction.

"Sorry. I'm a journalist. I've known almost from the beginning. You have all the signs."

"What signs?"

"Well, there's the fact that you hate injustice and —"

"Never mind, you can describe my tells to me another time. And you can pay me back whatever I've lost to you playing poker over the years."

Juan arrived with their drinks. "Want something to eat?"

Darius started to order something, but Mex interrupted him. "Give us a few minutes."

Mex folded his hands and bounced them on the table. "We lived in a little town south of Agua Prieta, on the Arizona-Mexico border."

"A dangerous place."

Mex ignored the comment. "The cartel was active. A lot of the once-good men were being bought or scared into acquiescence. But not me." Mex looked into Darius's eyes. "Not me."

"Oh, my God."

"I thought we were safe. We lived in the middle of nowhere on a small farm. We had protection. We were all careful." Mex was surprised at the tears forming in his eyes.

Darius listened.

"A few other lawmen were beginning to stand their ground as well. I'd received some emails of support. The cartel wanted to send a message to them." Mex wiped his eyes. "There were two of them. They probably assassinated my brother first, probably because he was the biggest threat. Then my father, my sister, who was seven-months pregnant...." He caught his breath. "It was her first baby. She was so happy. Then they went after my wife. Maria was also pregnant, but it was new and fresh and she wasn't showing yet. Still, they slashed her belly as if they knew what she carried."

"Mex..." Darius moaned.

"They murdered my three-year old son, Antonio. He was looking forward to being a big brother all over again. He was my little man." Mex realized his face was wet, the tears pooling on his chin and falling on the table and into his lap.

He grabbed the napkin Juan had left with his drink and wiped his eyes. His hand shook. "And my baby girl. My sweet, sweet baby girl."

"They were all at the house?"

Mex nodded.

"Where was Sedona?"

"She hid in the barn."

"And you?"

"I was working a B&E on the far side of town. A breaking and entering that looked staged to me. A diversion."

"They made sure you weren't around."

Mex closed his eyes and said nothing. When he opened them he didn't focus on anything. "After the funerals I went after the men who killed my family. The men who cut my wife. For two years I tracked them all around the world. The Senora-Ciento cartel may not have been happy with me before, but they grew to hate me. Everywhere those men went, I followed. And where I followed I caused them problems. I disrupted shipments, got local law enforcement personnel involved... whatever I could do to shake those men loose from their protectors. Finally, in Honduras, the trail stopped."

"They disappeared?"

"A tape was delivered to me while I was there. It took me two days to find a way to see it. It was a video of the two men I'd been tracking. They'd been gagged and trussed in a field. A man came up, smiled into the camera, then turned and shot both men in the head. Two other men came and began chopping parts off the bodies, the blood still flowing.

"As they worked, buzzards descended. Hundreds and hundreds of buzzards. Within a few hours, the bones of the murderers of my family had been picked clean. But that wasn't enough. The same two men who had chopped off some of the body parts to excite the buzzards, donned rain gear and grabbed huge mallets. They pulverized the bones and the heavy skulls, creating some weird kind of buzzard dessert. The bone fragments and blood splattered their plastic protection."

The men who were directly responsible were beyond his retribution. It would be impossible for an outsider to learn more. The cartel had taken care of the loose strings.

"After Honduras, I went back to my town for a few days, but it was lost to me. Hell, Darius, *I* was lost to me. I packed up a few things and literally walked across the border. Dual citizenship made it especially easy. The next place I stayed for any length of time was Aspen Falls."

"Damn, Mex. I'd imagined a few things, but I hadn't come close."

"My pride, my honor, was responsible for the deaths of the people I loved. I sacrificed them for an ideal."

"Sounds more like integrity to me."

"Pride, honor, integrity. It doesn't matter. Whatever it was got my family killed."

"I don't know how you've held it together."

Mex shrugged. "Well, sometimes it's not so good, as you've seen over the years. And now there's this."

Darius waited. When Mex didn't speak he said, "This what?"

"One of the leaders in the cartel I refused to bow down to is a man named Vicente Vega. He came to see me last night to ask for my help."

Ten minutes later, Mex had brought Darius up to speed about the missing young girl and the fear for her life.

Darius didn't hesitate. "I want in."

***

Mex wondered if Darius had gone off the deep end. This man had the family Mex once had, and yet he was saying he was ready to leave it. Again. "Are you crazy? You just got home."

"Pamela will understand. *She will.* When I tell her about this—well, I know I can convince her. This isn't like the last one, Mex. *You're* involved. I need this. I know a good story when I see it, and this one is begging for a book. And with my research connections I can be a huge help."

"You need to think about this. I'm willing to sit down with you after it's over and give you everything you need to write the great true crime story of the year."

"Not the same."

"Talk to your wife. I can always use your research connections without you being with me."

"Not as good and you know it."

"Check the contents of the lockbox. Make sure there is something inside other than my passport and will. Just confirm that there's something there. Respect my honor. Then talk to Pamela. Get her blessing. After you have it, call me."

***

Mex walked into his empty house. The house he'd built to forget his past life. The house he'd built to commemorate the dreams he'd had with his dead wife. The house he'd built to forget the intense pain. For a while, the project did keep his mind off his loss. But it didn't last. As it turned out, forgetting was a temporary thing.

God, the emptiness as he walked in about killed him. He needed a dog. Or even a cat. Or a guinea pig. *Something*.

The light on his landline phone flashed. He punched in the code for his messages.

Sedona. "Call me."

He thought about his sister. He paid all her expenses. Bought her the condo she lived in. Was free with the cash he gave her to spend however she wanted, all thanks to his early dot com investment and the investments that followed. She was all he had left in the world. His lifeline to his past and his promise of a future.

He punched in her speed dial number.

She didn't answer with hello. Instead he heard, "I was worried."

"About what?"

"You said you were going to help Vega."

"That's right. I am."

"Have you talked with him again?"

"I have."

"Teo, I think you are making a mistake."

"We're talking about a little girl, *mi hermana*. Dia Vega Arroyo may have the name of her father, but she also carries the name of her mother. And in the end, she's only *una niña*, an innocent child."

"Surely the great Vicente Vega has options. There is no real need to bring you into this." She paused. "Have you considered that maybe this is some kind of trap? Some kind of new way for him to get to you? Or me?"

"Sedona, you know I love you. You've always been here for me. You are all I have left in this world." He hesitated.

"But?"

"But nothing. That's all the truth. The rest of the truth is that I have entered into an agreement with the father of a missing young girl. And the father has thus far kept his end of the agreement."

"Don't trust him, Teo."

"Darius is helping. At least a little. If he tells me that it looks like Vega has kept up the most important part of our agreement, I'll begin looking for his daughter. If it's a sham—and you know Darius can smell nine out of ten bogus situations—then I won't worry about walking away and forgetting we ever had an agreement."

"When did Darius get back?"

"Recently."

"And was he successful in his latest pursuit?"

"Not this time."

"Maybe there's something wrong with his sense of smell. You should think about that, *mi hermano*."

CHAPTER SIX

He'd been about to go take a leak. Between the boredom and his bladder, this wasn't a job he loved at the moment. His cell phone rang. "Yeah."

"Do you see her?"

"She's still in her condo."

"Fuck."

"Chill. According to her neighbors, her shit is to leave sometime in the next half hour. Quit raggin' on me, will you?"

"I just want this to happen."

"I ain't never let you or Mr. Vega down, have I?"

"Do not let this be the first time."

"Unless you let me go take a piss, it could happen."

The line went dead.

Fine. One more job for the heir apparent. But first...

Just as he finished his business, he saw her walk out of the building. Perfect timing. And not another soul in sight.

He met her at the corner. He pulled out his polite voice. "Excuse me, miss?"

He watched as she looked in his direction. What she saw was what she was supposed to see. Nicely dressed. Engaging. Handsome in a blond and preppy kind of way. Everything about him shouted trustworthy and well... at this point, harmless. Give him a little time between the sheets and the harmless shit would go to the curb. That too, was part of the vibe he'd worked on over the years. Women loved bad boys.

"Yes?"

"I was wondering, could you tell me how to get to the library?" Experience had taught him that asking direction were the safest kinds of questions. And the library? A sudden inspiration.

"The library? Let's see…"

Before she could come up with the directions, he placed the chloroformed towel over her mouth and after a brief struggle, began to walk-drag her down the walkway to his car. He opened the backseat and dumped her in, prepared with an excuse of taking care of a drunken friend if anyone had seen him. He looked around. All clear.

Sitting in the driver's seat, he turned the keys in the ignition, checked for traffic, and pulled out. Only then did he take out his cell phone and press the two numbers to connect him to Vicente Vega's son.

"Hey, VV. Got her. We're on our way to the motel."

"Just make sure no one sees you. We can't let this get away from us now."

"How many jobs have I done for your family?"

"Exactly none where the life of my sister was in the balance."

"Yeah, okay. No problem. I'll let you know when we get there."

VV's normal intensity had taken on a new edge in the last couple of days. Somehow the bitch in his backseat could mean the difference between Dia being saved or not. He liked Dia. VV was kind of a whack job, but still the boss's son. He always made sure to remember that, even when he wanted to smack the kid upside the head and make him think straight for a change.

He wondered if the boss knew what was going on but lacked the courage to ask.

Yesterday he'd checked into the motel. One of those dumps where no one looked at anyone else. The side entrance made it perfect to move in and out without anyone noticing—even if he was carrying some dead weight through the door. He'd made sure to get the room closest to that entrance.

He pulled into the nearest parking spot. Checked to make sure the bitch was still unconscious. Then he slipped through the side entrance and opened the door to his room.

Less than ten minutes later he'd bound his prize to the crappy chair that sat in the corner, a gag over her mouth ensuring she wouldn't shout holy hell when she came too.

He took out his cell phone and call VV. "We're here."

"Good."

"What do you want me to do now?"

"Keep her there and keep her quiet. I have a call of my own to make."

CHAPTER SEVEN

The messenger had dropped the videos off three hours ago. Mex watched all of them twice. Dia had, at one time anyway, been a totally happy little girl. He watched her at birthday parties, weddings, and other family gatherings. A lot of the focus of the videos seemed to be on her brother, but Dia truly brought light and laughter to all of the events. She and her mother. Mex confirmed with Vega that these were everything that belonged to him. If there were other videos, they were in the homes of others. It was telling of the family dynamics that no videos had been made after the death of Guadalupe Arroyo de Vega.

The first time through the footage was hard. The love and laughter and feeling of family cut into his heart. And Vicente Vega, somehow a part of these videos even though he was rarely seen in one, was part of the group responsible for Mex's lacerated life.

Mex absorbed everything without taking a single note. Notes were flat reports of an event. Instead, he'd always preferred to work as if he were a participant—even more than a witness. It didn't matter if it was a homicide or a fraud scheme or a runaway. He liked to figure out a way to *be* there in his head. Understand the dynamics. Inside every case there was something that was off, and when he figured out what, the solution wasn't far. He already knew from watching these videos that Dia being a simple runaway didn't feel right, but he couldn't put his finger on why. Not yet. He pushed the rewind button.

A rumbling in his stomach made him realize he hadn't eaten since breakfast.

His cell phone rang, interrupting his thoughts. He didn't recognize the number and almost didn't answer.

"Anderson."

"Mr. Anderson, this is Vicente Vega, Jr., and I have some information you need."

Mex sat up. If the caller really was Vicente Vega, Jr., that meant he was Dia's brother. Could he know something that could lead Mex to his sister? "I'm listening."

"It's in your best interest to accept my father's offer and find my sister."

"I—"

"You said you were listening, so listen. Listen carefully. If you ever want to see *your* sister alive again, you will find mine."

Mex felt his skin go cold. Spots filled his vision. "What are you talking about?"

"Sedona is now under my control. Whether she lives or dies however, is up to you."

"You don't understand. I'd already agreed to find your sister."

Silence.

"Did you hear me, VV?"

"How did you know what people call me?"

"I've been around a long time, son. And you need to let Sedona go. I've spent the last several hours working to find out what happened with Dia."

More silence.

"Okay, Mex Anderson, here's the new deal. If you want to see the lovely Sedona again, you won't just find out what happened to Dia, you will find Dia. And you will not, under any circumstance, tell my father that his agreement with you has been amended. If my father finds out that we have spoken, your sister's life is over. Do you understand?"

Mex knew a loose cannon when he ran across one. And Vicente Vega, Jr. was one of the loosest cannons he'd ever heard. "I do."

"Whatever you report to my father, you will also report to me. Am I clear?"

"Perfectly."

"I want my sister home, Anderson. I want her back where she belongs."

"How do I know Sedona is alive? You will need to provide me with proof of life whenever I request it."

"As long as it isn't excessive."

"And what happens if Dia left of her own accord?"

"You will still need to make sure she is brought home. She is too young to make these decisions on her own. Anything less than you bringing her back to our home is not satisfactory. Anything less than satisfactory will result in your sister's death. Are you willing to sacrifice your sister because of your failure?"

Sacrifice. Images of his family flipped through his head like a deck of cards. His own sense of right is what had cost each one of them their lives. He had *sacrificed* the people he loved because of his asinine integrity. Sedona was all he had left.

Mex took a breath. "I will find Dia."

"You will do more than find Dia, Mr. Anderson. You will bring her back home—alive. If you don't, you won't be happy with the repercussions."

***

This isn't right. Sedona's sense of smell confused her—stale, with some underlying mold. This was not her home, nor was it Teo's. The sounds were wrong too. She heard a muted television and the sound of a lighter flicking. As her awareness grew so did her confusion. She tried to open her eyes. A heaviness pushed against her eyelids and kept them closed. Then she smelled the tobacco.

Sedona tried to suck in some air through her mouth and gagged. Raw terror roared through her veins. Questions screamed in her head. Where was she? What happened? Why? She pushed against the pressure that kept her eyes locked down. One thing at a time. Shallow breaths. Stay still. Don't let whoever it was know she was awake.

Breathe. Steady. Find her strength. The most important thing in her life at this moment was to open her baby blues. Well, her baby grays. It was as if her very existence depended on her being able to see this strange smelling world. As if vision would answer all of her questions. She almost laughed aloud when the word "focus" came to her.

A slice of a room appeared at the bottom of the cloth that covered her eyes. Brown. Lots and lots of brown. She could make out a bedspread almost coming into contact with carpeting. The legs of a dresser. Plain. Nondescript.

Shit. Reality hit Sedona in a series of images. She was in a hotel room. A gag over her mouth was tied almost unbearably tight in back of her head. The steady throbbing in her ears promised a headache at the very least. Her hands and feet were trussed. She was mute and immobile.

Why was she here?

Her mind flashed to Vicente Vega. Why, after all this time, would he want to kill her? If it was Vicente, then why wasn't she already dead? It would not be Vicente.

A plume of cigarette smoke pushed into her face. "Ah, there you are." The voice loomed over her like a hovering aircraft. A rough jerk removed the cloth that covered her eyes.

"Where am I?" She muffled the words through the gag.

"Doesn't matter."

"Who are you?"

"Doesn't matter."

Sedona sat in silence while she considered her situation. She did her best to take stock.

She opened her eyes wider. "Thirsty."

"Damn. You have good looking eyes."

She resisted the impulse to close them. "Thirsty," she repeated.

The man stuck the cigarette in the corner of his mouth and squinted through the smoke. He gave a little nod before he rose and walked the few steps to the bathroom. When she heard water running, she tried to loosen whatever bound her hands. It didn't work. The water stopped and the man held a dirty glass in his hands, which were none too clean either.

He sat the glass down on the rickety table near her chair, and reached behind her head to loosen the gag. "Don't make me regret I gave you water." An ash dropped from the cigarette and rolled down her face.

When the rag slipped out of her mouth Sedona swallowed. "Will you untie my hands, please?"

"Nope." He held the glass to her lips and tilted it up.

She took some of the water and let the rest run down her chin. "Why?"

"Because I'm not gonna fight you. You're a lot easier tied up."

"That's not what I meant. Why did you take me?" It suddenly occurred to her that maybe this guy was after Teo's money. *Damn.* She knew that was it. Her life was being threatened because her brother had made a lot of money in a couple of internet investments. Thank God he didn't care about it. Thank God she was all he had left.

"I took you because I was told to take you, lady. Now shut the fuck up or I'll stick the rag so far down your throat you'll never talk again."

Had they contacted Teo yet? Was he getting the money together? How much had they asked for?

CHAPTER EIGHT

The bar was more crowded than usual this afternoon. The day laborers who hadn't found work would sit for hours nursing cheap beer and eating peanuts.

Juan, busy taking an order, nodded his head a couple of times in the direction of Mex's booth. Good, Mex thought. Darius is here. He held up two fingers in Juan's direction and hurried to the back of the bar.

Mex had called Darius Johnson from his house and asked him to meet him right away. He also asked the newspaperman to bring everything he could dig up on Vicente Vega, Jr.

"Hey, man." Mex slipped into the booth. "Sorry for the short notice."

"I couldn't search and print and get here, but here's what I've found." Darius swiped his index finger across the tablet screen he'd brought and spun it around to face Mex.

Juan brought two cold beers and a bowl of peanuts to the table. Mex was too engrossed in the information to acknowledge him.

"Thanks," Darius told the barman. "Could we get some nachos or something? I'm starving."

"Beans and tortillas work for you?"

Darius nodded, but Mex looked up from the tablet. "Would you bring me a couple of burritos? Beans and tortillas won't make a dent."

As Juan walked away, Mex signaled with his hand to Darius. "Talk to me."

"Vicente Vega, Jr., known as VV to his friends, holds dual-citizenship between the United States and Mexico. He was actually born in San Antonio when his parents were on vacation. He's single, and although he's frequently seen with his father and his father's friends, he also runs his own business."

"Let me guess. Import and export?"

"Old school. VV buys and sells construction equipment."

Mex thought for a moment. "They're laundering money."

"Yep. A cartel operative buys the equipment for cash. Someone else fronts as the seller and the equipment gets sold at auction."

"And if they lose a little on the deal, who cares? The cost of doing business. And because it's clean money, they can send it right back to Mexico through the banking system."

"You could've been a crook."

Mex almost smiled. "It depends on who you talk to. Some people probably think that's exactly what I am."

"Why did you need this information? Is he in danger too?"

As much as Mex trusted Darius, telling him about Sedona's abduction wasn't going to help, and might even add to his sister's danger.

"VV is a player. He contacted me directly and made some threats. Told me not to say anything about our conversation to his father. Right now he just wants to make sure I'm on board to save his little sister. He must have thought I'd turn down the offer from his old man to find Dia." Mex took a sip of his beer. "Apparently he wasn't aware of the extra enticement of information regarding the murders of my family."

"Did you tell him?"

"He wasn't interested. The kid has his own plan to be a hero and that's all he cares about."

"Have you told Vega?"

"Not worth the time."

"Do you think he'll get in our way?"

Mex considered. "Our primary focus has to be Dia. Not who might or might not be a problem." Mex thought about Sedona and his heart hardened. "But we need to learn as much as possible about VV and his equipment business. His private life. His habits. His vulnerable spots. I don't want to be surprised." I don't want Sedona harmed, he thought. Because if she is, I will kill the little bastard and show no mercy.

"Could VV be behind Dia's disappearance?" Darius asked.

"I thought about that, but to what end?"

"Rattle the old man?"

"Why?"

"So he could take control?"

"Unlikely. First, VV is already being groomed, and pretty fast. Second, Vega wouldn't hesitate to kill his own son if he even thought VV was making some kind of power play."

Darius nodded. "What do you need me to do first?"

"Right now, it's all about Dia. We need to interview all of the household members of the Vega family. Full-time and part-time staff. Also all of her friends, or as many as we can find."

"Are the staff Hispanic?"

"Probably, but from what I can tell in the family videos, most of them are black."

"I should interview them. They might be more willing to talk to me. You take the friends."

"Your Spanish up to speed?"

"No problema."

"I was hoping you'd say that. We fly to Monterrey tomorrow." Mex looked carefully at his friend. "Your wife good?"

"She will be."

***

THE SACRIFICE

Dia's head bounced against the backseat window. At first she thought she was still dreaming, but gradually her memory returned. How long had they been driving? They'd spent the first night at someone's home, sleeping on the floor. Then they'd gone to the pretty farm house with the trees and the river. It had been dark when they'd left that place and it was still dark.

She was lucky to have such good friends who were willing to do anything to keep her safe from her father. They understood her. They got how terrible it had been to lose her mother and live under the iron rule of a man who didn't love her. A man who would kill them if he knew they'd helped her leave. She'd heard enough to know her father had done bad things and worked with people her mother never would have allowed in their home.

Her father must suspect Pilar. If anything happened to the nanny who had become her best friend, it would be all her fault. Dia squeezed the thought away.

Pilar and Luis spoke quietly in the front of the car, and Hector gazed solemnly out his window on his side of the backseat. Pilar and Luis were speaking English, probably so Hector couldn't understand them. She was proud of the English she'd learned, both at school and from watching American movies.

No one noticed she'd awakened so she closed her eyes and tried to listen. She'd learned that often adults were more likely to tell the truth if they weren't talking to someone they considered a child. Noise from the dirt road they were on made it hard, but she picked up a few words here and there. Enough to know that they'd be at their new destination for at least a few days and maybe longer. Someone was expected to join them. They kept saying the diviner, like it was a person's name. The Diviner. And someone else they knew had *prepared* the place for them. Dia thought that was a funny thing to say. Prepared how? Probably just cleaned it up a bit and brought in some food. Pilar and Luis probably didn't know another English word for what they meant. Who cares? They were going to be at one house for a while. She could hardly wait.

Her head bounced again. Hard. She'd gone back to sleep even while she'd been trying to eavesdrop. The fuzzy kind of silence from the background noise filled her head when the car was finally stopped and the engine turned off. Car doors opened and closed.

She felt a nudge on her shoulder from Hector.

"*Despiértese, estamos aquí*—wake up, we're here." Hector opened his door, but looked over his shoulder to make sure she'd heard him and was moving.

Dia's awareness of her surroundings grew as she walked to the back of the car to take a bag from the trunk. *Green*. Everything was some shade of green. Or brown. Even the air looked green. It felt heavy and without a breeze of any kind, it sucked up close. It smelled like an old, unclean fish tank, with undertones of wet wood and old, rotting lettuce. She wrinkled up her nose and swatted at a mosquito that lit on her arm.

Hector met her at the trunk. "Here. Take this one. The others are too heavy for you."

She hauled a duffle toward her. "I can handle my regular bag, Hector. You've seen me carry it before. What are you talking about?"

Hector pointed. She glanced toward the house and gaped in surprise. Long poles held it high above the ground. Who would build a house that way? It was kind of like a giant tree house without the tree. A set of steep rickety-looking wooden steps climbed to a porch. It looked like those steps were the only way in. Without another word she exchanged loads with Hector.

"Stay with me," Hector said. "There are dangers here and you're not familiar with them."

"Are you?"

"Not really."

Pilar and Luis were already inside the house. Dia heard them laughing and calling out to one another in a language she'd never heard before. For the first time since Dia had known Luis, he no longer sounded like a grump.

She stuck right behind Hector as he picked his own way toward the structure. He seemed to be as much in awe of their surrounding as she was. The ground stretched flat with odd-looking slime toward equally odd-looking trees with seaweed hanging from their branches. Birds called from the distance. They sounded wild. More wild than any birds she'd ever heard back home in Monterrey.

Dia saw something and stopped in her tracks. The slimy covering on the ground was moving. *Dios!*

"Hector!"

Hector turned around and looked surprised not to see her at his heels. Then he saw the shifting water. The angle was away from them, toward the back of the house.

"Hector!"

A wide arc of movement indicated a change in direction for the monster beneath the smelly water. It was now coming right at them.

"Hec—"

"Hush, Dia. *Silencio*. Hurry now, in front of me. Quick. Get up those steps."

Dia couldn't move. She wanted to run but her legs—her feet—held her firm to the spot where she stood.

Hector dropped the two duffels he carried and ran back to her, throwing her over his shoulder like a sack of feed. Dia was aware of his sweaty smell and the way his shoulder dug into her stomach. She lifted her head and watched the water part, faster now as the monster closed in on the path. A sharp jolt caused her to grab Hector's shirt. He'd hit the stairs and begun to climb them quickly. Before they reached the top, Dia watched the alligator emerge from the murk, break the water in one swift move and grab one of the duffels before disappearing deep under the surface. The slime settled quickly, as if nothing had ever happened. But Dia had seen the jaws open, teeth like sharpened cones.

CHAPTER NINE

The plane touched down at Monterrey's General Mariano Escobedo International Airport only about five minutes behind schedule. Mex and Darius had taken a puddle-jumper out of Aspen to Denver International early that morning, then transferred to a major carrier to Monterrey. Mex hated airports. It didn't matter how much they tried to cater to travelers, he found them sterile and completely lacking in imagination. Even their VIP lounges could use some improvement. The rest? Like herding cattle.

He thought about Sedona—what she must be going through. He would have helped find this young girl regardless of who her father was. There was no need for VV to bring his sister into this. To put her life at risk. He would deal with VV when this was over. He would make sure nothing like this would ever happen to Sedona again. Vicente Vega, Jr. didn't know who he was messing with.

Mex and Darius grabbed their carry-ons and made their way through customs without incident. Mex had made arrangements earlier through an old and trusted friend to pick up a couple of weapons. His contact was meeting them at the Safi in a couple of hours.

The Safi Royal Luxury Towers were thirty minutes from the airport, in the heart of the city. The security was superb. The hotel had a strict "no visitation" policy. No one other than registered guests were allowed into the rooms. If you wanted to see someone, you arranged to meet them in the lobby bar or restaurant. Perfect for Mex's needs, but he still wouldn't put it past someone to circumvent the stringent safeguards.

As they walked into the reception area, Mex saw a man in a chauffeur uniform carrying a sign that said "MEX ANDERSON" in huge block letters. Vega had apparently sent his driver. On one hand it could prove convenient, on the other it could prove intrusive or even worse. Deadly.

Mex considered his options. He could approach the driver and risk that Vega had his own agenda, or completely ignore him and plead ignorance if the question came up. But maybe the driver had some insight he could use to find Dia. After all, she was the mission.

Darius had clearly seen the sign but waited for Mex to make a move. Satisfied that his journalist friend was more than just a pretty face, Mex decided to get a feel for this employee of Vicente Vega. He waited until they made eye contact, the uniformed man clearly recognizing him, then angled his walk to meet the driver. Darius followed.

"Hello. I'm Mex Anderson," Mex said in English.

The man nodded, but his eyes squinted in the direction of Darius, obviously an unexpected surprise. A second man when there should have been one—and a black man at that. Mex knew what the driver must be thinking. Anything out of the norm was a threat—to both him and his employer.

"This is Darius Johnson. He's working with me."

Darius gave a little nod, but remained silent.

"*Un momento.*" The chauffeur pulled away a few steps and pulled out a cell phone. No doubt to call Vega.

Mex looked around. Most of the passengers from his flight had gone to baggage claim, the others had either been reunited with their families or hooked up with other limousine services. The area around them was almost deserted.

Except for two men. One on either side of the reception area. Two men who were not there to meet passengers and who quickly tried to focus their attention elsewhere in the terminal when Mex looked in their direction.

Mex turned his back to the driver and got Darius's attention. A quick flick of his index finger, side-to-side, and he knew his friend had also picked up on the surveillance. This wasn't good. Especially since Vegas' man didn't seem to think anything was out of place.

A motion to Darius to follow, and both men made a quick exit out of the airport.

"I'll call my weapons contact and arrange to meet him somewhere else. In the meantime, you go to the hotel. I'll meet up with you there. It's best we travel separately, at least for now."

"What about Vega? Won't he wonder why we didn't ride with his driver?"

"I didn't like the way his driver looked. If Vega is offended, he can go screw himself. He needs to know that I'm running this operation, not him."

***

A masked state police officer, standing in the middle of the road, signaled Mex's cab driver to pull over.

Monterrey, the wealthiest city in Mexico, had once been considered among the safest. Now roadblocks and checkpoints were a part of daily life. The drug lords who once kept their families safe in Monterrey had instead made the entire city a target. More than eight hundred people had been killed in the state of *Nuevo Leon* in the first six months of the year. Not a huge step up from the previous year, but a definite upward trend. Law enforcement was doing their best to stay on top.

The driver complied and rolled down his window. "*Buenos tardes.*"

The driver was probably innocent of any wrongdoing, but Mex watched as he began to cough nervously anyway.

Shit. This guy was gonna delay him even more. Mex resisted the impulse to lean forward and dive into the conversation.

The police officer, dressed all in black, from combat boots to hooded ski mask, stuck his head in the window and stared hard at Mex. "Who is this?"

The cab driver shrugged. "Just a fare."

"Where are you taking him?"

"Starbucks."

The officer circled the vehicle. Mex was acutely aware of the long automatic assault rifle that dangled casually at the officer's side. He looked like he was about to ask more questions when his radio crackled to life. A moment later, he extended his arm. "Go."

Monterrey was far from the modern, wealthy enclave he'd experienced when he'd visited here in the past. There was a bite to the air. A certain current of electricity that held power over the residents. Any sign of a potential threat and people withdrew. Some behind front doors that barely kept out the cold winter air, and others behind eight-foot tall brick walls topped with razor-wire and including armed guards and trained dogs protecting their property. The city had exchanged its veil of affluence for one of fear—or worse, resignation—the idea that this was just the way things were. Get used to them or get a new life somewhere else.

The cab ride took Mex past ghost structures. There was the boarded up hotel where more than fifty people had been murdered, makeshift memorials still beckoning with their piles of wilted and dead flowers from family members who had nowhere else to grieve. The Casino Royale was the death site of fifty-two people who had been killed after suspected drug traffickers had torched it several years ago. But it remained standing, another ghost to haunt the city and a monument to greed. For some, a monument to loss.

As the cab drove through various neighborhoods, Mex could hear some of the new music, a fusion of old and new, defiant and hopeful. The electronic beats melding with Columbian *cumbia* to form tribal *guarachero* resulted in its own element of urgency. Some compared it to reggaeton. Mex reflected that as long as music served as an expression of the people, Mexico would not be lost. At least he hoped.

Mex went through one more checkpoint before they reached the Starbucks where he'd meet his contact. He and Darius had been on the ground less than two hours and already their mission had run into complications. Mex hoped the early glitches with the chauffeur and the checkpoints weren't a sign that they'd be unable to accomplish what they'd come to do.

As the cabdriver pulled up to the curb, Mex searched for anything out of place. Two women were walking into the coffee shop, a man holding the door for them as he exited. No one was sitting in a car in the parking lot, but he needed to be sure.

"I want to sit here for a minute, if you don't mind." Mex spoke in rapid Spanish.

"It's your dime." Somehow that phrase was the same the world over.

Mex watched the street traffic for a car passing more than once. After about five minutes, he was satisfied and handed the driver some cash. "Keep the change."

"You want me to wait?"

"No thanks." The fewer people who could track him here and then to his hotel, the better. He could even walk from here if he chose.

He took his duffle and slung it over his back. Mex had already spotted a familiar old car in the parking lot. Where the vehicle wasn't corroded and rusty, dull red paint—almost a sepia tone, like dried blood—struggled to hold on to whatever primer might still be there. Mex smiled. The car had looked the same for the last fifteen years. Underneath the hood was where the real muscle slept. This dilapidated looking, deathtrap-looking vehicle could probably outrun anything on any track in America today. Among certain groups of people, it had its own reputation for speed, control, and endurance. The anti-theft mechanisms the owner had installed kept anyone curious about the car from getting too close.

Mex swung the door open and watched the now breast-less Starbucks mermaid smile at all her customers. He wondered what she had to smile about. Mex savored the smell of rich coffee and moist air.

Shit. His contact wasn't alone. And the man sitting with him at the tiny table was not one of the good guys.

CHAPTER TEN

Sedona could not figure out what was going on. Over the last several hours—twelve? twenty-four? she couldn't be sure about anything anymore—she'd begun to understand that money was not behind her kidnapping. A practical woman, Sedona knew she might be beautiful to some but she was no longer young. Trafficking was unlikely.

What then?

She was left alone for hours on end. But it was always the same piece of white trash who eventually returned. He brought her food that initially she'd hated. She was a good cook and to have to eat the crap he brought was almost as horrible as the ties that bound her. But eventually the Chinese food and English muffins with ham slices and cheese became tasty and even desirable.

Going to the bathroom was another issue entirely. Her captor had finally come back with a package of cheap underwear that he allowed her to change into whenever she'd lost control when he was gone for too long. She hated herself for being grateful. She hated him for making her hate herself.

Sedona had been alone now for a long time but her body had not turned against her and she felt a strange mixture of gratitude and pride. A little bit of courage sat around the torn edges of her psyche as if it was looking for a reason to attach itself.

She was a survivor. She'd demonstrated it over and over again. She'd kicked all kinds of habits over the years, and with each successful recovery she'd proven her strength. She'd shown everyone that she wasn't someone to take lightly. She'd come out of a love that was all wrong, and she'd come out stronger.

And now... now she was the one who held her brother together when he was sinking into the abyss of depression. Teo needed more than medication—he needed her.

The door to the room opened with a bang. Two men entered, in the middle of a conversation. One of them was the one she'd come to know as her captor. The one who only followed orders. She watched him carefully as he pushed through the entry.

"—he's already doing what your father wants."

"Not good enough. Without the results I demand, nothing will ever be good enough." Sedona heard the door close. "I want my sister back."

Sister? What the hell was he talking about? *She* was the sister. She was the one who...was there something familiar about that voice? She fought to remember where she'd heard it.

Screw this. She kicked out as far as she could, moved her arms to their fullest—albeit constrained—position, and grunted and moaned through the gag her captor reapplied with infuriating regularity.

The sudden silence of the two men's conversation scared her. What were they about to do? Had she set them off? She tried to pull into herself, feel less like an animal on display. Feel less vulnerable. Become smaller.

Sedona heard a slap as someone hit the surface of a piece of furniture. "Never question what I ask you to do again. I have killed for less." The second man's voice was familiar but she couldn't place...

"I wasn't questioning you. I just thought maybe you weren't aware—"

"I'm always aware."

Sedona heard her captor blow out a sigh. "VV, what I mean is..."

A roar filled her head, like thousands of waves hitting the shore at the same time. She didn't hear the rest of the sentence her captor spoke. Whatever those words were no longer mattered.

Oh, God. Realization slammed her heart against her chest.

VV. As in Vicente Vega, Jr. Sedona felt her world constrict. She knew, beyond any worst possible scenario, this was not going to end well.

***

Dia let out a yelp and bolted upright in her bed, convinced she was about to be gator food. Her tiny cry sounded loud in her head and forced her eyes to open. She saw the bed around her and the solid floor beneath it. No ripples. No bumpy skin. No teeth.

Moonlight filtered through the windows in a green-yellow tinge. It seemed to stick to the thick air. The mosquito netting around her bed, kind of romantic at first, now made her feel like a caged animal. She wanted to shove it away, but Pilar had warned her that the mosquitoes in the Honey Island Swamp were ruthless from dusk to dawn, and unless she wanted to be miserable she'd best keep herself as protected as possible.

Dia pulled the sheet up to her shoulders, checked the floor one more time for any signs of movement, then laid her head back down onto her pillow.

This place was all so different, and it didn't help that she'd somehow lost her Justin Bieber backpack. She must have left it at the last little house where they stayed. They made her leave so fast.

She looked up at the netting. It seemed like the real netting was a lot easier to get away from than the one her father had created. The only time she ever got out from under his net was when VV lifted it up for a few hours. Was VV worried about her? Probably not. He was likely so busy learning their father's business that he didn't even know she was gone. She resented that just because he was a boy he got all of the attention. At least from their father. Mamá had been a different story. She'd treated them the same. Still, she thought maybe there was a possibility her brother missed her and worried about her.

And her father? How did he react when he found out she'd run away? Dia was certain someone would have had to give him the information—he would never have noticed on his own. Relief that she was no longer his responsibility was probably quickly replaced by anger that she had defied him. And deadly anger toward anyone who had helped her. She owed a tremendous debt to Pilar and Luis. Without them she would still be under her father's thumb.

Without Pilar and Luis she would never have learned about Santeria.

CHAPTER ELEVEN

Mex moved cautiously into the coffee shop. He approached the counter where baristas held court and he refrained from looking directly at the two men sitting at the table. His awareness, however, engulfed the entire Starbucks. If his contact sent a signal, Mex needed to receive it. He had to trust that if there was a problem, his old friend would let him know.

Physically, the man sitting across from his friend hadn't changed much in the ten years since Mex had seen him. A muscleman for La Familia, the rival group of Vicente's Senora-Ciento cartel, was known as *Dejar*—so named because many people he was seen with *dropped* out of sight. Dejar had been part of the protection the day Mex told a La Familia boss he would not play their game either. There was something decidedly different about him. He'd put on a little weight. Who hadn't? But there was also something about his shoulders. More stooped. Mex straightened his posture and immediately felt taller. More fit and in control. *There.* That was the big difference. Dejar's swagger was gone. The arrogant confidence of the drug cartel member was now a misty memory.

What had happened?

After Mex bought his coffee, he moved to a location where he was in the line of sight of his contact while Dejar's back was to him. People might change, but he wasn't prepared to bet his life that this man wouldn't stand up in the middle of Starbuck's and finish the job he'd started years ago. Even if ordered by a different cartel. Another cartel that Mex had refused.

Mex's contact barely glanced in his direction and gave an almost imperceptible shake of his head. Mex sat down at an empty table, watched, and waited. A few minutes later, the cartel member stood up, put on some designer shades, and shoved a package toward the other man. In almost every other city in the world, this action would have brought at least a few whispers but in the new Monterrey, it was a common occurrence. Nobody wanted to get involved.

The contact slipped the package into an inside jacket pocket and pushed back his chair. He waited for Dejar to leave, then he went to the counter to order another espresso and joined Mex. "It's been a long time, Gray Eyes," he said in excellent English as he slid into a chair.

Mex raised an eyebrow and sipped his *caramel macchiato*. What he wouldn't give for one of Juan's Cubans right about now. He set the cup down. "It has been a long time. Things change." Mex sharpened his observation of his old friend. "What was your business with Dejar?"

The man shifted in his seat. "Merely a matter of expediency."

"Yours or his?"

"What does it matter?"

"I need to know whose side you're on. I'm in Monterrey, dealing with some sensitive issues, and I want to know who I should be watching."

"You have been away a long time, *mi amigo*. Today, in Monterrey, you need to watch everyone."

"You haven't answered my question."

"I truly wish Dejar and I had been able to finish our business before you arrived. You know me, Mex. I like to keep things personal."

"When your 'personal' has the potential to impact me, it's no longer private. It no longer belongs to you." Mex pushed his cup to the side. "Now answer my question."

More shifting in his seat. A sip of his espresso. A tiny cough.

Mex waited.

"You know my parents were killed in a plane crash when I was thirteen, right?"

Mex nodded.

"*Mi tia*, my father's sister, took in the four of us. They already had three children of their own, but they were determined that our family would stay together. It was crowded. It was difficult, but she was determined to make it work."

Mex understood the concept of family. He waited.

"The woman who saved us, who wrapped us in her arms, is ill. She's dying. The cancer brings her unbelievable pain. The painkillers her doctor prescribed don't touch her agony. But these," he patted his jacket, "these bring her relief and allow her last moments on this earth to be filled with family and friends rather than darkened rooms and mind-numbing drugs."

"Dejar provides them?"

"For the last three months."

"And what do you provide in return?"

"I pay him."

"And what else?"

His friend sat up straight and stiff in his chair. He looked directly at Mex. "I don't arrest him. It's a small price to pay to help my aunt." His chin lifted. "Don't judge me until you find yourself in my shoes."

The moment the words were out of his mouth the man seemed to realize what he'd said. "I'm sorry. Your loss..."

Mex thought about Sedona. He thought about Dia. He reached across the little table and clamped his hand on his contact's arm, his eyes hardened. "Screw my loss. Do you have what I want?"

***

Mex walked into the lobby of the Safi Valle. The magnificent hotel never failed to impress him. Between the luxurious surroundings and the attentive staff, he understood how this hotel had stayed around as long as it had. The efficiency of the front desk had him registered and on the way to his room in less than three minutes.

He liked the hotel's visitation policy. Not exactly private, but the odds of someone unexpected popping up at his door were diminished—which was a good thing. All thanks to the new Monterrey.

He put the keycard into the door and pushed it open. He'd arranged for a two-bedroom suite. Mex required a certain amount of privacy, but he and Darius needed a common area to work and compare notes.

Darius walked into the suite from the terrace, his cell phone held firmly against his ear. "I promise. Yeah, just a couple of days. This is important, or I wouldn't be here." He held a finger up in Mex's direction. "Gotta go, honey. Mex is here. I'll call you later."

The journalist looked at Mex. "Where the hell have you been? I've never been in a city that was this much of a war zone, unless I was in a war zone."

Mex laid two weapons on the table. "Yep."

Darius picked up the 9mm Glock and expertly dismantled the weapon in three swift steps. "This'll help."

"I thought you had a green light for this trip."

"I do."

"Didn't sound that way."

"Pamela gets to this point with every pregnancy. There's nothing I can do that's right. If we agree on something one day, it's a fight the next. Believe me, this is the best thing for our marriage." He reassembled the weapon, leaving the magazine on the table. "Did you get some bullets?"

Mex pulled a box out of a cloth bag and sat it down on the table. "Load both mags. I need a shower."

His cell phone rang. "Anderson."

"Why didn't you go with my driver?"

Shit. Vega. "I'd made other arrangements."

There was a pause. Obviously Vicente Vega was not used to people thinking and acting for themselves. He wondered how that translated to his parenting.

"And you didn't come alone." He sounded accusatory.

"I never said I would."

"You brought this Egbert Darius Johnson who has the safe deposit box key."

Egbert? "Yes. He's my partner."

"Can he be trusted?"

"Look, Vega. You don't need to trust him. I do."

Another pause. "When will you arrive?"

"Darius needs a shower, then he'll get a cab to your home. I want him to begin interviewing your household staff, starting with those who have been with you the longest."

"And you?"

"I'll be talking with Dia's classmates and friends tomorrow."

"I do not want this Darius in my home without you."

"Darius will have a better chance at getting answers." He didn't say it was because Darius was black.

"He will be here all night, and I do not want him in my home without you."

All night? "He'll interview your staff, the main ones, and then leave. How many are we talking about? Three? Four?"

"Fourteen."

Shit.

"I can send a car."

Mex considered whether they would be more or less likely to be pulled over riding in an armored limo driven by someone associated with a cartel. "No, thanks. We'll catch a cab."

"My driver will know which routes to take where you won't be bothered by checkpoints."

The system hadn't changed. It had just spread.

"Fine. Have your car outside of the Safi Valle in fifteen minutes. And tell whoever is driving to answer all of our questions while he takes us to your villa." Mex disconnected.

Darius cocked his head. "Looks like tonight has turned into a two-man job. How large is the staff? Five or six?"

"A few more, *Egbert*." Mex watched as his friends face stained with embarrassment. "Hey, your name's got nothin' on mine. It's just a new piece of information about you is all."

Mex moved to his bedroom and called over his shoulder. "Send your wife some flowers. Pamela might just welcome you home."

CHAPTER TWELVE

The worn mat underneath her was familiar. She'd been sitting on it, or one like it, as a diviner for years. For such an important client, she had one assistant, two attending priests, and two attending priestesses who joined her on the mat. Her client sat directly in front of her on a low stool.

Within reach, she had a *jicara*, the gourd filled to the brim with water. A lit cigar and a lit candle provided the grace and the power for the diviner to consult the spirits to get answers for her client.

The man on the stool was impatient, which always made the divining difficult. As they worked through his questions, he would be given certain symbolic items to hold in his hand. They included a smooth black stone, various shells, a bone taken from the left hind leg of a goat, and a tiny doll's head that would fit in his hand.

She sprinkled three dashes of water from the *jicara* over the sixteen cowrie shells she held in her hand, and said the special words intended to prepare them. "Fresh water, freshen the road to the orisha, refresh my power. Freshen my home. Freshen Elegguá of Eshu Loroye. Bring us freshness that has no end."

The diviner rubbed the small bits between her palms. Over and over, around and around. Then she leaned forward and tapped the hand that held the shells to the mat three times.

After the third strike, she lifted her hand and opened it to allow the shells to spill on the mat, ready for her to read. Divined. The Diviner.

The client spoke for the first time. "Can't you hurry with this? You know what I want to know. I just need confirmation."

"We spend one session a week together. It is unlikely anything has changed in that time. Settle. Relax. Let me employ my powers to assure what you are doing will succeed."

The Diviner had determined months ago the weaknesses of her client—his deepest desires and his deepest fears. She could play them. She *had* played them. For the first time in her life, she knew the security of a roof over her head, all the food she could eat, and the promise of more. All from luring an outwardly strong man into her power. She'd taken his. Used it. Made him believe in the future she divined from the shells. From her *diloggún*. She had moved beyond the mundane religious concepts of the Santeria practitioners who had been her early mentors. She could taste greater power, and greater power was exactly what she wanted.

Five times in the past eighteen months, her client asked her for advice on what course of action he should take in order to achieve his goals. Four of those times, she told him to stand strong and move forward. One time she advised him to cut his losses. Each time she had been proven right. After the second success, she had been invited to move into his villa—be a part of his inner-circle. She had learned all of the ways this man could be controlled. Beyond sex. Beyond money. It all centered on her influence. Her divinations would determine what this man did.

He approached her to begin a sexual relationship two nights after she'd moved in, but she was too smart for that. She didn't intend for him to ever tire of her, and if either of them was going to do the using, it would be her.

Regal, beautiful by any standard, the Diviner compelled attention when she entered a room. Both men and women were aware of her presence, and the power she held over their lives.

She knew men dreamed about her but awoke soaked in the sweat of their fear. She learned early to use her assets—all of them.

The Diviner barely looked at the cowrie shells splayed before her. She realized she had only a moment to keep his attention. "The direction I gave you before holds true. You are on the verge of destroying a significant enemy and sending a message to all of your other enemies. You are perfectly placed to assume your rightful position as the leader of the largest and most formidable drug cartel in all the world. Your strength will be compounded while the other is weakened beyond recovery."

"So the sacrifice is as you've foreseen?"

"All the elements are as I've foreseen. If they are to differ, it is your doubt that will make it so."

"I don't doubt you, Diviner. If I did, one of us would die."

She straightened her back and rose from the mat in one fluid move. "You need to travel to Honey Island soon."

"I have other matters to take care of first. The girl will keep."

CHAPTER THIRTEEN

Based on the directions Mex checked on the Internet, the Vega property was about thirty minutes out of town—longer if they were stopped for any reason. That would give them some time to question the driver.

"What's your name?" Mex asked in Spanish. Darius also spoke the language fluently, so Mex wasn't worried about him not understanding.

"Arturo Gonzales." The driver had obviously been given instructions to cooperate.

"Have you worked for Vicente Vega long?"

"Twelve years."

That meant he had been an employee while Dia was growing up and her mother was still alive.

"Have you always worked exclusively for Vega, or do you occasionally spend time with the rest of the family?"

"My primary responsibility has always been to Mr. Vega. But I was assigned to drive the late Mrs. Vega, may she rest in peace, from time to time. And whenever I was with Mrs. Vega at least one of the children was always with her."

"What was she like with the children?"

"She was loving and attentive. Nurturing. Almost..."

"Almost what?"

"Mr. Vega often thought she was too soft with the children."

"His was a firmer hand?"

Gonzales gave an almost imperceptible nod. "He deals from a place of strength in all aspects of his life. His children would become strong only through firmness and a certain aloofness. Mr. Vega made sure the entire staff was aware of his position. The only person who paid him no heed was his wife."

"Did that cause any problems?" Darius asked.

"Vicente Vega is a hard man who demands obedience. There were some arguments between them, but in the end he always indulged her."

"What do you think happened to Dia?" Mex asked.

Silence.

"Well?"

"I'm sure I don't know."

"I didn't ask you what you know. I asked you what you think."

"What I *think* is that my opinion hardly matters. What I *think* is that I need this job, and you should do yours without bringing me into things I know nothing about. Things I *think* nothing of."

"Well, then. It seems like we're done for now. Mind if we talk later?"

The driver rolled down his window and spat. "Can't stop you."

After a few more minutes they pulled into an entrance, armed guards on either side. A visual of the car and driver weren't good enough. Gonzales stopped and gave a code word—probably one that changed daily. Mex thought about living this way and felt grateful for his comparatively idyllic life in Aspen Falls.

The guard waved them through.

They drove up a short hill, then descended onto a circular drive. The main house was magnificent, Mex thought, if you like formidable. Another armed guard stood at the door.

Mex was not impressed—he'd seen this all before and then some. But Darius was eyeing the weaponry, his right elbow surreptitiously pulled into his waistband, confirming the position of his stowed Glock. *Damn.* Mex caught his eye and shook his head. They didn't need to get all jumpy and ready for action. They were here as friends of the family. More or less.

Gonzales pulled the car to a stop, but didn't put it in park. Clearly he was not going to open their doors. Fine. Mex and Darius got out and stood in the portico. As soon as they'd closed the car doors, Gonzales pulled away. As the limousine left the covered area, two other guards appeared, standing close and tight to the newcomers.

"Lift your arms. Now. Over your head." The man next to Mex spoke loudly. "Both of you."

Within seconds their weapons were removed. "You'll get these back when you leave the compound."

A man dressed in khakis and a polo shirt stood at the front door. "Please. Follow me."

Mex and Darius entered the building, the two guards following close behind. The ornate decor made Mex want to cringe. He'd learned a lot from both Maria and Sedona, and this was like overdosing on frosting.

He glanced at his friend. Darius kept his eyes in front of him, giving no clue as to what he was thinking.

Good. Apparently Darius's background was kicking in. As a journalist who always went after the big story, his job had taken him all over the globe and thrown him into questionable situations, but Mex had never seen him in action. Maybe the man simply had innate survival skills. Something. Until this moment, Mex hadn't been completely sure how the journalist would respond under stress. He breathed a little easier.

Mex followed Darius into a large dining room. Darius stopped dead in his tracks and turned to shoot an accusing look at Mex. "Why didn't you tell me there were this many people to talk to?"

"Would it have made you happy?"

The casually dressed man nodded to them. "These are the immediate household staff. They are all prepared to speak with you." Fourteen pairs of eyes trained on them.

"It's going to be a long night," Darius whispered.

***

Mex stood and stretched. He and Darius had taken only one break since they began the interviews. They'd walked outside and paced the estate grounds for a few minutes in silence, each lost in their own thoughts.

Darius rolled his head on his neck and Mex could hear the pops from across the room. They were exhausted.

"We have one more interview to go. Tomorrow we'll talk to Dia's friends." Mex didn't sound hopeful.

"We need something, Mex. All we've got is a loving mother who died, a distant father, a brother who stands ready to step into the shoes of his father, and a succession of nannies with the last one apparently aiding and abetting a runaway."

"Find out what you can about the nanny."

"I've already got my sources on it."

Mex nodded, put his water bottle to his lips, and emptied it in one long pull. "You ready?"

"Let's get 'er done." Darius walked to the door. He opened it and signaled for the last staff member to enter.

"Thank you for waiting," Darius said. "We appreciate your patience."

The middle-aged woman nodded. *"No problema.* I am not expected anywhere." She settled herself at the table.

"Can we get you something to drink?" Darius asked.

"Not right now."

Mex sat across from the woman. "How long have you worked for the Vega family?"

"Almost two years."

So, she'd begun working around the time Dia's mother had died. Mex was hopeful.

"And do you know why we're talking to you?" Mex had asked this question fourteen times tonight, and it felt obvious. Stale.

"Dia is gone and her father wants to know who is responsible."

Mex nodded. A little more direct than they'd heard from the others, but essentially the same. "Do you have an opinion? Why do you think Dia is gone?"

The woman's eyes scrunched to small slits. "After talking to thirteen others, you have received no ideas?"

Mex felt a chill propel through his body. They might have something here. "We're not here to tell you what others have said. Tell us what *you* think."

"People must pay for their sins." The woman folded her hands on her lap.

Pious. Mex could play pious as well as the next guy. "I agree. There is such a thing as atonement in this life."

The woman looked at him, her eyes shining brightly. "And Dia is at the age of reckoning."

"Did she make a bad choice?"

The woman crossed herself. "There are wrong people involved here."

"Wrong people?"

"Miss Dia was suggestible."

"And these wrong people suggested what?"

"They led her away from the God her mother loved."

"Explain that to me."

"There are people who take any religion and twist it."

"Are you saying that Dia got involved in some kind of religious group? A cult?"

"Dia got involved with her nanny. Her nanny was involved with a religion that could charm a little girl who had lost her mother."

"What religion?"

"There are a lot of practitioners who follow the good ways. There are others who make their own way."

"What religion?" Mex pushed back into his chair, forcing himself to stay out of the woman's face—where he really wanted to be.

"Some call it Yoruba. But most know it as Santeria."

"You said something about people who twist a religion. Twist it how?" Darius asked.

The woman cast a long stare in Darius's direction. "Personal gain. The desire for power changes hearts."

Darius met her gaze. "Sometimes it's changed hearts that create the desire for power."

The woman continued to look at Darius, but her eye twitched and she blinked. Then she dropped her eyes.

"Pilar is a practitioner of Santeria?" Mex asked.

"She is. But I think that it's her boyfriend who has turned her to a darker way."

Mex looked up. "Do you know his name?"

"Luis Alvarez. He has people in the U.S. The gulf part."

Darius cleared his throat. "What do you mean by 'darker way'? Is there something specific you can put your finger on? Something that might help us find Dia?"

The woman grew visibly smaller. Curled into herself. Mex thought she looked like one of those scared rabbits who sat in the middle of the sidewalk, still as statues, as if they didn't move, they'd be invisible.

Damn, I need to get more sleep.

Mex reached out and touched her arm. "Please. Anything. Help us. We need to find Dia before something terrible happens to her." If something hasn't already happened, he thought.

The woman popped a bit as she uncurled. "I believe this boyfriend, Luis, is connected in some way to another cartel, and that cartel uses Santeria to protect them."

"Protect them how?" Mex asked.

"Keep them safe from the law, from their enemies."

Mex fell silent.

Darius, his voice just above a whisper, asked, "And how do they do that?"

"With sacrifices greater than goats and chickens." The woman barely got the words out before she strangled a cry and buried her head in her hands. She'd clearly said all she could.

CHAPTER FOURTEEN

Awareness flooded Mex in an overwhelming wave. Dark room. Monterrey. Cold, wet pillow. Face awash in tears. He'd had another dream he couldn't quite remember now that he was awake. The dream might be gone from his memory, but the sadness lingered. It burrowed, made him want to stay in bed. The same sadness followed him every day of his life. Some days, he could stay ahead of its shadow. On others, the darkness poured into his skin and there was no escape.

Today was one of those days.

He tried to fall back to sleep but knew he wouldn't succeed. Mex shoved the covers off and sat on the edge of the bed. *Damn.* All he wanted to do was lie back down and pull the blankets over his head.

But there was a missing little girl he'd promised to find.

Mex pushed off the bed and walked into his bathroom. Without flipping on any lights, he reached into the walk-in shower and turned on the water. Then he went to the Nespresso and popped in a pack without bothering to check the flavor. At this point it didn't matter. Caffeine was caffeine. And to have whatever flavored coffee ready for him when he stepped out of the shower made life a little more bearable—especially since he'd made a personal commitment and had to function on some level. He swallowed a couple of pills.

More than anything, he wanted to be in Aspen Falls. In his bedroom. Alone.

He pushed aside the crushing weight of depression and stepped into the shower. He was under the water for two minutes before he registered the fresh tears adding to the liquid flowing down the drain. He allowed himself one horrendous, awkward cry, then rinsed out the shampoo, washed off the soap, and reached for a towel.

His sister's life and the life of a young girl depended on him. He had to keep moving. He had to care.

Fifteen minutes and two cups of coffee later, Mex walked into the still dark common area of the suite. About to knock on Darius's bedroom door, he changed his mind. Let his partner sleep a few minutes more while he bought a paper. They didn't need to get to the school this early. Vega had made arrangements with the headmaster and they were to be given free rein. He'd grab a paper and some pastries and then haul Darius into the program.

The door pulled open. "Hey, man." Darius rubbed his eyes. "I'm ready."

"Yeah, you and the sandman."

"No, really. Are you ready to roll?"

"Roll?" Mex snickered at Darius's attempt to be hip. A tiny sliver of darkness turned to gray.

"Fuck you."

"Take a leak. Grab a shower. Have some coffee. We'll *roll* after I get back."

Mex thought some fresh morning air might help. But he'd forgotten that Monterrey was a major city with major cars and major pollution. He hit the sidewalk and whatever energy he'd managed to conjure up vanished in one breath.

Damn.

He walked to the Starbucks he'd been to yesterday, grabbed a paper and a couple of muffins, then made his way back to the hotel. On the way, he spotted a man who seemed out of place.

He shook his head. He'd hoped they would fly a little more under the radar, but it wasn't really a shock.

They were being watched.

Who was behind the eyes? Vega was naturally suspicious. Was it him? Was he keeping tabs? The Mexican Federales might have reason to watch Vega's activities, but why waste their resources on him? Could the watchers be connected with the disappearance of Dia Vega?

Or could they be another part of Vega's cartel responsible for the deaths of his family?

Mex forced himself through his suspicions and continued to his hotel. They already knew he was here, where he was staying. His one-up was knowing they—whoever they were—were watching.

When he walked into the room, he tossed the muffins on the coffee table. Darius was out of the shower, dressed, and enjoying some coffee while he watched an international news program.

"We've got at least one tail."

Darius reached for a muffin. "Not surprised." He took a healthy bite. "You got a plan?"

"Play it tight and get out of Dodge."

"That's it?"

"Well, how about this—don't get killed."

"Are we still good to talk to Dia's friends?"

"Yeah, but I'm gonna take those myself. I need you to dig into this Santeria thing. Use your news sources. Get us some information. And dig up everything you can find on the nanny."

"Do you think the girl is still alive?"

Mex didn't answer.

***

Mex pushed away from the table and watched the young man saunter out of the conference room. This was the eighth friend of Dia's he'd talked to and they all said pretty much the same thing. While Dia had every reason to run away because of her father, she could never have done so without help.

He wondered about the role of Santeria. Had Darius been able to find anything?

And what was happening to Sedona? Mex shook his head. Couldn't think about that right now. He had to believe that by focusing on saving Dia, he'd save Sedona.

Vicente Vega had instructed the headmaster to provide him access to Dia's friends. Mex knew that there was a good possibility the parents of several of the children at the private school were also involved, at least peripherally, with the drug cartels. Vega's prominence apparently held more sway over the educator than the parents of the other students. Mex's main concern was the presence of people connected to rival cartels, especially La Familia. It was a risk he felt they needed to take.

Mex tried to impress on each of the kids that this was a sensitive matter and they should not discuss any of what they talked about with each other or their parents. In the United States there would be no way of pulling this off without parental permission. In Mexico, even if such a law existed, Vicente Vega could make justice truly blind. Asking the kids not to talk to their parents made Mex uncomfortable, but it was necessary. Being followed was one thing, but details of questions he was asking were quite another. Although the kids assured him they would keep the nature of their discussion confidential, Mex figured he and Darius had three hours maximum to get a strong enough lead to make their next move.

He grabbed his phone and called his partner. Voicemail.

Mex stuck his spiral notebook in a pocket, followed by his phone. He loved the notebook for interviews because it kept him focused on the conversation. Kept him tight. Gave him something to do with his hands. But he'd learned that recording the question and answer sessions on his phone was a good idea. Insurance.

He stood and stretched. Tried Darius again. Voicemail. "I sure as hell hope you got more than I got this afternoon. I'm on my way back to the hotel. I'll grab some beer and sandwiches. We're there until we can figure out our next step."

Mex left the conference room and walked down the short hallway to the headmaster's office. He stopped when he heard the man talking to someone. The words he heard were rapid, more stage whisper than sotto voce, and Mex only caught a few. *Vega. Cartel. No choice.* Mex listened to ascertain whether or not the man was alone. Only one voice. Must be on the phone. He moved to the office door and waited. He listened. He moved into view.

The headmaster was busy spouting something to do with it being a privilege to have the son of such a prominent man in their school and didn't see Mex standing behind him. He promised the man he would personally see that the American left and did not return. He went on to assure him that the Vega family did not control the decisions he made.

Yeah, right.

Mex cleared his throat. The headmaster whipped around with such speed that his glasses spilled off his nose and onto the desk.

Mex raised his eyebrows and motioned for the beet-red educator to hang up the phone. Then he watched as surprise, fear, and embarrassment fused and solidified, pressing the human being in front of him into a non-moving statue of flesh and dripping sweat.

Mex walked over, removed the phone easily, and pressed the off button. He laid the phone on the desk and reached for the man's glasses. "Talk to me."

"It was nothing. Just a parent who heard you were talking to students."

"Heard from who?"

"Another parent. Their child received a text message."

Shit. The three hour window he'd hoped for had seriously closed.

***

On his way back to the hotel, Mex stopped for some cold beer and soda and fresh sandwiches. When he walked into the hotel room, Darius was hunched over his laptop, fingers flying over the keyboard. He'd somehow gotten hold of a printer, and there was a stack two inches deep of research piled on the edge of the table. Mex put the bags down and reached for the paper.

Darius waved him off. "Wait. I'm almost there."

Mex shook his head and grabbed the top few pages anyway. *Remains of Headless Goat, Roosters Cause Stir in Miami's Affluent South Beach* read the headlines on the first page. *Mexico Drug Cartels in Regions Steeped in Witchcraft, Demonic Influence* topped the page for the next article. Darius had been busy. Mex grabbed the next few pages and began to read.

Oh, God. Mex pushed down a fistful of fear and anger. VV had his sister. Was he subjecting Sedona to this shit? The papers shook.

"I said wait. I'm about to save you all kinds of time." Darius leaned in closer to his screen.

"Saving time is good because we're running out." Mex continued to scan the pages held in his hands. What he read sent chills down his spine. "Human sacrifice? Are you kidding me?" *Sedona.*

With a flourish, Darius typed the last few keys and turned to Mex. "No joke, amigo. But that's a cartel thing, not all of Santeria."

"And since we're operating in the middle of a cartel…"

"Yep. It could be bad for Dia, unless she's bait or something."

"Either way, she's a kid. She doesn't know what she's doing." Mex didn't like the "or something."

"That, kemo sabe, is exactly why I have rounded up not only an expert in non-traditional religions and cults, but Santeria in particular. This expert knows all about extricating people from groups and deprogramming them. What the politically correct people now call "exit counseling.""

"Good. Is he local?"

"Not exactly."

"Don't tell me he's in Central America." Mex did not want to go back there. Not ever.

"Louisiana. We're booked on two flights out of Monterrey tonight."

"Why two flights, and why can't we just call this guy and talk to him from here?"

"I booked us separately because I assume we still have unwanted company keeping an eye on us. It seemed like a good idea to split up." Darius grabbed a sandwich and popped open a beer. "And this is why we need to leave tonight." He handed Mex a large flat envelope.

"What's this?" Mex asked as he looked at the front. It had both of their names on the front in block printing.

"Take a look. It was delivered by a bellman about twenty minutes ago. He said the front desk found the envelope sitting on the counter. No one saw who delivered it."

Mex opened the envelope and carefully pulled out two photographs. One was Dia with a pretty woman and a surly young man. The woman and Dia were smiling. The young man glowered. He turned it over. Nothing. The second picture was grainy. It looked like it had been taken in poor light and on the move. A dark, older, four-door sedan was centered but it was the background that drew Mex's attention. A row of structures that reminded him of the dollhouse Sedona had as a little girl. He turned the second photograph over. NEW ORLEANS was printed in block letters.

Mex nodded. Louisiana. Something about it... damn. He was tired. "Tell me about this deprogrammer." He took a bottle of beer and opened it while he stood and paced. He knew he should have chosen a Coke when the depression was on him, but a cold one felt right.

Darius took a quick gulp and sat the bottle down next to the sandwich. He rifled through the stack of papers and handed several to Mex. "I don't know too much. Cade LeBlanc's name appeared in three or four recent articles about kids who'd been brainwashed into some crazy religious cult. The parents didn't have any luck in getting their kids out, so they hired LeBlanc to kidnap and deprogram them. But like I said, they call it exit counseling now. Same shit, nicer name."

"And the Santeria angle?" He took a pull on the beer while glancing through the articles Darius had printed out.

"One kid in Mexico, one in Florida. Both of them hooked up with Santeria through friends. Both of them *counseled* by LeBlanc. One of them was the nephew of some cartel boss. The background on the cartel kid is included. Unfortunately, both the kid's parents were killed less than a year later and he was sent to live with his uncle. LeBlanc's good but can't control the kind of lessons the cartel dishes out, as you know."

"Is he expecting us?"

"Some crab shack at midnight."

Mex sat down and looked at him. Relief that they had a plan and were moving forward without wasting time mixed with a twinge of uncertainty about meeting someone associated with cults and cartels at midnight in an unfamiliar location.

Darius nodded. "I get your reluctance." He closed his laptop. "Apparently LeBlanc knows the owner."

"Where in Louisiana?" Mex wanted to know if he had a contact in the area for backup.

"Outside of New Orleans."

Damn. He knew a guy in Texarkana. Had the meet been in Shreveport, he might have been able to arrange something. "Give me your gun."

Darius looked at him.

"We can't carry on the plane and even if I had somewhere to ship them to, they wouldn't get there in time. I'm going to rent a safe deposit box here in Monterrey. At least if we need to return I won't have to buy more weapons."

His phone rang. Vega. "Anderson."

"What have you found?"

"It looks as if your daughter has become involved in Santeria."

"Dia? No. There is no way she would—"

"It also appears she's a runaway as opposed to a kidnap victim."

Silence. "And do you know where she is now?" The bluster had left. Now his words were quiet, almost timid. Mex *almost* felt sorry for the man.

"We're working a lead near New Orleans."

"Wha—"

"And we're likely to be out of pocket for the next couple of days."

"Out of pocket?"

"Unavailable. I'll call you with updates."

"That is not acceptable." The bravado was making a comeback.

Mex answered by ending the call.

CHAPTER FIFTEEN

Sedona felt as if she were fighting to get to the surface. The surface of what, she had no idea. The air was thick and hot and it was hard to breathe.

They'd drugged her. When her brain wrapped itself around that realization, things cleared faster. Because she'd learned that Vicente Vega, Jr. was involved in her kidnapping, if not behind it, she knew that it wasn't Teo's money that had put her in danger. But she also knew that somehow her brother was the end target. The one who could set her free.

Damn. She prayed Teo wasn't disabled with depression. Her fate would be sealed. Teo had been known to spend days, even weeks, isolated and oblivious to the rest of the world. She squeezed her eyes tight.

"Well, lookey here. Look who's coming back to the land of the living." Her captor had the inevitable cigarette hanging from the corner of his mouth.

"What did you give me?" Even though she was no longer gagged, she fought to form the words.

"Nothing serious. I just made you a little more convenient."

She wanted to wipe her eyes. She wanted to pee in private. She wanted to let this *pendejo* know that all *idiots* lose in the end. Instead, Sedona tried her best to smile.

The man hacked out a laugh. "You don't fool me none. I know a problem when I see one, and my eyesight is crystal clear."

"Why? Why did you take me?" Sedona struggled to stay focused. This man's physical presentation did not match his current crude behavior and poor language skills.

The man scratched the stubble on his cheek, new since she'd first seen him. "I told you once. I took you because I was told to take you. Up to me, I don't see no upside."

"And um... um... is VV a part of the reason?"

"Sweet cakes, VV is the whole shittin' shebang of the reason."

"Is it because of my... my..." Sedona's words just couldn't come.

"Girlie, I don't know why the hell VV wants you. It ain't to fuck you, or he would have by now. It ain't for money, or I would have been told and maybe even been offered a cut. I just don't want no problems. Not from you, and 'specially not from VV."

She swallowed. "Does my brother know? Does he know where I am?"

"He was the first call."

"Did you... does he know—"

"It don't do you no good to ask me anything. I just needed to nab you, hide you, and keep you alive. That's all."

"So you aren't gonna kill me?"

"Don't know yet. VV hasn't said."

Sedona closed her eyes. What had happened to bring her to this point? Why in the world would Vicente Vega, Jr. want to bring this on her now? She blamed her brother. Teo was at the root of all of this. Teo was the root of all of their problems—including the loss of the rest of her family. There could be no other answer.

***

"You actually eat this?" Dia looked up at Pilar. She tried hard to keep her face from screwing up in distaste. She didn't want to look judgmental. But mostly she didn't want to look immature.

"Honey, it's not like it's from outer space or anything. It's alligator. Plain old simple gator. It won't hurt you, and it's what we've got on hand."

Dia thought about the monster that had threatened her when she was walking to the house. Plain, old, or simple didn't apply to the creature hell-bent on grabbing her for its own meal. Didn't even come close. But maybe eating it would make her feel like she had the upper hand.

She brought the fork up to her lips and sniffed. Took a nibble. *Chickeny.* Not bad. "Oh yeah, gator. Sure. It's been awhile." Dia finished up the piece on her fork and cut off another.

"We're going to have some special visitors, Dia."

"For a ceremony?"

Pilar's face pulled tight. "What makes you think they're here for a ceremony?"

"You're kidding, right?" Dia's eyes went to the kitchen counter where several small bowls held the *íbo* tools for special ceremonies. Smooth black stones, representing immortality clustered in one, crushed eggshells for a positive answer in another. Cowrie shells, used for financial ceremonies bunched in a third bowl, and broken china for use in divining things related to wars and feuds was in a fourth.

Pilar's face relaxed, but only a little. "You have learned well in a short time."

"When will the visitors be here? How many are there? Does that mean we're staying in this house?" Dia thought of the alligator again. But since she'd eaten alligator and no alligator had eaten Dia, she felt more confident. She would learn how to deal with the creatures.

"So many questions, Dia. You'll have your answers when the time is right."

CHAPTER SIXTEEN

Mex and Darius reasoned that if they were going to continue to be watched, Darius was the least likely target. He got the direct flight from Monterrey to New Orleans, and was already at the Hilton where they'd arranged to meet up. Mex had taken an earlier flight, one with a short layover in Dallas. He checked his watch. They'd touched down five minutes early at the Louis Armstrong International Airport, and with only his carryon to contend with, he should be at the hotel inside of twenty.

There'd been some talk of a tropical storm forming but no one had any idea where it might be going. At least their flights hadn't been delayed.

His phone rang. Darius. "I'm on my way."

"Good. A freelancer I know was just here."

Mex closed his eyes and took a deep breath. "What for?" All they needed was for more people to get involved in looking for Dia. He would never see Sedona again.

"He's an old buddy of mine and wrote a couple of the articles I found about Santeria. Turns out there's quite a group right here in N'awlins."

"What have you told him?"

"Just that I was chasing a story on non-mainstream religions and cults and Santeria came up."

Mex realized he'd been holding his breath even as he had a death grip on his phone. He forced himself to relax.

The next words from his friend were like flint. "Hey, man. You know me better than that. And I know you." Darius sucked in a breath of his own. "Is there something you're not telling me?"

"Can you not be a journalist for a change?"

Darius didn't respond. Finally, he spoke softly. "I wasn't being a journalist, Mex. I was being a friend. A friend who, by the way, left his pregnant wife and kids to be your partner in finding a little girl."

Mex began to speak, to apologize. But his words sounded hollow and flat without a live connection. Darius had hung up.

Fifteen minutes later, Mex walked in to his side of the adjoining rooms. Darius had made the reservations under false names. He was Martin Riggs and Darius was Roger Murtaugh, the two main characters in the *Lethal Weapon* movies. Mex was kind of surprised no one seemed to have caught on. Probably because neither Mel Gibson or Danny Glover frequented the Big Easy's Airport Hilton.

He tossed his duffle on the bed and headed to the bathroom. He needed to take a leak and throw some water on his face. It was going to be a long night.

He was toweling off when he heard a knock.

Mex pulled the connecting door open and began the apology he'd tried to say earlier to dead air. "I trust you, Darius. I just get a little obsessed from time to time. It gets in the way of my relationships."

"No worries." Darius avoided eye contact. He pushed into the room and tossed a battered looking Glock on Mex's bed. "The best I could do. I knew we couldn't go to this meet without protection."

Mex looked at the banged-up gun and cringed. "What's yours?"

"I could only get one from my connection. I didn't want him to think there were two of us."

Crap. Darius really did know what he was doing. Mex felt like an ass.

"I cleaned it and checked it out. It looks a lot worse than it is." The journalist shrugged his shoulders. "At least I hope so."

"Hey buddy, I—"

"I said, no worries." Darius turned and looked him dead in the eye. Mex couldn't read his expression. "When you want to fill me in, you will. I'm guessing that whatever it is you're keeping to yourself you think you have to keep to yourself. I'm also guessing that it's what's making you lose your perspective."

Mex decided they didn't need to go there. He picked up the phone in the room. Hotel room phones these days were pretty much expensive internal communication devices. Did anyone use them to dial out any more? "You hungry?" Mex knew his friend—he was always up for food.

Darius gave a shrug. "We're going to a crab shack in," he looked at his watch, "three hours."

"Kitchen will likely be closed."

"Yeah, okay. Let's eat."

Mex hid a smile. "If you're sure. We can always wait and see."

"Probably shouldn't risk it. Hard to get down to business if we're hungry."

Mex, wanting to make up a little lost ground with his friend, ordered two full steak dinners with every available side dish.

***

Darius replied to an email from Pamela, then closed his laptop and pushed it aside on his bed. He stretched out and checked his watch. He had about fifteen minutes before they needed to head out to the crab shack. He considered his relationship with Mex Anderson. Their friendship went back to the first days Mex had turned up in Aspen Falls. From the beginning, Darius's journalist antenna had registered an ethical, if troubled, man. In the five plus years he'd known Mex, his initial impression had not proved wrong. They'd become close friends and shared a lot of their histories.

So what was going on now? What secret was Mex keeping? Could it endanger him simply by his association with Mex? If Darius didn't have a family things would be different. His responsibilities wouldn't be the same. What the hell had he gotten himself into?

And then he thought about the story potential. This could be huge. The rescue of a young, innocent girl whose father was a drug lord? The possible twists were mind boggling. This could make his career. This could be the story that raised him from the ranks of "who wrote that?" to "I never miss his column or his books." Whatever he was digging himself into could make a huge difference in his family's finances.

A solid story here, and Pamela would forgive everything. Especially if it brought in some money to pay the extra bills and take a few family vacations. Hell, Darius thought, might as well think big.

Then he thought again.

Yeah, they were walking into unknown waters tonight. Darius just hoped there weren't any gators.

CHAPTER SEVENTEEN

"We good?" Mex asked as Darius slid into the passenger seat of the rented SUV. The interior overhead light glowed dimly in the darkness.

Darius looked briefly in his direction. "Wouldn't be here if we weren't." He closed the door and the light slipped away.

"Just checkin'."

"Know where we're going?"

"I've programmed the GPS gizmo. Other than that the answer is no."

"Better than I'd hoped for."

"Fuck you."

"You taking your meds?"

"What? Just 'cause I cuss you think I need drugs?"

"It's a sign is all."

Mex looked at his friend. Didn't see any subterfuge. "Yeah. It hit me a few days ago. I'm on 'em."

"You feel yourself slipping, you need to let me know."

"I wouldn't be here if I wasn't good."

"Well, good then."

"Good."

It didn't take too long before they were out of the city. Mex imagined that if he could see past the headlights, he'd see the flat swampland the region was known for. The air was heavier here too, the humidity making it crawl with a life of its own.

The two travelled in companionable silence for several miles. According to the GPS they'd be on the current road for twenty more miles.

Darius cleared his throat. "I spoke with Pamela."

"I would expect you to speak with your wife." Mex wondered what was coming. "She good? Kids good?"

"Yeah, yeah. All good. She's just... I don't know. Pregnant."

"Look, if you need to get home, I understand."

"Nah. Not right away. You know Pamela. She gets that this is important."

"But?"

"But nothing'. She just misses me. Her hormones are kicking places they shouldn't be kicking and she's reacting."

"Sure?"

"Hell, I don't know, Mex. Pamela's at that point where she wants me around and doesn't want me around. She doesn't know what she wants. And I know I want this story." Darius shifted in his seat, pulled his seat belt away from his chest and let it resettle. "Just thought I'd tell you we talked is all."

The two friends fell silent for a mile or so.

"You've read more about this Cade LeBlanc than I have," Mex said. "What do you think makes him tick?"

Darius popped his neck. "I just skimmed but I think a family member—a sister maybe—got involved in some cult and ended up dying. I don't remember the details."

For a moment he thought of Sedona, then shook it off. "What cult?"

"I told you, I was skimming." Darius turned his head away from Mex and looked out the window.

"What aren't you telling me?"

Silence.

"Darius?"

"Nothing much else to say. Except that along with the anti-social behavior—the whole cult thing and all—the sister also had trouble with depression."

Silence.

"Shit, amigo. Unless the dead sister's depression is significant to our case, what the hell do I care?"

"You don't. I don't. Unless it affects how Cade LeBlanc responds to you."

"What? Like I'm carrying a sign or something?"

Darius waited for Mex to take a breath and look him in the eye. "Or something."

"Fine. I'll try and play nice. Anything else?"

"Just that he's been doing this for a long time, knows what he's doing and has had a lot of success."

"Which is why he wants to meet us out in the middle of a swamp at midnight?"

Darius didn't bother to answer.

A few minutes later the GPS had them pull off the dark road on to an even darker road. One made of dirt and not exactly smooth.

"Are you sure about this?" Darius asked.

"Like I would know. I just input the information. From that point forward it's a relationship based on trust."

"Which we all know you have very little of."

The dark road had so much gravel build-up that he fishtailed twice and grimaced as flying bits of rock hit the rental. The last time he'd been on a back road in Louisiana, it had been made of ground up seashells from the gulf. Gravel was probably cheaper and maybe more ecological, but he missed the idea of driving on shells.

Mex slowed to a crawl, peering out the windows to try and see past the headlights. This can't be good. Based on the activity in the lights in front of them, they were outnumbered a gazillion to one by bugs, most of which probably bit and sucked.

A few yards later the road leveled out to an even grade. A large parking lot stretched in front of a building with a sign that had the smallest spotlight in the world angled on it. It took Mex fifty more yards to be able to read the thing. *Boudreaux's* was all it said.

There were two vehicles in the parking lot. One was on the side of the building: a beater with more rust than paint. The other, a brilliant red BMW SUV that was so clean it caught a fragment of light from the spotlight and spilled it back into the night like stardust. Mex figured the clean machine belonged to LeBlanc. A part of Mex wondered how the hell a guy who pulled kids out of cults could afford a high-end Beamer, but the other part knew there were more than a few people back home who questioned his own wealth. Because he was Mexican, they assumed it was drugs. Because he kept to himself they *knew* it was drugs.

Screw 'em.

He pulled up next to the BMW, angled so that although he and Darius had easy access, the driver of the red luxury vehicle would have a hard time getting in the driver's side.

The two men sat and took in the view of the crab shack.

Suddenly, there was a pop as the door to the restaurant flung back and hit the siding. A man stood there, eyeing them right back. Three hundred pounds of muscle. Hair tied back in a pony-tail. Fierce. Challenging. A shotgun in his right hand.

***

Shit. We haven't even stepped out of our rental car and Genghis Khan stands ready to pick us off. This meet was a bad idea.

Before Mex could stop him, Darius pushed open his door and squeezed out.

His friend held his hands high, palms forward. "We're expected. We're here to see Cade LeBlanc."

Mex wondered if he was going to have to haul Darius back into the SUV and peel out of this dark and desolate spot before they were both obliterated from the face of the earth. He was glad he hadn't killed the engine.

The giant seemed to consider Darius's words, then rested the shotgun at his side. Took one step back. Bowed his head. That was the best they could hope to get, and Mex decided they had no other choice but to take this opportunity.

Mex tweaked the ignition key, and the silence was deafening. At least until the night insects took up their songs. He stepped out of the vehicle, closed the door and moved toward the restaurant. Darius fell into step behind him. Mex was comforted by the gun secured in the back of his waist, but he seriously doubted that both of them would survive if Mount Etna decided to fight.

They walked steadily toward the restaurant, neither of them giving into the urge to swat at the deluge of insects. Mex kept looking for a Plan B and wasn't happy with any of the options.

There were five steps up to the deck area, then another ten feet past the sentinel to the entrance. Mex stilled his thoughts. Decided that if he were killed, he'd be with the love of his life. That would not be so bad. He missed Maria every day. But what about Darius? A wife waiting for him in Colorado. Kids. Another on the way. He pushed those concerns away. All that was important—the only thing that mattered—was saving Dia, and by saving Dia he could save his sister.

No more sacrifices.

Mex swallowed.

As the two men cleared the top step the giant held up a hand and twirled a finger indicating they were to turn around. Mex felt his gun slip out of his waistband, and after quick pat-downs—the man had obviously done one or two—he signaled them to enter the restaurant. "Gun be your' when you lea'. Righ' now, it be mine." The man-mountain's Cajun rolled like honey out of his mouth. Mex barely got the gist. The guard didn't enter with them but stood sentry, presumably what he'd been doing when he and Darius had pulled up.

Mex wondered what the lookout was for. Was there more danger here than he'd considered?

The interior of the crab shack was murky. Light filtered through a window in a swinging door to the kitchen and blended substance and shadow. Weak moonlight messed with things from another angle. Well-worn tables stood empty and clean, scattered throughout the room. Several tables lined the glass wall that ran the width of the room at the far end. One caught his attention. A lit candle reflected off the glass, but not enough to reveal the features of the lone figure who sat waiting.

Mex and Darius took a few steps and stopped. Waited.

The shadowed form stood. In greeting or preparedness? "What's your business here?" Soft. A little sexy with business mixed in.

A woman! How many people does this guy have set up for them to get past?

"We're here to meet Cade LeBlanc." Mex felt as if he was a little too loud. A little too official. He dialed it back. "We have an appointment."

Although he couldn't see her face, Mex swore the woman smiled as she spoke. "Then I suggest you get yourselves over to my table before you're late and I decide I don't want to wait any more." Yep. Definitely. She was smiling. Mex could understand her smooth cadence easier than he could the giant's, but it still sounded like honey to him. Honey, with just a little bourbon.

He and Darius walked across the restaurant. Mex forced himself to look straight ahead, acutely aware of what he could and couldn't see peripherally.

"Please, gentlemen. It's just me and Boudreaux and Little Ray, aside from the two of you. Since Boudreaux wouldn't hurt a fly that was yammering at him for hours, I'm forced to bring Little Ray with me in case there's trouble."

"Little Ray?" Mex asked.

Cade LeBlanc laughed. He found himself drawn to the husky sound. "When we were kids, we grew up in the same neighborhood of camelbacks, and Ray was the tiniest kid around." She noted the questioning looks from both Mex and Darius. "A camelback is a house that's one story in front and two in back. Ya'll aren't from around here, are you? Anyway, he hated being called Little Ray, but there was nothing he could do about it. One night we went to sleep, and the next morning he'd blown up to giant-size."

"But you still call him Little Ray."

"Nothing he can do about it. When you live in a small place with big imagination, names stick."

Mex looked Ms. Cade LeBlanc over. Wavy hair, brown with a few streaks of red the flickering light picked up, but even more of gray. Average in just about every way except for a pair of enormous eyes. It was hard to tell in the candlelight, but he guessed they were green with some amber tossed in. Just a guess, but it felt right.

When all three were seated, Cade LeBlanc put her elbows on the table and leaned forward. She looked directly at Mex. "You've got a missing girl who is connected to a drug cartel."

"I do."

"You think Santeria is involved."

"I do."

"Then she's in trouble."

CHAPTER EIGHTEEN

Dia woke with a start and listened hard. She'd heard a noise. Where had it come from? What was it? *There.* A thump and voices. Outside. She pushed the light blanket off, pushed aside the mosquito netting and stepped to look out the window.

Pilar, Luis, and Hector were swaying and chanting. Sparks from the fire they stood around flew off into the night. What were they doing? If this was a Santeria ritual Dia wanted to be there.

Where did she leave her shoes? Come on, Dia, she thought. You would think in this small room she wouldn't lose anything. She dug around in her clothes bag. Nothing. Maybe if she stood on the deck it would be okay. She wouldn't need shoes if she didn't go down by the fire.

Dia padded barefoot to the door that led from the main area to the back deck and eased the screen open. She tried to be quiet, not because she was trying to be sneaky, but because she didn't want to interrupt a religious ritual. Softly closing the door behind her, she moved to the edge of the deck where she could more clearly see and hear what was going on.

It was a ritual all right. But the words were different from any she'd ever heard before. She'd have to ask Pilar what they meant.

Luis held something in his hand and raised it over his head. Dia gasped out loud when she realized it was a dead rooster. The man spun in her direction, the firelight carving angry lines in his face as he looked at her.

"You! Leave at once!" The venom of the words stung Dia and pushed her back from the deck rail. She knew Luis had mostly just put up with her, but now he sounded like he hated her. She sought Pilar. Their eyes met and Dia could not understand the expression on her nanny-turned-friend's face. Then Dia dropped her gaze down to what Pilar held in her hands.

My shoes.

***

Sedona couldn't sleep. She'd overheard her captor talking on the phone earlier. It sounded like he was talking to VV but she couldn't be certain. Whoever it was, they were making plans to move her. Something about the motel getting suspicious because Cigarette Breath told them he didn't want maid service.

Yeah, right. Like a maid ever touched this room. Oh please, God. I don't want to die here. And I don't want to go wherever they're going to take me. If this place was their first choice, she didn't want to think about what might be next.

She remembered the advice from the experts who said never let someone take you away from the place of first contact. She was already too late for the first move, but maybe there was something she could do about the second one.

At least if they were talking about moving her, they weren't going to kill her. Yet. She tried to push those thoughts away.

"C'mon, Princess. Here. Swallow this." Cigarette Breath forced a pill in her mouth.

She spit it out.

"Bitch, you forget who you're dealin' with. You think I don't have an option to a freakin' pill?" He bent over and plucked it out of the dirty carpet. Wiped it on his jeans. Sedona figured a needle probably wasn't any cleaner. The next time he stuffed it between her lips, she accepted the glass of water he held up and swallowed.

"We're relocatin'."

Great, Sedona thought. He'd wait until the sedative took effect and she was unable to fight back.

Teo, where are you?

CHAPTER NINETEEN

Mex pushed his chair back from the table. Confirmation of his worst fears made him want to take action. Do something.

"What can we do?" Darius asked the woman sitting next to him.

Cade LeBlanc looked from Darius to Mex and sighed. "Tell me everything you know about the drug cartel her father is involved with, including their rivals. I need to know names as well. Who was the nanny close to outside of the family? If you don't have this information now, get it by noon tomorrow. If what I suspect is right, we don't have much time. We might already be too late."

Mex stiffened. "What do you suspect?"

Cade looked away.

"Ma'am. We're tired. We've come a long way. What do you suspect?"

"Call me Cade."

Mex nodded.

"It is not unusual for drug cartel members to be involved in what I call extreme religions."

Mex waited.

Cade took a long pull from the bottle of beer sitting in front of her. "They include animal sacrifice. It can be horrific."

Mex waited.

"And within the cartels especially, the sacrifices often go beyond animals. We know that people have lost their lives in rituals where cartels hope to protect themselves from law enforcement."

Mex waited.

"Or to gain the upper hand over rival groups." Cade pushed the bottle away from her. "I suspect that a rival cartel is hoping to kill two birds with one stone by sacrificing the little girl. On one hand, in their minds, they might gain some elevation of protection or success, but most definitely they'll send a message."

Mex and Darius spent the next hour detailing everything they knew to Cade LeBlanc. She asked a lot of questions and they knew they had more research to do.

"I need you to find out whatever you can about the nanny's boyfriend. Luis is the key. He will lead us to the people responsible for the abduction of the girl."

"Why don't you use her name?" Mex asked. "Why don't you call her Dia?"

"Because I can't go there yet. It's how I remain professional. Clear-headed. Detached."

Mex squinted his eyes as he considered her words. "Why did you get involved in this line of work?"

Cade crossed her arms. "That's for another time, when and if I feel like sharing."

"Are you usually this easy to get along with?"

"Usually."

***

Mex wanted nothing more than to fall into the room and close the door to the rest of the world. To close the door to everyone and everything that took a breath. He had to focus hard to remove his clothes and crawl into bed. It had been all he could do to remain "in the moment" at the meeting with Cade LeBlanc.

His pattern rarely varied. He remembered his family as he'd seen each of them the last time they were alive. Then he saw the blood. Smelled it. Finally, he imagined what they might have been doing today if not for his choice of integrity—and a certain amount of arrogant pride—over their safety. Then the Sexy Siren of Void would seduce him. "Leave those thoughts. Come with me to a place where there is absolutely nothing."

But tonight was different. Even through his dark thoughts, even through the total numbness, he sensed there was something about Cade LeBlanc he might find interesting. Later. A sort of hopeful interest he wasn't quite ready to accept. Another day. He swallowed some more pills and sought the emptiness of dreamless sleep.

Which didn't come.

Mex finally gave in to a sleepless night and popped open his laptop. He sent off an email to Chase Waters in Aspen Falls. Chase was one of the few people he trusted, and the fact that he was a detective didn't hurt. He'd have some of the same contacts, or better, than Mex had and would be able to get the current cartel information Cade needed. Darius would probably run into a bunch of walls, and if Mex began asking the right questions their danger would increase. Besides, Darius was busy contacting his own sources to research Pilar and Luis, and asking Chase to fire up a search on Pilar and Luis would bring in a lot of law enforcement action they were better off avoiding. Chase was his man for the cartel aspect.

He checked his watch. Three o'clock. That would make it two o'clock in Colorado. He doubted if Chase would still be up, or if he was awake, on his computer. He was about to try a text when his phone rang.

He smiled when he saw who was calling. "You're up late."

Chase sighed. "Yeah, working on a case where I needed to talk to a guy in London first thing. He wanted to Skype before he left for work."

Mex considered his depression and insomnia. "Skyping with someone like me would be a bad idea. Don't think you'd want to see my mug tonight."

"I don't want to see your mug on a good night." There was a pause. "You're not doing any better since the night at Juan's?"

The attempted robbery at the bar seemed like years ago. "Not much."

Mex heard a dog barking. "Is that McKenzie?"

"Yeah, he's decided that since I'm still up there must be something nefarious going on."

"You need to keep better hours so your dog can get some sleep."

Chase laughed. "You want to meet for breakfast and catch me up? I might be able to have some of the cartel information you're looking for by then."

"Can't. I'm in New Orleans."

"You're there on the cartel case?"

"Cartels are involved, but it's not the main focus. The initial one, Senora-Ciento is the beginning point. As I said in the email, the key person connected to my case is Vicente Vega. I need to know what you can tell me about personal rivals inside his cartel, and who the outside challengers are. Has there been any bad blood spilled? Who would have it in for Vega? Also keep an eye out for any connections to religious cults, especially Santeria."

"This is all in your backyard, Mex. I mean, you know these guys. You could probably get information a lot faster."

"I can't afford to have it get out that I'm interested. And who knows who's been turned in Mexico? When I left they were falling like flies."

"Someone's life is at stake?"

Mex considered. He knew that Chase would connect any agreement to the "life at stake" question to Vega, but he also knew that his affirmative answer might make the father of three remember his own particular loss not too many years ago. Chase had lost a son. And almost lost a daughter. "Yeah. A little girl."

"Do I need to get official on this?"

"I'm trusting that you won't."

Chase paused. "I'm on it. Sleep is for wimps."

"Thank you, my friend."

"I'll have something for you when you wake up tomorrow."

"Like you, sleep is probably not coming any time soon. I owe you."

"I can never repay you for everything you've done for me. We're far from even, let alone you owing me. I'll talk to you tomorrow, in person or through email."

Mex sat his phone on the hotel desk and plugged in the charger. No way would he miss a call because of a dead battery.

Funny. Talking to Chase had lifted some of the darkness he'd been feeling. It was good to have someone else on his team digging up information. Someone he could count on.

Without even thinking much about sleep, Mex found his eyes shuttering. Knowing better than to question their heaviness, he moved quickly to his bed, pulled up the covers, and fell into a deep, dreamless sleep.

CHAPTER TWENTY

Mex pushed his eyes open to a darkened room, forgetting for a moment where he was. Once oriented, he threw off the bedding and plodded to the bathroom. He splashed water on his face before looking in the mirror.

"You look like hell."

He was in the shower when he remembered his conversation in the early morning hours with Chase Waters. He grabbed a towel and hurried to his laptop.

He powered it up and waited impatiently to access his email account. When he finally got in, he was gratified to see an email from Chase that had come in about two hours ago.

You are in the middle of a bad deal, Mex. The Senora-Ciento cartel has made a lot of enemies over the years. Vicente Vega has been grooming his son to take his place in the leadership. Trusted LEOs in the area tell me that Vicente Vega, Jr. is an entitled bad ass who's made enemies both inside and outside his own cartel.

Their main rival is a fairly new group called La Familia. LF has overpowered and absorbed three smaller groups in the last two years. There have been several standoffs between S-C and LF and a couple of nasty retaliation-type shootings.

I'll have to let you know about the cult thing. I've got a couple of contacts I made last year who might be able to help. One in particular is a Santeria guy who lives in Aspen Falls. He doesn't like me much but since when has that stopped me?

Stay safe and keep your cell on. I'll call you when I have something more.

***

Mex and Darius met for breakfast in the lobby restaurant. Café La Salle boasted a twenty-four hour buffet but neither man felt up to the effort a buffet required. Coffee came quickly and they placed their orders. Clearly the staff was used to dealing with the flying public.

Mex rubbed his hand over the stubble that covered the lower half of his face. "What did you find out?"

Darius took a sip of his coffee and watched Mex. "We'll get to that in a minute. You okay?"

I have a headache that would cripple an elephant, Mex thought. I have a river of dark water flowing through my mind that wants to pull me under, and I'm thinking that's not a bad thing. Instead of sharing his bleak thoughts, he said, "I'll be better when we get that little girl back where she belongs, whether she wants to be there or not. Now tell me what you've got."

Darius pulled out his tablet and keyed in a few prompts. "Where do you want me to start?"

"Cade LeBlanc."

"Good. She was easy. You know what we found searching Cade LeBlanc, but Acadia LeBlanc brought a whole new element to the story. Acadia was a smart little girl who grew up poor in a small parish outside of New Orleans. One of her first teachers took an interest early on and became a mentor. He even published a series of articles on the "Gem of the Gulf." I couldn't find the details but something must have happened to make an intelligent young girl give up a promising future to do what she does."

Darius paused and Mex took a sip of his coffee. He understood about turning points. "And then?"

"Then there's a gap until all of the recent data on her."

Mex waited.

"In addition to the news stories about people she's pulled out of cults, she's attended fundraisers for suicide awareness and depression. Whether or not there's a connection, I can't tell."

The depression piece froze in Mex's mind. It had touched Cade LeBlanc. Hell, it's touched most people if they just open their eyes. People with loved ones who suffered from this disease often developed radar. He would need to be on guard around her in the future. There might come a time soon when he would need her to trust him and not have a ghost from her past make her second-guess his choices.

Darius hit a key on his tablet and moved on. "Pilar Estrada Velasquez Villanueva was born in a tiny village in Cuba. She came to Florida when she was thirteen and was raised by relatives. She excelled in school, graduated early, and took evening classes at a local community college."

"What types of classes?"

"Psychology, family health, parenting. Those seemed to be her main choices."

"All good picks for someone who later became a nanny. Any other courses?"

"Funny you should ask. One titled Island Religions. Santeria and Santa Muerte factored heavily in the course."

"Would have thought she'd gotten all that in Cuba. Why take a class?"

Darius laid his tablet down. "I thought about that. She was only thirteen when her whole life changed. Maybe she didn't get all that much indoctrination in Cuba and wondered if she was missing out on something. She could have been missing home, ya know?"

"Where's her family?"

"Dead."

"All of them? How?"

"Mostly natural causes, but two brothers were gunned down in Nogales, Arizona. Their murders were never solved."

"Cartel connection?"

"Unknown. If they were in a cartel, they were pretty damned low on the scorecard. But given the odds, it's safe to say that drugs were involved. And if drugs were involved in that part of the country, the cartel had to be close."

"Do me a favor, Darius. Don't play the odds or make assumptions. When we do that, we run the risk of missing something important."

"Sorry, but other than background, I don't see these deaths having any direct connection to what's happening with Pilar. Consider my comment speculation and not assumption."

Mex nodded. "What about Luis Alvarez?"

"I'm coming up with nothing on him."

"What does that mean?"

"It means I haven't been able to find anything. No social networking, no public records, nothing."

Mex felt his anger rising. "How hard have you tried? You get info on everyone and everything. A girl's life is at stake." *Not to mention my own sister's*, he thought.

"Look, I know you're in a bad way, and you're frustrated."

Mex could not have heard any worse words at that moment. He squeezed the hostile feelings he wanted to unleash deep into his gut, right next to the ulcer that was surely forming. His fingers bit the edges of the table until they turned white. *Let it go. He's right. I am in a bad way. Breathe. I know how depression affects my reason. Breathe.* "I need some answers."

"I can't give you answers I don't have, Mex."

"I need someone I can rely on." Mex regretted the words the minute he said them.

"I have a hormonal wife and a psycho friend. Where the hell did I go wrong?"

Mex couldn't bring himself to apologize. He wanted a fight. Even if it was with one of his best friends. "If I can't count on you, I don't need you around. You can just go piss off somewhere else."

"I've dug up pertinent information for you. I've spent hours away from home to help you. I've even put myself in dangerous situations for you. Where the hell do you get off questioning me?"

"I will find out about Luis Alvarez myself. All you want is a story—a book deal. If Dia is killed before I can get to her, you will be as much to blame as me." Mex threw a few bills on the table and left, swallowing another pill as he walked out the door.

CHAPTER TWENTY-ONE

Once Mex left the hotel restaurant his steps faltered, his shoulders sagged and his head drooped. He was at the end of the road. He'd found himself unable to appreciate his friend. A man who had always been there for him. If he was totally honest, it was he who was failing. Not Darius.

He punched the elevator button and waited.

A little girl named Dia deserved the chance to grow up, and his own sister had already sacrificed so much of her life to take care of him.

Sacrifice. That word again. He had to stop this pattern. Sacrifice never led to anything positive.

He needed to pull himself together. Find a way. Find Dia. Was Luis the key, as Cade thought?

When he arrived at his room, Mex pulled out his phone and keyed in the number. Waited. Cursed. Waited some more while it rang.

"Did you find her?" Vicente Vega almost gasped.

"Not yet."

"She's dead then."

"We don't know that. We really don't know anything yet."

"If she is still alive, every minute marks itself as one moment closer to her death."

Mex waited for the cartel head, the father, to calm down.

"Why are you calling me?"

"I need you to look inside your own organization. I have a name. Before I give it to you, I need you to fully understand that if you don't keep this quiet, your daughter could die. Do you understand?"

Silence.

"If you breathe this name to the wrong person, Dia is dead. There are a lot of wrong people, Vega, including those you may have no reason to suspect. If you don't have anyone you can trust, then you're better off not asking about him. Do you understand what I'm saying?"

"Is this the name of the man who has my daughter?"

"I don't know."

"But he's connected?"

"He could be."

"What's his name?"

"Luis Alvarez."

"This man has my little girl?"

"I told you, I don't know. I think there might be a connection."

"I don't know the name, but I'll find out who he is. Is he in my organization?"

"I don't know that either. I want to find out as much as possible. He could be a key. But if he's a really big key, you have to understand you could be signing Dia's death warrant if you're too overt."

"I understand."

"I also need to know who in La Familia might want to do this to you. To Dia. And if not La Familia, then who?"

Silence.

Mex hardened his tone. "La Familia, Vega. Who?"

"There is intense competition between our cartels. Some have died."

"Yeah, and?"

"Most wouldn't dare to bring me harm. I'm too powerful."

"But someone might be as powerful as you are, and willing to take the risk."

"Let me think about this."

Mex ended the call.

Now what?

He sat down and started going through all of his notes and printouts again. There had to be something here. Twenty minutes later he had a theory. But it needed to be checked out. Fast.

And Darius already had the connections.

Damn. When would he learn how to keep his thoughts to himself?

Mex walked through the adjoining door. Darius was sprawled out in the corner armchair, the remote control for the television in his hand. A glass with ice and amber liquid twirled in his other hand. He was watching a news stream from the BBC about a bold jewelry store heist. A part of Mex's brain registered that the UK seemed to have a lot of exceptionally brazen thefts. With a click, the Denver Nuggets battled to maintain their narrow lead in a rare playoff game. So what else was new?

Mex slipped into the room and sat on the edge of the bed. Darius clicked back and forth between the channels without acknowledging Mex's presence.

Screw this. He and Darius would take care of the details later. The make-up shit. Right now he needed information. "Do you have access to the student registrar where Pilar was taking classes?"

Darius clicked the remote, moving from a weather map of the gulf area to a scene featuring Leonard Nimoy in his Spock role.

"Do you?" Mex asked again.

"I could probably get in."

"Can you access a list of previous students?"

Darius clicked back to the basketball game. Watched one of the Nugget players pass the ball to a teammate, then move to receive it under the basket. The crowd didn't explode as Mex thought it would at the two-point score. He checked the time left. A lot. No wonder. Close wasn't close until it was the end of the game.

He and Darius were at the end of *their* game.

"Can you?" Mex repeated his question.

"If I can get in or connect with an insider, I can probably access anything." Darius clicked back to the BBC channel. He hadn't looked Mex in the eye once since he'd come into the room.

"I want you to look for a student, or a staff member. One that would have completed that Island Religions class before Pilar, or maybe they were the instructor or assistant."

"Name?"

Mex worked to soften his voice. "Luis Alvarez."

CHAPTER TWENTY-TWO

Mex and Cade sat at the same table they'd sat at the night before. Mex figured it was probably Cade's table, similar to his booth at Juan's. Storm clouds were forming. Another New Orleans soaker was about to break loose.

He looked around and was impressed. For being out in the middle of nowhere, Boudreaux's did some damn good lunch business. His law radar had beeped when he saw the steady stream of customers, and he spent several minutes watching them. His experience said this much traffic had something to do with drugs. Or money laundering. Or both. Apparently all of these people were here for the food.

"Yat." A voice called from behind him.

"Yat." Cade replied.

Mex decided it must be some kind of greeting.

"What'll you have?" A waitress stood next to their table. A hundred pounds soaking wet, she looked to be in her mid-forties. A few wrinkles and kind eyes.

Mex pointed to Cade. "Ladies first."

"I already know what Cade is having. She's having whatever I surprise her with. It's our tradition." The waitress grinned.

Cade leaned in. "You can't go wrong at Boudreaux's. They make everything from scratch and from fresh. And it doesn't matter who's cooking, it's done right."

"It's done right, with good *lagniappe*, or my granddaddy's ghost gets downright mean."

Cade laughed. Mex thought he might like hearing that throaty sound every day.

"Bring my friend a sampler. A little bit o' dis and a little bit o' dat. Let him see for himself. And bring both of us a home brew."

When the waitress left, Mex arched an eyebrow toward Cade LeBlanc. "Am I still in America?"

"You're in the *best* part of America."

"Yat?"

That laugh again. "Ah... you question our language. *Yat* can work itself into our conversations in a couple of ways. It's a standard greeting, a conversation opener. It's also used to describe a true native of N'awlins."

Mex nodded. Just as he thought. "And land app?"

Cade screwed her face up. "Say again?"

"Land app. Or lawn app. Something like that."

This time she laughed louder. A few diners looked their way and Mex felt himself blushing. Good thing it didn't display very well.

"Lagniappe. It's when someone gives a little extra that the customer doesn't pay for. A thank you—like a baker's dozen. Something to sweeten the deal."

The waitress returned with two frosted glasses holding a dark amber liquid.

"Home brew?"

"If you've ever tasted beer this good anywhere else in the world, I'll eat the next gator raw and all by myself."

Mex stuck his nose into the glass and sniffed. Took a tiny sip. Then a bigger sip. Finally he swallowed. "Damn."

"Boudreaux's knows more than just a little cookin'."

"Is this legal?"

Cade stiffened a little and jutted her chin into the air. "They have a license."

He'd erased a lot of the goodwill he'd been building. "Sorry."

She sniffed. "It's okay. You probably can't help it."

It was Mex's turn to laugh. "Yeah, you've got that right. Once a lawman, always a lawman."

"Since you brought it up, why are you helping out a member of a drug cartel?"

Sobered, Mex replied, "A little girl's life is at stake."

"Maybe I should rephrase my question. Why would a member of a drug cartel seek your help? Why would he even think you'd say yes? I checked you out. You don't need the money."

Touché. He guessed she'd probably figured out that he knew about her past as well. "It's personal."

"Yeah, well. It gets real personal when I'm in the middle of a large number of hostile people trying to pull out someone who thinks that's exactly where they are supposed to be. Someone who thinks I'm the enemy. So excuse me if I have a few questions."

The waitress drew up with two platters filled with the best-smelling food Mex had ever experienced. The presentation was elegant. Beautiful. If this was a crab shack, he wondered what a four-star restaurant in these parts might have to offer. He had to keep swallowing or he'd drool.

"See what I mean? And you haven't even had a taste." Cade unfolded her napkin onto her lap. "You might want to consider hooking yours into your neckline. Unless you're used to this, things can get a little out of hand."

Mex considered, then stuck the napkin inside the top of his shirt. The food—this fabulous food—was acting as a mediator for their discussion. A conversation bordering on things he wasn't ready to talk about.

He took a bite of something he couldn't quite identify. "This tastes a little like chicken, only better." He thought she'd say something about frogs or alligators.

"Well, my new friend, that's because it *is* chicken. But done the Boudreaux way. You won't taste any better, even from your mama."

Mex remembered his mom. She was beautiful but not the best cook in the world. Thank goodness for cheese and salsa. He took another bite. What the hell did they do to make chicken taste so... so... extravagant? If he finished this case, and finished it well, he would be back here to talk to the cooks—hell, the chefs—at a little crab shack out in the swamps of Louisiana.

After indulging in a most sumptuous meal, he pushed his chair back and relaxed.

"Are you ready to answer my question? The personal bit?"

"Do you know what happened to my family?" Mex wiped his mouth with the huge napkin. Boudreaux's took care of every need of their customers.

Cade shook her head.

Mex waited while strong black coffee was served, then told her his story about that horrible day in Agua Prieta.

"I'm sorry, Mex. No one should have to deal with that kind of loss."

He closed his eyes and forced the images away. "I hunted their killers. I tracked them through Mexico to Venezuela and finally to Honduras."

"Did you find them?"

"They were killed before I could get to them."

"Killed? How?"

"By their own cartel. It involved hatchets, mallets, and buzzards. The only way I know for sure it was them was someone videotaped the killings and made sure I got a copy. There was no evidence left, not even a skull. It seems I was getting in the way of their daily operations. It made sense to get rid of the two people I'd been hunting half way around the world so they could focus on the business at hand."

"Why didn't they just kill you?"

Mex blew out air in a half laugh, half grimace. "I asked a friend of mine, an old time Federale, the same thing. He said there was one message in a dead lawman, but a bigger message in the death of a lawman's family and the world watching him fall apart. Making me the walking dead suited their purposes at the time."

"And now? Why are you doing this?"

"I told you. A little girl is in danger and because of my contacts I might be able to save her."

"Sorry. I'm not buying it. Why did her father come to you?"

Mex thought about the promise of information. Of a direct lead to the man who put out the kill order on his family. This was not the time to share. "You'd have to ask him."

"Fine. Be that way. Do you have all of the information I wanted?"

"Most of it."

"Give me what you've got."

Mex detailed the background Darius had received on Pilar. Cade took notes and asked pertinent questions.

"What about Luis Alvarez?"

"We're still digging."

"You can't think I'd ever be able to take any kind of action without knowing what I was up against. Even if I could find the exact location of Dia, going in without full data could be suicide. I told you I needed to know everything."

"And I've given you everything I have."

"It's not enough."

"Damn it, Cade. A girl's life is in danger."

"I get that. But going in without intel on the people involved doesn't help her, and could kill both of us."

"We need to formulate a plan based on what we know now, even though we don't know crap. There isn't much time." Mex would have grabbed her and shaken her if he believed it would help. "Do you get what's at stake?"

"I get it. I also get that if we go in half-assed, she's dead. I need as much as I can get."

"You should be able to achieve results even without knowing everything."

"What are you saying? Are you saying I'm overly cautious?"

"If the shoe fits."

"I'd like all of us to survive this."

Mex sat back in his chair and took a deep breath. In a moment, conversations in the restaurant filtered back into his awareness. He looked out of the large windows. Cyprus and tupelo gum trees spiked out of the water like green sentinels. A Louisiana heron zeroed in on some prey and made a strike in the murky water. As intriguing as this part of the country was, he had a momentary pang for the fresh air of Colorado.

Mex pulled his gaze back to the woman who sat in front of him. "I'm sorry. You didn't deserve that."

Cade narrowed her eyes and brought the beer up to her lips. Rather than taking a drink, she tilted it to the side. "I like your passion."

"Yeah, well. Passion is one thing. Action is something else. But thanks."

Cade took a long swallow and set the empty bottle back on the table. "Where are you looking for information on Luis Alvarez?"

"He and Pilar are a couple. They had to meet somewhere. Darius is checking out the community college Pilar attended. If we can get any bit of information, like an address, we can find out everything about him including where he might be right now. I've also got Vicente Vega doing some discreet inquiries within his own cartel."

"I have another idea."

"Yeah?"

"I can talk to a few of my own contacts. If they are deeply into either Santeria or Santa Muerte, someone might know who he is."

"Good."

Mex's phone rang. Darius. "What do you have?"

"You were right. Luis Alvarez was an assistant to a professor at the college the same time as Pilar attended the school. The address he gave isn't good any more, but the emergency contact is. And get this—she lives in Metairie."

Mex suddenly remembered what had struck him when the idea of Louisiana first came up. The gulf coast location had come up in their last staff interview at the Vega compound "What's her name?"

"Sanchez. Margarita. She's Alvarez's grandmother."

"Get me whatever you can on her. Find out who else is living there now, and get me some background on them as well." Mex paused. "Good work."

He ended the call and turned to Cade. "We've got a lead on Alvarez. And she's local."

A clap of thunder and rain fell to the earth, unleashed and wild. Cade barely seemed to notice. "You won't be going very far in this. If the parking lot isn't already a swimming hole, the road has turned into a river. Sit back and relax."

"Relax? You've got to be kidding."

"Humor me. Just don't get all anxious or depressed on me."

Mex sniffed. "Relax it is."

Rain slammed against the windows and the noise echoed in the large dining room. The powerful storm was at odds with the reflective mood he slipped into. The idea to relax must have worked.

Mex watched the candlelight wash gently over Cade's face in the storm darkened restaurant. He wanted to tell her she was a beautiful woman but he wasn't ready to go there. They sat in comfortable silence and listened to the tempest outside.

An hour later he was on his way back to the hotel and wondering if he'd missed an opportunity.

CHAPTER TWENTY-THREE

The next morning, Mex sat outside the small brick home and watched. Margarita Sanchez lived there with her daughter, granddaughter and great-grandson. He'd been surprised by all of the brick homes even in the poorest neighborhoods until he realized that frame homes would probably rot quickly in the damp.

The daughter and granddaughter had taken off for work. Darius found out they both had jobs at the Harrah's in New Orleans. That left the old woman and her great-grandson. Mex checked his watch. Then he called Darius, glad they had a friendship that pulled back together after one of them, usually him, acted like a jackass.

"The daughter and granddaughter have left," Mex updated his partner. "If we're right, when you call and start asking questions about Luis, she'll leave. If she takes the little boy, she'll never notice a tail."

Once they'd gotten the hit on Luis Alvarez's grandmother, they were able to unearth a ton of information. Most important, Chase had called to let him know that Luis was heavily involved in both Santeria and the La Familia cartel. Because local law enforcement officers had been shadowing him off and on for years, he'd developed an old-style way of communicating that had served him well. Like the spies of old, he had drop off points where notes could be left if someone had to contact him.

Depending on the urgency, he'd find a way to communicate verbally or in person. About the time the local guys figured this out their attention was drawn to more immediate concerns. A small time Santeria follower with ties to a drug cartel would have to wait.

Mex looked at his watch again. If their plan worked, Grandma should be heading out any minute now.

He waited. Nothing.

Three minutes. Five. Maybe they'd been wrong. He was about to call Darius to try and figure out what had happened when Margarita Sanchez emerged from the front door, a bright yellow and blue scarf over her head. She was tugging a reluctant boy down the steps to the driveway. The woman herded her great-grandson into the passenger side of an old Mazda, then glanced up and down the street before she walked around the car and got in. After a couple of failed starts, the engine caught and she backed out into the street. As she passed by him, Mex could see her fussing with her passenger. Good.

He pulled up and into the nearest driveway, then backed out to follow. His cell rang. Darius.

"It worked. I'm tailing her now."

"When you get to the drop, call me with the address. I'll run a program to find out the names of all of the property owners in the area."

"What if he's a tenant?"

"That'll take longer."

"I'm hoping Alvarez will come by and I can follow him. I don't want to have to wait for a damn database of names."

"Any idea where she's heading?"

"Into the city. That's all I've got right now."

"Let me know if I can help."

He ended the call and worked to follow the Mazda without appearing too obvious. The woman drove slower than a sloth and he was afraid she'd notice anyone who didn't pass her. When she exited I-10 onto Orleans Avenue, he had a good idea where she was going. He hoped the French Quarter wasn't packed with tourists. Even moving slowly, she could be easy to lose.

His phone rang. VV. "Anderson."

"Have you found my sister?"

If the man didn't have Sedona's life in his hands, Mex would have shared a few choice words for interrupting him while he was working to do exactly that. "Tracking a lead right now."

"This Luis Alvarez person?"

Shit. "How did you hear about Alvarez?"

"I have learned to take an interest in anyone who interests my father. When he wouldn't tell me why he was asking about this person—someone I'd never heard of before—I naturally assumed he might be connected to the disappearance of my sister. My father does not ask idle questions. I can assist you in locating him if you'd like."

All Mex needed was more people stirring the pot. "I think we're close. Thanks for your offer though."

"Hey, it's not only *my* sister's life at stake."

"If any harm comes to Sedona you and I will get to know each other on a very personal level."

Mex hung up. He had nothing more to say and the Mazda had pulled onto Basin Street and then into the parking lot for St. Louis Cemetery No.1. Mex pulled in behind her and found a parking space where he could watch the old woman's actions without being too conspicuous. This part of the cemetery hadn't changed since he and Maria had celebrated their anniversary in the French Quarter.

***

Margarita Sanchez sat in the front seat with her head bowed. Praying? Could be she was praying for Luis, could be she always said a prayer when she went to one of the cities of the dead. He wondered what the entity's name was she prayed to. She said something to the boy, then they both emerged.

The woman had her pocketbook looped over her forearm as she folded a piece of paper. She'd been writing a note, not praying. Smaller and smaller she folded the paper until it fit neatly into her palm. With her free hand, she grabbed the boy and pulled him to her side as they made their way to the entrance gates. Her bright yellow and blue scarf caught the sun like a spotlight.

A walking tour was forming and Mex debated whether to let them remain between himself and Sanchez. Tourists came from all over to see the tombs, or vaults, of the oldest cemetery in New Orleans. The unique method of burial, necessary because of the water level, made for some interesting history. He slipped out of the car.

Mex paused with the group and heard the guide say that the family tombs dated back generations.

"But they're so small. How can they hold all of those coffins?" a fanny-packed, umbrella-toting visitor asked.

The guide smiled. He'd obviously heard this question often. "Some are quite large, but you're right—even the big ones would run out of room after a few generations." The guide got a conspiratorial look on his face. "Once a body has been in there for at least two years, it can be placed in a specially made burial bag and removed to either the back or side of the vault."

Synchronized dying, Mex thought. He decided at the last minute that the group would probably be even slower than Grandma so he scooted around them while they were still gathering with their guide.

The old woman was brave to walk this cemetery on her own. Muggers often hid behind the freestanding tombs and relieved unwary explorers, also known as stupid tourists, of their cash and jewelry. Mex figured that Margarita Sanchez knew the twisted, narrow paths and would not walk into a dangerous dead end. She was marching with a purpose, not wandering around in awe of the surroundings. That, plus the fact she wasn't alone, probably made her less of a target. Even a young boy would make her less of an easy target, and the muggers he'd known were all for easy.

It had been years since Mex was last in this cemetery. Even before Katrina many tombs sat in a decayed state, chunks crumbling onto the walkways in piles of tired mortar and history. Post storm, even though he saw additional degradation, he was surprised not to see complete and utter devastation.

A few tombs had a voodoo connection. Piles of offerings that included flowers, Mardi Gras beads, liquor, cigarettes, votive candles, and just about anything else you could imagine were colorful invocations for favors to be granted by the occupants. Multiple triple "X's", which some think of as a voodoo mark, had been painted on every flat surface of the voodoo-oriented tombs. It was Mex's opinion that this practice began as an anonymous signature by people seeking to have their wishes granted. He wondered if one of these tombs was Grandma's destination.

Mex followed down a new aisle and felt a moment of panic. Grandma was gone. She must have turned again. *Where the hell did she go?* He quickened his step, peered down another path and caught a glimpse of yellow before it disappeared. He'd be lucky if he found his way out of here before some voodoo priestess became aware of his presence. He rushed to the corner, and feeling a bit like one of the muggers he'd heard so much about, took a surreptitious glance around a particularly decrepit family vault.

The woman and the boy had moved to the back of an ordinary looking tomb. All Mex could see were their shadows. He knew what they were doing and moved to the side of another ancient structure where he would be hidden from view. He heard them walking in his direction.

"Can we get some beignets? Please? At Café Du Monde?" The little boy asked in English, completely surprising Mex. He would have laid down a large bet that Great-Grandma only spoke Spanish.

"Yes, Marco. But not Café Du Monde. That is a place for outsiders."

"Please? I like to look at all the pretty people."

The woman grabbed the boy's arm. "Quit whining or there will be no sweets for you for the rest of the week."

The two passed and Mex found a small bench. He pulled out his phone and called Darius. "I've got the drop site. It's in St. Louis Cemetery No. 1. Run a two-mile radius, but focus on the Iberville Projects. They're right behind the cemetery."

"Got it. You okay?"

"I'll wait to see who shows to pick up the note from Grandma."

"That's not what I meant."

"I'm good."

"Yeah?"

"Yeah."

"Fine. I'll let you know what I find out."

"Don't call me. Even on vibrate the sound might carry. I'll check back with you in an hour."

CHAPTER TWENTY-FOUR

Darius set the phone down and booted up his computer. He'd begin with the easily accessed public records. If he had to, he'd play his journalist card with his contact in the local media—an old newspaper guy who knew how to keep his mouth shut and wait for a kick-ass story. No way would most of the television journalists he knew understand the importance of patience. And trust. And IOUs.

Thank goodness for stand-up guys like Martin Van Buren. Darius smiled. He remembered how Van Buren had introduced himself the first time they'd met at one of the many journalist conventions around the country. Van Buren had looked Darius dead in the eye. "Yeah, I know. He was an asshole. But I'm not—unless the story requires one." Then he'd winked and raised his drink.

Too bad journalists like Martin Van Buren were becoming relics.

Darius logged in to the property rolls and hoped that the Napoleonic law particular to Louisiana wouldn't hinder his search. Real estate laws in this southern state required a law degree of their own. After twenty minutes of nothing, he decided to give Martin a call.

After the usual jibes about each other's heritage and limited chit-chat, Martin asked Darius why he'd called. Darius gathered his thoughts. His old friend was not apt to miss a note, and he didn't want to hit a wrong one.

"I need to find someone who might be hard to find. He has relatives in the area, but that doesn't mean he's anywhere around."

"It's important?"

"It's important."

"You've got the story?"

Darius hesitated. "It's important enough that I'll give you the quick shot—the immediate story—but the book is mine."

"Talk to me."

With "off the record" on the record, Darius laid out the pertinent facts, omitting all the names except for those of Luis Alvarez and Margarita Sanchez. "Finding this guy could lead us to the missing girl. And we need to find her fast."

"Time frame?"

"Yesterday."

"Got it."

"Look, my partner is calling me in less than an hour. I need to have something for him."

"Then let's hang up the damn phone so I can get to work."

Darius went back online. He was tempted to continue his research efforts, but decided he'd wait to see if Martin came up with something before Mex contacted him. Research at this point might lead to attempted hacking, and a hacking charge, even if he was able to do it, would be time consuming and expensive.

He went to the fridge and pulled out one of the beers Mex had brought earlier. When he got to the sofa, he pushed his laptop closed and propped his feet on the coffee table. He wished he could think of a way to permanently help his friend get well.

Aspen Falls almost six years ago. He'd spotted Mex as a fish out of water at the E-Lev 2, a popular Aspen Falls restaurant, almost immediately. But Darius's already keen sense of a story told him the gray-eyed Mexican was an *interesting* fish out of water. They'd connected, Darius offering up a community tour of sorts, and a friendship was born. It was the kind of friendship only guys could form. Firm. Fast. But with limited sharing of history. It went from tentative to a version of "semi-solid unless you give me reason to dump your ass" in almost record time. And since there'd been no reason to dump one another's asses, they'd been friends ever since.

And still, Mex had only recently told him about what had happened to his family. The pain he'd come from. The pain he'd lived through. Now the depression made sense. Darius couldn't imagine surviving that kind of horror. This explained the sudden bursts of anger that seemed out of proportion to the situation that had occurred from the beginning of their friendship. Darius had always let it go and they'd managed to go on.

He knew Mex well enough to know that Mex was holding something back. Hell, based on the story he'd told him, Mex might be holding a lot of things back. Still, he trusted him. When Mex was ready, he'd tell Darius whatever he'd been keeping secret.

His phone rang. He smiled when he saw who was calling. "My sweet, sweet Pamela. How did you know I needed to hear your voice?"

He heard his wife choke with tears. Gasp for breath.

He froze. "Pammy?"

"Oh, God."

Darius felt his heart rate double. "What's wrong?" He waited, feeling his world skid to a stop. "Are the kids okay? Is the baby okay? Has something happened?"

Please God, please God, please God. Oh, please God.

He heard her clear her throat. Suck in a breath. "We're fine. We're all fine." Another choke. Not like Pamela.

But he could breathe again. "Honey, what is it?"

"I got a call."

He waited, giving his wife time to pull her thoughts together.

"I got a call. On my cell. We were at the grocery store. He said... he said...." Her voice trailed off to more sobs.

"Shake it off, Pamela. Shake it off. I need to know what's happened."

"He said...that if you didn't let this hunt for the girl go... he said your family would pay the price. That he would make sure we all died and that you would know it before he had you killed as well."

Blood roared in his ears and drowned out all coherent thought. He closed his eyes and willed it still. Darius waited for his wife to catch her breath.

"And that's not all."

Darius hadn't realized he'd been pacing like a madman until he stopped. "What else?"

"By the time we got home, I'd managed to calm down a little. I didn't want the kids to see me freaking out, you know?"

Darius nodded. "Yeah, baby. Good thinking."

"I thought I'd just get the mail, put on some mac and cheese, then find a quiet place to give you a call."

"That's my girl."

A wracking sob ripped through the phone, straight to his heart. Pamela said something he couldn't understand. "Pammy, speak slower. Tell me slowly."

"I reached in the mailbox without looking." Her voice shook. "Inside was a headless chicken."

CHAPTER TWENTY-FIVE

Dia wanted to know what was going on and no one would talk to her. She might as well be back home. She stomped from the deck into the house, making sure the screen door slammed as loud as she could.

When she'd walked outside five minutes earlier, Pilar, Luis and Hector's conversation stopped. And then Pilar started some lame thing about her list of what she wanted Luis and Hector to pick up for her when they went to the city. Like she was a little kid who would never pick up on the fact that they were keeping a secret from her.

Did it have anything to do with the ritual she'd seen the other night? The one where Pilar had her shoes? Pilar had told her she'd found them on the deck and was hanging on to them to remember to bring them to her. Dia wanted so badly to believe her friend she actually thought maybe she'd left them outside for some reason, even though that didn't feel right.

They were obviously preparing for some other visitors. She figured it must be the ones they'd been talking about the first night they got here—when she'd overheard them in the car while they thought she was asleep in the backseat.

She was getting tired of all the secrets.

***

Sedona knew she was back in Mexico before she opened her eyes. She heard Spanish being spoken outside a window that brought in the smells she'd grown up with in Agua Prieta. But there was more noise here. More energy.

Then she knew. VV had brought her to Monterrey. Does Vicente know she's here? *Oh, God. Help me.* Anything could happen to me now and no one would know.

Would anyone care?

Why move her here? The answer to that question was simpler. More control. More cops in his pocket. He must have border guards on the payroll as well. She felt the beginnings of a headache.

The sheets surrounding her were soft and fresh. This was definitely not the same kind of motel room where she'd first woken up...when? She'd lost all track of time. An eyelid opened enough to see her nearest surroundings. Tile floors. A white dust ruffle. Colorfully painted furniture legs. She shifted. White baseboards, yellow walls, white curtains billowing in the breeze.

She popped both eyes open. An open window! At the very least she could call for help. She moved to swing her legs over the side of the bed only to find she was strapped down. If she screamed, what would happen?

"Help! Help me! I've been kidnapped!" Immediately footsteps crossed the floor and pulled the window closed.

"I was trying to make you comfortable." VV swung around. His cold eyes softened and she knew he remembered the infrequent, but special, connection they'd had in the past. He'd only been a boy, but she'd taken the time to talk to him, even given him a hug when she felt he could use one. "I could always have you gagged again."

"No. Please don't."

"Promise not to scream?"

"I promise."

VV moved to the window and threw it open wider. The ceiling fan grabbed the fresh air and spun it around the room.

Would this supposed to make her grateful? *Please let me survive and get back to my life.*

"Why am I here?"

The young man put his hands on his hips. "You are my insurance."

"Insurance? Insurance for what?" Maybe they were after Teo's money after all. *Damn him. Damn his money.*

"You are my insurance that your brother will do everything possible to bring my little sister home where she belongs."

"Dia? I'm here because of what happened to Dia? What did happen, VV?"

"We don't know. She's gone missing."

"She ran away?" If Dia ran away, he couldn't possibly hold her prisoner. That would be a family matter, not something either she or Mex could be expected to resolve.

"Listen to me, woman. We. Don't. Know."

Sedona fell silent as she processed this new element of the little boy she once knew. He would never have been this disrespectful when he was younger.

"Does your father know I'm here?"

VV turned his back on her and paced to the door. He turned, hand on the knob. "Someone will be here shortly to address your needs." With that he was gone.

Vicente Vega did not know she was here. For some reason, VV was acting on his own.

What the hell was going on?

CHAPTER TWENTY-SIX

Mex rubbed his stiff muscles. He'd never been good on stakeouts, and now that he was older there were more reasons to hate them. He keyed a button on his phone and waited. "Hey, Darius. What do you have? Can you pinpoint Luis Alvarez in this area?"

"He had an apartment in Iberville until about a week ago. The manager said he just turned in his keys and took off."

Mex felt a twist in his gut and he squinted. Something was off with Darius, something in his voice, but now wasn't the time to talk about it. "We've got a meet-up scheduled with Cade at seven to review everything. At Boudreaux's. I'll stick here in case Alvarez shows, but I'm not confident. Especially since he's apparently moved on."

"Yeah, but it's a recent move. He may not have had time to tell Grandma."

"Good point."

"Meet you at the shack?"

Mex sensed there would be more coming when they finally met up. "Yeah. Seven. See you then."

Darius ended the call without saying goodbye. Not a good sign. Mex knew his friend had been blindsided by something that was throwing him off his game. They'd talk about it tonight.

Mex rolled his neck and shoulders. Stretched his legs. He needed to be quiet and hidden. Should a tourist wander back here, he didn't want to create a stir. He'd stake out the drop until he needed to leave for the meeting. Not too hopeful that anyone would actually show up, his mind worked to find something engaging.

Brief family moments, like movie clips, flashed through his mind. He and Sedona as kids, the first time he met his wife, Christmas celebrations with the entire family. Flashes of funeral services inserted themselves. The loss and devastation. Then short shots of his home in Aspen Falls. The one he and Maria had dreamed about and designed. The project that had kept him sane when every day was a battle to survive.

He shifted and stretched his muscles, one at a time. Waited. Listened. Stretched. Watched.

Late afternoon clouds began to fill the sky and Mex could smell rain. The heavens were about to dump on this part of town, and he didn't want to get soaked. He figured he had just enough time to get back to the hotel and put on a clean shirt for the meeting with Cade and Darius.

He rose to his feet and froze. Someone was nearby. Mex looked around the edge of the tomb. A hooded figure was behind the same tomb Margarita Sanchez had stood at only a few hours before. Mex backed up and waited. When he heard the footsteps begin to recede, he moved to follow.

Fat raindrops hit the ground like water bullets. The hooded figure broke into a jog and Mex matched him. All the visitors were jogging toward the parking lot and their cars and no one noticed anyone else.

Was he trailing *the* Luis Alvarez? Or someone Luis had sent to check his drop? Or just some guy who happened to hit the spot while Mex was watching?

The clouds opened up and threw down so much water it was hard to believe they'd been through a big rainstorm yesterday. While Mex moved to his rental, Hoody hopped into the passenger side of a four-door sedan.

Shit. Mex doubled his running speed and had the key in the ignition before he shut the door. He was pulling out even before he located the windshield wiper switch. He saw the sedan turn.

Umbrellas were blooming everywhere in the parking lot and because of that people were acting momentarily brain-dead and not paying attention to two-thousand pounds of metal coming in their direction. Mex had to break twice before he got to the exit and turned to pursue the car.

The driver and Hoody weren't in a tremendous hurry, which was good because the rain was so heavy the windshield wipers weren't keeping up with the deluge. Mex pulled out his cell and thumbed a key.

"Hey. Raining where you are?"

Darius laughed, but he still sounded off. "I'm trying to locate Noah's descendants. Figure they might have had a heads up."

"Need you to meet Cade without me. Someone showed up at the drop and I'm following them now."

"Them?"

"Guy in a hoody was at the drop. Someone else is driving."

"Direction?"

"You're kidding, right? It's all I can do to follow the damn car in this rain."

Mex watched the car pull to the curb about a block ahead of him and another person dashed from the shelter of a storefront into the backseat.

***

The sedan took I-10 east toward Slidell. Traffic was terrible, but Mex was able to stick pretty close without being too conspicuous. Drivers were dealing with rain and forward visibility, not so much what or who was in their rearview mirrors. Still, he allowed a couple of cars as buffers between them.

He didn't even know for sure that he was following anyone connected to Luis Alvarez, let alone Alvarez himself. It was just a damned guess. But it was the best damned guess he could make.

Frustration pushed his patience to the limit. Sedona was being held against her will. He tried not to imagine what might be happening to the only surviving family member he had in the world.

Where the hell were they going? Based on the highway signs, and assuming he was able to see, about now he'd be looking out over Lake Ponchartrain.

When the sedan neared the Slidell exit, Mex hoped this was the destination. He was tired. Hungry. And really needing his meds. But they passed Slidell. *Shit.*

And then all hell broke loose. A tanker truck, driving too fast for the conditions, had to brake suddenly to avoid hitting a stalled car. Even though it was in the far right lane, the back end swung in front of the other traffic lanes and forced every driver to apply their brakes. Hard. The driver of a red SUV, following too close to the Volvo in front, managed to pile into it, further spreading the chaos. A rusted and battered Chevy pickup tried to avoid hitting them and skidded sideways onto the shoulder. Beyond the shoulder were dense trees.

"Damn it!" He hit the steering wheel hard, then sat helpless while the sedan sped ahead of the accident. The multiple accidents effectively closed down the highway. There was no way he could follow them beyond Slidell. Assuming of course, they were worth following.

But he felt in his gut they were.

Sedona, don't give up on me now.

Mex maneuvered into the median to bypass the accident that way, but the strip of land had barriers that stretched between the east and westbound lanes where there was a bridge. Heavy traffic heading toward New Orleans meant he couldn't try to go the wrong way on the highway either.

The heavy rain had turned the median into a mini-swamp. When Mex tried to pull up onto the west bound side his left rear tire sunk into the mire. *Great. Just great.*

Emergency responders were already making their way through the jumble of vehicles. Mex got out of the SUV and stepped carefully back to the other side of the median. A tow-truck, trailing behind the police cars and fire engine edged toward the median. Mex flagged him down.

"You stuck?"

"I just need you to get me onto the shoulder."

"I got cars to tow, buddy."

"It'll take you ten minutes. I'll pay you cash."

"How much?"

"Hundred dollars."

"I 'spect I've got a minute or two to spare ya."

Twenty minutes later Mex was on his way back to New Orleans with nothing to show for the last hour.

CHAPTER TWENTY-SEVEN

Cade spoke quietly into her phone. "Thanks. I owe you."

A plate of crawfish sat on the table, prepared the way only the chef at Boudreaux's could prepare them. Because the chef knew which of the three sauce choices was her favorite, there was an extra bowl. Cade loved this place for more than the food. They loved her. Accepted her. In the past, they'd taken care of her when she had no place else to go.

Some nights she felt more weary than others. And tonight was one of them. How much longer could she do this? She'd been working with families in the middle of pain and guilt for years. She'd been successful more often than not, but it was the nots that haunted her. Theirs were the voices she heard when she tried to sleep at night, the tears of their loved ones waking her up in the morning. Her failures. Her losses. Her battered spirit bound with history.

Cade checked her watch. Straight up seven. Mex and Darius should be here any minute. She signaled the waitress. "Three private brews, please, Maddie. And something crunchy. Surprise me."

The waitress moved to another table and Cade saw the handsome black man walk in, looking around for her. She didn't need to raise her hand before he saw her and moved to join her. She couldn't help but glance at the entrance to watch for someone else to walk in. When he didn't she had to work to hide her disappointment—from herself.

She rose to greet Darius. "Hello, Mr. Johnson."

Darius looked at his watch before giving her a brief, if awkward, hug. "Darius, please." His tone was pleasant enough, but something didn't seem right.

After sitting, Darius looked at her. "Mex is kind of tied up. He's following a lead on Luis Alvarez."

"A lead?"

"Well, it could actually be Alvarez. He doesn't know."

"And by 'following' you mean...?"

"Literally. We found a family member, his grandmother, who apparently keeps in touch with her grandson via a drop site. When we tested it, we got all the right answers. It's active and now in play. Mex couldn't give up that lead."

"I understand."

"Have you found anything?"

"I just got off the phone with one of my sources," Cade said. "Luis Alvarez has more family in the area. They've lived here for years. On the secretive side."

Darius's eyes flickered. It looked to Cade like the journalist knew a subplot when he heard one.

"Secretive?" Darius asked.

"Most of his family are your ordinary, routine folks. Just like our maiden aunts and widower uncles. Know what I mean?"

"Yeah. Boring."

"Pretty much."

"Except?"

"Except a sister of Luis Alvarez thought she could showcase some brutality and make a difference."

"I'm not following you."

"The less boring members of the family, the people who are particularly secretive, are involved in Santeria. Luis's youngest sister didn't like the animal sacrifice her family indulged in and blogged about it."

"So she outed them."

"In a big way."

"And she thought that would make them stop?"

"She did. She was fifteen at the time and naive. That was about four years ago. The family, and Luis in particular, have been on the authority's radar ever since."

"Where's the sister now?"

"Believe it or not, college in New Hampshire."

"Why Luis? Why now? Why is he so high up on the cop's radar?"

"The local cops have reason to believe he's involved in the La Familia cartel. It matches the information Chase gave us."

"Damn."

The way Darius said that word gave it double meaning if Cade had ever heard it. "Look, Darius, I barely know you. But something is going on. Do I need to know what it is? Is our working together likely to be jeopardized because of something that's happened? Is Dia's life?"

Darius's body tensed and his eyes snapped to Cade's. "Once again, I'm not following you."

"I don't want to get in your business but if it impacts mine, you have to come clean."

He took a swallow of beer and seemed to consider her request. Another swallow. He nodded. "You're a pretty wise woman, Cade LeBlanc. Mex could do worse."

In spite of herself she felt her face get hot.

"What do you mean?"

"Only an idiot could miss the clues. You two are dancing around romance like it's a snake that might bite."

Cade cleared her throat, putting an end to the topic.

"Do you know my wife is pregnant?" Darius asked.

"Congratulations. What does that have to do with what we're doing here?"

"This afternoon when she went to get our mail out of the box she found a headless chicken. A note was pinned to the carcass."

Cade barely blinked. "What did the note say?"

"It said 'Bring your husband home or your family dies'." Darius fidgeted with his napkin. "I'm booked on a flight later tonight."

"We must be getting close for them to step up and make these threats. The timing sure sucks. Is there someplace your family can go to be safe?"

"I'm not going to put my family in jeopardy. Not for you, not for Dia. Not even for Mex."

"But you've got to know your turning tail and running is not going to save them. There's only one way to kill a snake and that's to cut off its head. And in our case, I believe the head will be severed the moment we save Dia." She took a breath. "Have you told Mex?"

"Not yet."

"How the hell is he supposed to finish this without your help?"

His tone was tight. Controlled. "I'm not going to try and make you understand. Obviously your family is not a target. Mine is. Do I feel good about this? No fucking way. Do I have a choice?"

Darius stood up and shoved his chair into the table a little too hard. "I will not sacrifice my family the way Mex sacrificed his."

Soc Au' Lait! What the hell? Cade watched him storm out of the crab shack before she could tell him the rest of what she'd discovered.

***

Darius immediately regretted his words. Cade had dug just enough that his fight or flight response was all messed up. He felt like he'd let Mex down in more than one way. Betrayed him twice.

Mex would understand that Darius had to protect his family. He knew that. Even so, he felt like crap leaving in the middle like this. He also hated leaving the possibility of having a first-hand account, a great story, in the New Orleans mud. Boots on the ground was huge, even if the ground was slippery. Still, compared to his wife and children, there was no contest. Family had always come first to him and this was no exception.

What Darius's journalistic side wanted to know was why his family had been threatened. What had he turned up that would create such a reaction? What was he close to discovering?

On his way back to the hotel, he called Pamela for the fifth time since she'd called him that afternoon. "Just checking."

"We're fine. Everything is normal. I know it was horrible, but maybe I overreacted. Do you think? I mean, maybe they wanted me to freak out and there's really no threat at all. Maybe we just fell into some kind of trap. And here you are, leaving Mex to go it alone and leaving the possibility of your big true crime book in the dust. All because your hormonal wife went over the edge."

"Honey, first of all, you didn't overreact. You found a frigging headless chicken in with the electric bill. I can't even imagine. Second, Mex can handle himself. There's a woman we met here who seems to know her stuff and I'm pretty sure she'll be able to watch his back. And third, I'm not letting the book go. It just won't all be first hand."

"Have you told Mex you're leaving?"

Why does everyone ask him this? "Not yet. He's chasing down a lead. I expect he'll be back here before I need to leave to catch my plane."

"A little short notice."

"Can't be helped. And not your fault."

"I love you, D.J."

"Back atcha, P.J."

After he hung up, he tried to think about what else he could do for his friend before he cut bait. Darius forced down his feelings of guilt. He'd take a look at them later. Not now. Not when his family had been threatened.

Back in his room, he packed the last of the things for his flight back to Denver. From there he'd catch a commuter to Aspen that would put him home about two in the morning.

His phone rang. "Johnson."

"Mon cher."

Darius tugged at his collar. The caller was a local contact he'd used for years. A *beautiful* local contact he'd used for years. He'd searched her out to see what she could dig up on the Alvarez family. She wasn't subtle in broadcasting her interest—in a decidedly unprofessional way—despite him explaining that he wasn't available.

"I have some interesting things to share with you."

The double entendre couldn't be missed. "You know I'm happily married."

"Then why did I even tickle those thoughts?"

"Because I'm a man. But Deirdre? As gorgeous and delectable as you are? Ain't gonna happen. I love my wife. I value my marriage."

"Can't blame a girl for trying."

Well yes, he could. But that wouldn't get him anywhere. "What do you have for me?"

"Aside from my luscious body and insatiable sex drive? Aside from the things I can do for you—to you—that you've never even dreamed of?"

"Yeah, aside from those." *Damn, this woman was over the top.*

"Too bad. We could have made some fine memories, you and me."

Darius held his comment. She'd gotten the picture. He wasn't interested.

"Okay, fine. Be that way."

For a brief moment, Darius was afraid she was going to hang up on him. Then he heard her sigh.

"Luis Alvarez's involvement in Santeria eventually exposed him to the local arm of the La Familia cartel. It was a match made in hell, if you know what I mean. He convinced them that through the power of Santeria—and his power as a priest—they could find protection from law enforcement and their rivals."

"We kind of figured that out."

"The protection ritual must be strong. Powerful."

"We get that."

"It requires human sacrifice."

Darius fell to his bed. *Shit*.

"But he was recently assigned a new challenge. One that, if he fails to meet it, could mean his death."

"What's the challenge?"

"Are you sure you don't want to come to me?" Her emphasis was on the word 'come'. "Or would you rather me come to you?"

"Deirdre, you are a temptation. Another moment in time, another situation, (*another man*, he thought), things might be different. But for now, what was the new challenge Luis received?"

"La Familia, Luis's cartel, is making plans to take over the Senora-Ciento cartel. Luis's challenge is to protect his people and assure victory through the strongest and most powerful ritual he's ever attempted."

"How do you know this?"

"I am a woman with many contacts, mon cher. You should know that. Have I ever given you inaccurate information? Have I ever been wrong? Have I ever given you any reason not to trust me?"

"What in the world would Santeria practitioners consider stronger than human sacrifice?"

"Therein lies the challenge."

Darius already had the answer: a human sacrifice that was also a child of the rival drug cartel.

CHAPTER TWENTY-EIGHT

Mex wanted a shower. And a drink. And some good news from Darius. All the way back from Slidell he'd cursed his bad luck and the good luck of the driver of the sedan in which he was sure Luis Alvarez was riding. But he felt in his bones that he'd been close. Not far from Slidell. After all, Alvarez, or someone close to him, had made it to the drop.

He let himself into the hotel room, threw his keys down and stripped off his clothes, dried mud still clinging to both his boots and his jeans. He was tired. The depression clawing at his consciousness like it had never clawed before. He badly needed to decompress. To find some hope.

The shower's warm water flowed over his head, a soothing element for his soul. Could he just stand in here for hours? Days? Until everything was fixed and he could emerge from this cocoon of liquid gold into a world with compassion and ready justice? Death would happen when a person was ready to move on—not before. He'd know where Dia was and be able to extricate her without incident. And having done so, Sedona would be freed. All would be right with the world.

He turned the water off and reached for a towel. As he dried off, the real world began to reinsert itself. The disappointments, the cruelty, even the horror. But the healing waters of a warm shower had fortified him. He could handle this. He would find Dia. He would free his sister. He was feeling better than he had in months. Now, for that drink and Darius who should be back from his meeting with Cade.

Mex drew on some clean jeans and knocked on the connecting door, shoving it slightly open. "Hey, Darius! Let's go get a drink and catch up." He pulled open the dresser drawer and grabbed the t-shirt on top. "I swear I was following Luis Alvarez from the cemetery but there was a friggin' accident just past Slidell and I lost him." Mex pushed open the door and walked into Darius's room.

Darius stood over his bed, his carryon open and almost packed. Mex watched as his partner stuffed in his shaving kit and zipped the bag closed. Darius nodded to a bottle of Mex's favorite scotch sitting on the dresser. "We need to talk."

Mex tried to smile, but he knew he wasn't pulling it off. "Looks like it."

"My family has been threatened."

"Threatened how? Because of what we're doing?"

"My wife doesn't get threatening phone calls while at the grocery store with our kids as part of her normal routine. And oh yeah, when she goes to collect our mail, she doesn't usually expect to see decapitated animals in with our bills sporting a note pinned to the carcass talking about killing her family. And yeah, I sort of figure there's a connection."

"Anything else?"

"What the hell else should there be, Mex?"

"I get that you're upset. Really, I do. But we're so close. I know we are."

"Which is exactly why this has happened."

Mex moved to the bed and sat. He closed his eyes and put his head in his hands. What was he doing? How could he be so driven? "First a little girl, and now your family." And Sedona. He looked up. "I'm sorry, man. I had no right to involve you in this."

Darius moved to the dresser and poured two glasses of scotch. "I would have been pissed if you hadn't. This is still something I want to be involved with if I can. But I need to do it from the sidelines. From Aspen Falls. I can't risk my family."

"What time's your flight? Do you have time for one last brainstorm?"

Darius handed Mex a glass. "We have time. Let me fill you in on my meeting with Cade. By the way, I owe her an apology so it might be a bit sticky when you first talk with her again."

Mex took a breath. "Given your afternoon, I can get why there might have been some friction. I'll handle it."

They went over the information they'd gathered during the day, Darius with far more to offer than Mex. Especially via Cade. Cade LeBlanc was looking more and more interesting and Mex wasn't quite sure how he felt about that.

After refilling the glasses, Mex and Darius sat back in their chairs. A comfortable moment of silence passed before Mex spoke. "If you're not down with this, with being a research source for me, I get it. I do. I'll still get you as much of the story as I can for your book."

"Thanks, man. I think that maybe my bailing on you tonight might signal the assholes responsible for the threats that I'm out of the picture. Safe. Off their radar. I'm pretty sure I can handle the situation once I'm home where I'll have a better feel for what's going on. And I still want to be there for you. I'll pick up a disposable phone tomorrow and get in touch."

Mex respected the choice Darius had to make. He also recognized that he was losing some important backup.

Things could easily go south.

CHAPTER TWENTY-NINE

The Diviner settled onto her mat. The *jicara* was filled with water, the gourd carefully balanced on her divination surface. A lit cigar wafted its pungent fragrance into the air as it sat on the plate next to the candle. All of her other *ibó* were scattered around her; the eight symbolic items needed to gain a reading. Her fingers trailed through the white powdery chalk of *efun*, a smooth black stone, two bound cowries, a seashell, a piece of bone, a *guacalote* seed, a doll's head, and a piece of broken china.

Regardless of her client's seemingly aloof and casual attitude about the necessity for him to get to Honey Island Swamp, she knew it was critical he be there. And so did he. She'd already made her own travel arrangements.

The Diviner could not control the choices of others, and that included her powerful client. What she feared was that he would not respond appropriately, and her divinations would be in error. The position of her client meant that her life could be in jeopardy, regardless of whether the negative results were because of his actions, or lack of action. It might not matter that she had made it clear that he was the one who could alter the outcome.

She prayed the *mojuba*, naming herself and invoking her ancestors. She was desperate to know the course that would serve her best. The tightening she'd been feeling in her chest needed release, needed assurance, needed the proper resolution that only Santeria could provide. Tomorrow morning she would sacrifice the goat she'd procured that afternoon. The one that stood tethered and bleating under the shade tree in her yard. She needed the potent divinity the killing could afford her.

Forty-five minutes later, she pushed off the floor and reached for her phone. She punched in one number and waited. She sat in a chair, crossed her legs and her foot began pumping the air as she listened to what she considered the meaningless and impersonal message when someone isn't available—for whatever reason. She hated voicemail.

"You need to listen to me. I will be at the Honey Island house tomorrow. You must be there. Cut your other business short. I've performed some divinations tonight to confirm my earlier position and nothing has changed. The girl might be there whenever you decide to pay attention, but I can't guarantee the results will be what you're looking for."

CHAPTER THIRTY

Dia sat quietly in the corner of the deck. Her direct questions got her nowhere. She had figured out that she could learn a lot more if her new family forgot she was there. In that way it wasn't too different from her old one.

Luis paced in circles. His arms flew up in the air and then down to his sides as he spoke to Pilar who was sitting on the bench swing. Dia couldn't understand all of the words—they were speaking a mix of English, Spanish and Cajun—but she understood enough of them to know that where they were was supposed to be a secret. She couldn't figure out how someone asking Luis's grandmother how he was doing could be such a threat and thought maybe some of the words she didn't know probably explained the problem.

Pilar let Luis walk in his silly little circle until it seemed like maybe he'd come to the end of his rant. Then, her voice soft, she spoke. "It will all be fine, my love." She reached up and placed her hand on his arm. At her touch, Luis crumpled next to her on the swing. "The Diviner will be here soon and it will all be over. We will be able to move on with our lives and have the freedom to make decisions for ourselves."

"What if we're wrong? What if something happens?"

"We aren't. It won't."

Dia knew about diviners. They were the ones who knew how to tell what the future held. Only a few people were true diviners. There were a lot of fakes who got lucky or who knew how to lie well enough that no one could exactly blame them. But if Pilar was talking about a diviner, Dia knew this one had to have some genuine power.

Dia also took to heart the idea of moving on and having more freedom. The images that flashed through her mind cheered her. The promise of a real future with her friends made her smile. She pictured herself and Pilar sitting around a dining room table loaded with food. They'd celebrate holidays together, and Luis and Hector would be there along with other faceless, as yet unknown, friends. Dia knew there would be a lot of people there who enjoyed being around each other. Completely different than her old home. At least since her mom died.

Hector stepped out onto the deck. When he got Luis's attention he gave a jerk of his head toward the front of the house where the car was parked. Luis said something to Pilar and the two men were gone.

Pilar rubbed her arms as if she were cold and stared off into the swamp. Pilar had told Dia the names of all of the swamp's trees they could see, but the only two she could remember were cow oak trees and turkey oak trees. She'd never heard of a tree named after an animal or a bird before.

Pilar turned and saw Dia. "Sit by me. I have a swamp story to tell you."

"Where are Luis and Hector going?"

"Our guests have begun to arrive. Luis is meeting them in Slidell." Pilar shifted on the bench. "Come. I will tell you about the Honey Island Swamp Monster."

"A monster?"

"Yes. A real one."

Dia looked across the water to the turkey trees. "Here?" She squinted. Did she see something?

"Yes, here."

Dia moved quickly to sit as close to Pilar as possible. Her friend's arm around her shoulders made her feel better. Protected. Safe. "Okay. Tell me."

"Are you sure?"

Dia nodded but snuggled closer.

"There is a creature who has long lived in this part of the swamp. He's part Cajun and part Indian and part something else. Many folk have seen him, some closer than others."

"Something else? What kind of something else?"

Pilar gave a little smile. "The monster is tall, seven feet at least, and walks almost like a man. He's four hundred pounds of fury and stealth, able to hide for decades in the bowels of Honey Island without being killed by a hunter or a gator. He's covered with short gray hair, all over his body. Everywhere except for his face. The hair on his head is also gray, but long."

"Does he have fangs?"

"No one knows for sure. But he does have razor-sharp claws on his feet. Claws that can rip flesh with ease."

"Is there only one of him?"

"Not according to those who've seen the tracks."

"Have you seen him?"

"I've seen movement and shadows. And I've heard noises that aren't part of any normal voices of the swamp. I believe these creatures are around. I believe they see us easier than we see them."

Dia shivered.

"Do not worry, sweet Dia. We are working with our Santeria *orishas* to keep us safe."

"You and Luis?"

Pilar blinked, then nodded. "Yes. Me and Luis. You are not to worry. But now you know about our new rituals."

"And the guests? Are they a part of the rituals?"

"Yes, my darling. They are very important to the ceremony for which we are preparing."

"Will you let me be there this time?" Dia thought about watching her new family chanting around the fire the other night without her. The image of Pilar holding her shoes while the flames bounced and sparked into the night tucked into her head.

"Of course. We will make sure and include you."

***

Sedona sat in a chair out on the lanai and sipped her mojito. She was in VV's home and not Vicente's, so she could relax a little. Relax? What the hell was she thinking? She was being held here against her will and even now her feet were lashed to a post, the padlock mocking her.

She'd had a lot of time to think. To remember. Dia was a wonderful, happy little girl who adored her brother and her mother. Sedona had been in and out of their lives in Monterrey. They were both great kids with a devoted mother. She couldn't say the same about Vicente Vega.

She could understand why Dia might run away but it had been too long. Vicente Vega would have found his missing daughter within hours after he'd been told of her disappearance. He had an army of skilled and persuasive people at his disposal. Someone either helped her or kidnapped her. Either way, she was a little girl who had been protected all of her life and would not be equipped to deal with any kind of reality.

"Can I get you anything else?" VV's trusted housekeeper walked toward her. "I am sorry for the safety measures," she pointed to the padlock.

"Do you know Dia?"

"She has been around." The housekeeper's tone was wary.

"Do you know what's happened to her?"

"She's missing."

"Yes. And that's why I've been taken. I'm here until my brother can find Dia."

"That's my understanding."

"Don't you think there's something wrong with that? I mean, I haven't done anything wrong and my brother is only trying to help."

"It is not my place."

Sedona clenched her jaw. "It is not your place? *Not your place?* You have been under the Vega family thumb for far too long. Can't you frigging think for yourself?"

"You misunderstand. It is not my place to judge the Vega family any more than it's my place to judge the Anderson family." The housekeeper paused. "Do you understand now, Miss Sedona?"

Sedona stared at the woman and wondered where their conversation had gone wrong, but she didn't want to ask. "I would like some paper and a pen."

"I'm sorry. I cannot provide you with any means to communicate. Anything else to eat or drink? That I can assist you with. Mr. Vega sent one of the other housemaids to buy some clothing for you. Of course, she doesn't know why. I will bring the clothes up to you for your approval when she returns."

She was a prisoner. In elegant and comfortable surroundings—but a prisoner.

"First, I need to use the bathroom, and then I'd like another mojito if you don't mind."

"Certainly."

Might as well get drunk. Oblivion. Kind of like when she was younger.

Sedona held her hands behind her back to be tied until they reached the bathroom. Her hands would be bound before her feet were released. She would be locked in the room until she knocked on the door, the housekeeper waiting there for her to repeat the process. Strange how quickly she'd gotten used to the loss of her freedom, the routine of her restraints. Three days? Four at the most? She wasn't sure she liked what that said about her personality.

On the way back to the peacefulness of the lanai, VV stormed into the hallway. "Get her to her room. Lock her down. Lock the windows. No more moments for pleasantness."

The housekeeper's face showed a brief moment of surprise but was replaced with one of quick compliance. "Yes, sir."

"Why, VV? What has happened?"

"Your brother's arrogance cannot be taken out on him at this moment, but I can make you pay. No one, *no one*, hangs up on me."

"Were you just speaking to my brother? Is he close to finding your sister?"

"His disrespect for me has expressed itself and I've decided what price is appropriate. I've been considering how to handle it. From this point forward you will not leave your room. If your brother displays some recognition of my position that might change."

"I wouldn't count on it."

VV's slapped her face so fast she didn't have any time to react. The sting brought color to her cheek where he'd connected, and tears to her eyes.

"I'd forgotten how impudent you could be."

She bent her cheek to her shoulder. "Impudent? I think you mean strong."

VV hit her again.

CHAPTER THIRTY-ONE

After Mex dropped Darius off at the airport he called Cade. He was going to need some local backup and he wanted to see if it could come from this woman he'd just met, or if he'd have to find it elsewhere.

"LeBlanc."

"Hey, it's Mex Anderson."

He could hear her hesitate. "Darius is gone?"

"Yeah, but he needed to go home." Mex surprised himself by defending his friend.

"I'm afraid we didn't part on the best of terms and I regret that. I hope the two of you are okay."

"We're cool. Can we meet for a drink? I want to make sure we're both up to date and be sure my next move is a good one." That won't get anyone killed, he added to himself.

"Yeah, it would be good if you didn't get yourself killed."

Mex sucked in a surprise of air. The coincidence was a little eerie. Having someone echo his thoughts was disconcerting. But he was tired. Everything seemed a little eerie.

"Great. Boudreaux's? An hour? Will it be open?" He knew better than that. The first time they'd met at the crab shack it had been hours after closing.

"I'll meet you there."

On his way to meet Cade he thought about his sister. For the first time Mex considered how sad it was that probably nobody else would miss her. Her life had revolved around him for years. As much as she looked after him, he'd also taken care of her ever since the murders. Even so, they'd always led pretty independent lives. But everything changed for both of them in one afternoon.

Before the bitter darkness could take hold, Mex had another thought. He wondered if anyone would miss him if *he* went missing. Panic hit first and then he realized that Darius or Chase Waters would eventually know something was up. They spoke every week or two on a regular basis. If he didn't show up at Juan's after a few days, the bar owner would probably get curious, along with members of the Hispanic community in Aspen Falls who relied on Mex to be their unofficial lawman and mediator. Surely someone would ask questions.

Close call, Anderson. He made the mental commitment to connect with more people when he got back to Aspen Falls. Probably.

Well, maybe.

***

Mex pulled into what had become a familiar parking lot. Cade wasn't there yet, but he could see The Mountain waiting at the door. He wondered if Amazon Man worked for Cade or the owner of the restaurant. He suspected the latter. If the owner was willing to keep his place available for Cade LeBlanc to meet people, he cared about her. And if he cared about her, he was going to provide security. She was involved in a business that required a certain level of force some people might find objectionable.

He threw the transmission into park. Maybe, if he worked it right, he could find out a little bit about Cade from these people who knew her. He sat a moment while he figured out his best approach.

Mex stuffed the keys into his jeans and smiled at the giant bouncer. "Hey, man. Good to see you. I'm a little early." He walked up the steps. "Can I buy you a drink?"

The mountainous man grunted.

Mex kept talking as he walked past the armed gorilla. No pat down this time. No confiscation of his weapon. Mex had moved one step up the ladder. "It's been one helluva day. How 'bout you? Yours okay?"

Another grunt, but the big guy followed him into the restaurant. To the right was a large room that housed the main bar. Mex walked in and sat on a stool. An older man with long gray hair pulled into a ponytail stood behind the bar, polishing glasses.

Mex looked at the huge man. "What would you like?"

The bartender spoke without looking up. "Little Ray likes my Cajun martinis."

"One for, um, Little Ray, and one for me."

"You used to some heat?"

"I can handle it."

"Something you should know about your new friend here."

"Yeah?"

"Liquor won't loosen his tongue none. If anything, he gets quieter." The bartender put two martini glasses on the bar. "Figure you might've had a different expectation."

"I did. I was hoping to learn a little bit more about Cade LeBlanc. You know her?"

"I do."

"I'm sorry. My name is Mex Anderson." He reached across the bar and shook the old hippie's hand.

"I know."

"And you are?"

"Folk just call me Boudreaux."

**

Cade hated this part of her job. She'd spent the last hour with people suffering a devastating loss. A month ago she'd been asked by this family to intervene and provide exit counseling for their son. The problem was, they should have called her three months ago. Stephen had been one of six others who committed suicide. It happened two days after the family had asked for her help. She knew from personal experience that no amount of counseling would come close to assuaging their guilt. Still, she'd had to try.

The father had remained silent during every session they'd had together, crouched into his own world of suffering and self-blame. The mother, inconsolable at first, had finally begun to respond to her youngest daughter who begged her to think about the rest of her family. After an hour Cade felt comfortable enough to leave, satisfied the required grief that led to healing had begun, at least with the mother and other children. She couldn't be sure about the father.

Cade remembered her younger sister, Delphine, and felt the sadness weigh her down. Only so far though. The raw power of her determination to make a difference, thanks in part to her ancestors, always stopped her from toppling into the abyss.

The strength and spirit of all of the women in Acadia LeBlanc's lineage filled her, forcing her to move forward. Take a step. And then another. She could not deny her bloodline, nor did she want to.

She put today's heartache behind her as she prepared to meet with Mex Anderson at Boudreaux's. She'd give anything to put this meeting off. She was exhausted. Drained. Wondering if she had anything left to give.

There was more than her simply experiencing a bad day. The man troubled her. Not only the situation, which of course was critical, but the man himself. She sensed a lot of the same darkness that had engulfed Delphine. Cade struggled to understand why her sister never found the strength to climb out of the shadows.

While the man with the odd name both intrigued her mentally and appealed to her physically, she felt a wall go up as she registered the complications he lived with. She didn't need any more "complicated" in her life. She courted enough on her own.

Could she put their meeting off? Even for a few hours? That's exactly what she wanted to do. Time to regroup and refresh. Then she thought of the young girl whose life was very possibly on the line. The seriousness of the Santeria group she'd likely gotten involved with, and the exponential threat of the drug cartel connection.

While Cade had no children of her own, every parent's child she sought to save became hers in some way. She'd lost one. She didn't intend to lose another.

Her phone buzzed. Because she was driving she didn't try to read who the caller was. "LeBlanc."

"I'm hearing shit you should know about."

It was one of her Santeria connections. "What kind of shit?"

"Something about a sacrifice so that one drug cartel can gain victory over another."

"Sacrifice? A little girl?"

"A very special little girl. One who, in the minds of the people offering her up, would ensure they would come out on top. At the very least, they would send a message. And it's going to happen soon."

Shit. "Where did you get this?"

"Can't say. But I believe it."

So did she.

Cade hit the disconnect button and immediately punched two more buttons. "Is he there?"

Boudreaux spoke with his gentle Bayou drawl, "Yeah, *ma chere*, he's sitting in front of me now, choking down a Cajun martini."

"Do not let him leave. I don't care what happens. He and I need to—"

"Maybe you and he need to do a lot of things, things you're not ready to talk about, but he's not going anywhere. There is no need."

"Okay. No more of your martinis. Promise? I need him to focus."

"He's had a bad day and one of my martinis is not likely to penetrate or create a problem. For you though, I will stop. A late dinner?"

"Yes, please. Nothing heavy. We have a lot to talk about."

Cade clicked off the call. Though not especially religious, she was spiritual. Hell, how could she be anything else in her line of work? So she shot up a prayer.

Keep my strength coming. My mission is not complete. I need to help this pour soul from Colorado save the life of Dia Vega Arroyo. Nothing else matters. Whatever transpires between Mex Anderson and me later is for later, and as long as it doesn't impact my future missions, I'm good with whatever happens.

She crossed herself in a totally non-religious way and continued to the restaurant. She thought about how tired she was but said, "Screw this. I've got work to do."

CHAPTER THIRTY-TWO

Mex looked at the man who earlier he'd thought of as the bartender and smiled. "Boudreaux. I'm sort of leaping to a conclusion here, but are you the owner of this establishment?"

"That would be correct. If you have any complaints about the food or the service, I'm your man. If you're a creditor I'll need to have my accountant contact you. Tomorrow, I promise, if the storm isn't on us." He smiled.

"What storm?" Mex thought about the weather map he'd seen flash on the television screen.

"Ah, just some silly little rain-maker trying to find some muscle."

Mex nodded.

"So I'm guessing you're a longtime friend of Cade's?"

"Yep."

"And probably not willing to share any of her secrets?"

Boudreaux nodded, then winked at Mex. "Not unless I think it's in her best interest. She's one woman whose bad side I never want to find myself spending time with."

"Can you give me a clue to the best way to deal with her? You know, on a personal level?"

"*Deal* with her? Are you under some kind of voodoo spell? You respect her. You establish trust." Boudreaux tossed a towel over his shoulder. "I don't know you from Adam, but I'll tell you this, you don't ever want to *deal* with Cade LeBlanc. She's got a bite quicker than a snake and a memory longer than an elephant."

"But she has a story, right? Some reason that makes her do what she does? More than what's been made public, I mean."

"She do."

"And?"

"Her story is hers to tell. Not mine."

Little Ray put down his empty martini glass and moved to the entrance door just as Cade pushed through.

Boudreaux began to make another martini. "You look like hell."

"Always the charmer. Give me some home brew. I don't want to wait for a martini."

The hippie bartender/owner/chef pulled a cork out of a long neck bottle and handed it over.

"Bad day?" Mex asked.

"You could say that." Cade took a long pull on the beer then rolled her shoulders.

"Want to talk about it?"

"Nope." She took another swig, her bottle less than half-full, and signaled Boudreaux. He uncorked another home brew, she grabbed it and walked through the darkened restaurant to her table, a beer in each hand.

Mex sent a questioning look toward the man who knew her best and mouthed, *is she okay?* The man behind the bar shrugged, then nodded. Apparently this had happened before.

After procuring a second Cajun martini—a man-to-man promise with Boudreaux that the martini would remain between them—he trailed Cade to the table with one of the best views in the place. A less exhausted Cade would notice the second drink. Mex felt safe, but he hoped that Boudreaux would get them some food faster rather than slower. He wondered that he'd never seen Cade slip the man either cash or a credit card. Maybe he should offer to pay something.

"So you were after Luis Alvarez today?" Cade's gaze never left him as he settled into a chair.

Mex nodded. "He's our best lead to Dia. I don't know for sure it was him, but he's both Santeria and cartel connected, and he's the boyfriend of the nanny."

"I dug up some information that could be useful. I was about to tell your partner when our communication sort of broke down."

"I heard. He extends his apologies, by the way."

"We were both tired and stressed."

"What kind of information?"

"A family member of Luis Alvarez has a home in Pearl River. It's just past Slidell, right on the edge of Honey Island Swamp."

Mex felt a stab of disappointment. Luis could be here for no other reason than to visit family, if he was here at all. "We need to go there and interview whoever is living there. This could be where they're holding Dia."

"I know you want to get up on your white horse and rescue the damsel in distress, but we can't go in guns blazing."

"Then we'll question the neighbors first."

"Not a good idea. These old neighborhoods are filled with old friends who are suspicious of any strangers asking questions, even informally. Since everyone has secrets, well... our presence wouldn't be secret very long."

"What do you suggest?"

"I have an idea. Did you bring a suit?"

"No. I'm not even sure I own one."

"Well, you need to get one. You can donate it later if you want."

"I'm not wearing a damn suit."

"You will when you hear my plan."

CHAPTER THIRTY-THREE

The next morning Mex selected a table where he could watch people enter the restaurant while he waited for Cade. He didn't want any surprises. Aidan Gill for Men didn't open until ten, so they would eat breakfast first. He ordered coffee and spread the cloth napkin on his lap.

A damn suit. The last time he'd worn a suit was at the funerals.

The coffee came, hot and strong, and he thanked the waiter. The place was busy. Guests were engaged in conversation at almost all of the tables. It seemed to Mex that all people did in New Orleans was eat. Or maybe it was just him.

He looked at his watch. Although she wasn't late, he'd been waiting for what, five minutes now. Cade hadn't given him the address of the house in Pearl River or he'd consider chucking this idea of hers and getting his butt over there to find Dia by himself. If she was even there. This whole suit thing was—

Oh my God. He stood, placing his napkin on the table. Walking in his direction was *not* the same woman he'd been meeting with. That woman was all casual clothes and flowing hair. This one wore a form fitting, if severe, navy blue suit with a crisp white blouse opened low enough to provide for some nice cleavage. His gaze traveled from her tied-back hair, wavered a little on her neckline, then followed shapely legs down to a pair of sensible black pumps. If she hadn't let loose her deep-throated laugh he would have wondered if this really was Acadia LeBlanc.

"Do you approve?" Her eyes glittered at his dropped-jaw expression.

Mex shut his mouth and cleared his throat. "Actually, my preference is your jeans and T-shirt look, but you do clean up nice."

"Merci beaucoup."

He pulled a chair out for her and gently eased her to the table.

"You have good manners."

"Thanks to my mother."

Cade laughed again, low and bold. "Although I think it's thanks to these horrid nylons, I will be polite and give my thanks to your *maman*."

Mex warmed. He couldn't remember the last time a woman had made him smile this deep, this real. "My *maman*, if she were here, would take one look at your legs and nod in complete understanding."

"Why Mex Anderson, I do detect a compliment."

"With a little luck, Ms. LeBlanc, we'll be able to explore where this easily detectible compliment might lead. But in the meantime we have a job to do."

"Right. But before we proceed with our job, I could use some protein."

"Easily done."

***

They were at Aidan Gill's a little after ten. A quick twenty minutes later, Mex was stuffing his original clothes in elegant Aidan Gill bags and into the backseat of his rented SUV. He resisted the impulse to loosen his new tie. Nothing he wore felt quite right, but the tie was the worst. He felt less and less confident about this plan. What kind of fool was he?

A few minutes earlier, Cade had looked at him with wide eyes when he emerged from the changing room. Interested? He couldn't tell for sure. But she was definitely impressed.

"You want to see me in a suit again it will be at my funeral. And only then if someone who either hates me or doesn't know me decides what I should wear."

Cade settled into the passenger side. When Mex climbed in she said, "We need to make one stop along the way."

"Where and for how long?" The only reason Mex wasn't planning on speeding was he didn't want to waste the time it would take to get a ticket.

"There's a little motel just this side of Slidell. I'll need about three minutes. That work for you, cowboy?"

Cade gave him the address in Pearl River and he put it into the GPS. It had taken awhile, but he'd finally come to trust these things as long as his destination wasn't too remote. For remote he wanted a personal conversation with someone who knew the area and the landmarks.

They drove in silence for a while.

"You ever listen to Zydeco?" Cade asked.

"Once again I wonder what country I'm in. Zyda-who?"

Cade laughed and Mex felt an unexpected surge of pleasure. He loved being the reason for that laugh.

"Zydeco is a type of Cajun dance music. It combines traditional Cajun style, R&B and African blues." Cade reached to the radio and began pushing search buttons. "Here. Listen." She turned the volume up a little.

After a minute, Mex nodded. "Sounds like there's a little Tejano in there as well."

"Tejano? Now who's no longer speaking English?"

"Tejano is kind of a modern Tex-Mex mixture with a little blues of its own. And now that I hear some of your Zydeco, I'm feeling a little Tejano influence in there too."

Cade smiled and sat back. She looked comfortable. They were going to pretend to be something they weren't and she looked like they were out for a Sunday drive without a care in the world. Mex's estimation of her continued its steady climb.

"There. Off to the right. That's the motel."

Mex pulled into the almost empty parking lot. "Want me to go in with you?"

"No need. I'm in and out. And because I'm starting to like you, I'll make it less than three minutes so you can keep breathing."

"What's going to take less than three minutes?"

"You'll see."

CHAPTER THIRTY-FOUR

Sedona opened her eyes to a shuttered room and closed them again. She hadn't remembered VV as a volatile little boy but he'd clearly grown into an unpredictable and dangerous young man. That's what the power and money of his father's drug cartel had done for his son. What a legacy.

Teo, where are you? Do you know I'm gone? Do you care? Are you close to finding Dia? Did you say yes before or after they took me? Do you love me?

In the next moment she acknowledged her bitterness toward her brother. While he paid all of her expenses and saw to it she wanted for nothing, his money, and the very support he provided her, tied her to him in ways she never anticipated.

His money.

Her brother had gone to school at San Diego State University. Some fellow student of his had asked Teo for five hundred dollars to start up some silly internet company. He'd just sold his car to avoid needing a part-time job during the school year, so he had the money, and Teo's friend was very persuasive. He'd cashed in right before the murders that changed their lives forever. From then on, Teo's investment success would make Warren Buffet proud. Her brother had planned on building the home he lived in now, but he hadn't planned on doing it alone.

Sedona had no idea how much Teo was worth, but in her opinion he could be doing so much more with it. Instead he gave too much away, helping people who could help themselves if only they'd get off their butts and get jobs. Or better paying jobs. Then she considered what her life was like thanks to her brother and cut that line of thought off, but the thoughts wouldn't go away.

She didn't need to work, Teo paid for everything. It bothered her enough that she'd held a series of part-time jobs over the years since she'd been in Aspen Falls, but none of them for long. In Mexico it was different. Well, mostly in Monterrey. She'd been treated like a queen in the city and it had felt right.

Lying in the semi-dark room, she thought about Agua Prieta and her parents. Both of them had been mowed down with machine gun fire while going about a normal day. Her mother had been so lovely. A Mexican woman who stood taller than most. In her youth her full head of wavy black hair had reached her waist. Her mother had also been educated, an unusual thing for a Mexican girl in those days, at least in their tiny town.

And her father. Tall and smiling. That's how she'd always remember him. The American man who'd fallen in love with the most beautiful woman in the world. His life was perfect. Wait. No. The image of him when she'd caused them some trouble filtered through. Not anger. Sadness. Deep, deep sadness.

She'd made some mistakes. A tear tracked down from her eye to the tip of her nose, where it sat for a breath before finally dropping to the pillow.

She had made mistakes.

She couldn't think about her oldest brother or her pregnant sister, also murdered that day. Then there was Teo's wife, Maria, also pregnant. And her nephew and niece. If she dwelt on them, she'd surely die of a broken heart.

The Sacrifice

She wished she'd never answered the night Vicente Vega showed up at Teo's door. One more time, a cartel leader was making her and her brother's life hell. One more time, this particular cartel leader was impacting her life.

CHAPTER THIRTY-FIVE

Oh God, let this work. This man needs my idea to be successful. Cade hurried into the small motel's lobby. She quickly spotted what she wanted and moved toward the rack of tourist brochures that lined one wall.

Cade didn't see exactly what she was looking for, but found several that would do. She grabbed a handful and stuffed them in her purse. Took another handful for Mex.

As she'd done every time before what she called a "soft operation," she remembered her sister. Delphine could have been so much more. She should have fallen in love, had children, done something positive with her life.

Cade whispered, "Delphine, show me what I need to see. Help this young girl live to become a young woman. Don't let me lose her. I can't stand another loss so soon."

She never really knew if Delphine actually heard her, but she knew it made her feel better to talk with the sister who had meant so much to her—even if it couldn't exactly be called communication. When things went right in an operation, she liked to think it was because Delphine had shown her the way. When things went wrong, Cade burrowed the failure into her heart and felt its weight.

She walked back to the SUV where Mex waited. The man intrigued her. She'd tried to find out about him online but had been frustrated. There really wasn't much, at least not as much as she'd hoped for. She could tell by looking at him that he'd fought through his own share of pain, but exactly what it was and why, she hadn't been able to find out. He'd graduated from San Diego State University, been a lawman in Mexico, and was an early investor in an internet startup that made billions when it was sold, but other than those pieces of information, his life was a blank. The only odd thing she found was a link to a blog post that was entirely in Spanish and looked like it belonged to a drug cartel she'd never heard of. The name Anderson was easy to pick out because that's the only word she knew. She wondered if this wasn't the event that had changed his life. She marked it to have translated when time permitted.

Except for his involvement in bringing a particularly hideous case to a close in Aspen Falls a year ago, there wasn't much about his current life. Clearly he worked hard to keep out of the limelight. Her intuition told her, based on some of the details of the story, it was the trust the Hispanic community had for him that helped the local authorities bring down a particularly bad group of people.

Cade admitted to herself that she would really like to learn more about Mex Anderson. She also admitted that while she was clear about what she should do next to free someone from the clutches of a cult, she had no clue how to move a relationship along.

As an exit counselor she ranked high. As a relationship expert, she sucked.

She hopped into the SUV. "Miss me?"

"About to call the search and rescue team."

Cade checked his eyes to make sure he was joking and not frustrated because she'd taken too long. She read joking. "The more the merrier."

Mex put the SUV in gear and they drove out of the parking lot. "Can you tell me now why we needed to make this stop?"

Cade held up a handful of brochures. "We needed these."

"What the hell? We needed to know more about the French Quarter? The French Market? A frigging swamp tour?"

"What we needed, *mon cher*, was a little *gris-gris* for some *cunja*."

"Translate."

"Happy to. Even though it sounds like "gree-gree", g-r-i-s times two refers to an object that's used to either inflict evil or protect yourself from evil." She held up the brochures. "And if we're lucky, they'll help us in our attempt to create some good *cunja*, which is a spell that's put on someone else."

Cade put the brochures down and looked at him. "You really need to get out more."

"What I need are two things. I need to bring Dia back to her family and I need to lose all involvement with Santeria and any other kind of cult. This shit makes me glad I've never been ultra-religious."

Cade considered her next question carefully. By virtue of what she did for a living, Santeria would always be a part of her life, but it wasn't a part of her. "You're not religious?"

"Nope. Never have been."

"You don't believe in God?"

"Damn, Cade. I didn't say that. I do believe in God. I've seen too much not to. God and I have had more than one argument and we both know who we are. What I don't buy into is all the kneeling and raising of the hands crap. God doesn't give a shit about that. He appreciates people reading words attributed to him, but he hates them trying to confine and define him based on those words in the Bible or Koran or Torah or whatever."

"You know this how?" Cade had her own ideas about God, but she was more curious about Mex's.

"Like I said, we've argued a bit."

She decided to drop the subject. Tension between them would not be good while they were nearing the target.

A few minutes later they'd driven through Slidell and were on their way to Pearl River and to the home owned by relatives of Luis Alvarez.

***

As intrigued as Mex was with Cade LeBlanc, this *gris-gris* and *cunja* stuff could probably kill the whole thing. Did she have to think like this every day? Did she have to know about—try and live every day with the knowledge—of all of this darkness? What else did she think and know about? Mex wasn't sure he could continue to be involved, even on the sidelines, with beliefs that were so radical. At least to him.

But still, she had that laugh. And those eyes. And a certain strength of purpose that made her a presence. Maybe he could hold off a little before he made a decision. Just thinking that surprised him. He thought he'd never be remotely interested in another woman after Maria. He'd never imagined another woman could ever pique his interest again.

He'd been wrong.

Mex checked the GPS. Looked like they were now about five minutes away.

"Tell me again how we're doing this?"

"You and I are canvassing the neighborhood with a religious message. Haven't those people ever come to your door? They usually come in pairs, sometimes even teams, and they want you to know what their God can do for you—for your salvation. The implication is that if you don't jump on their particular bandwagon, God is gonna vent some wrath onto you. Anyway, we're out trying to save as many souls as we can from the fires of hell."

"Yeah, like a Santeria practitioner is going to give us the time of day."

"That's the beauty, Mex. I know more about Santeria than you do. All you have to say is that I was once a follower but have now found the truth and the light. Got it? I can take it from there."

"So I let on that we know they're Santeria?"

"Pull over." Cade's voice was more strained than he'd ever heard. "Now."

Mex moved the SUV onto the shoulder. "What did I say?"

"If you even mention the word Santeria, our cover is blown and the girl could be dead."

"I thought you wanted me to say you were a Santeria follower."

"Just a follower, Mex. Someone who fell into a cult. Do not get any more specific. If you mention the word Santeria, a family with secrets would know their secrets were out. And a family with major secrets, like a kidnapped little girl, could decide to cut their losses and move on before anything else became known."

Mex considered what she said. "Okay. I introduce you as being a victim of a cult when you were younger, who was later called to witness for your new religion?"

Cade sat in silence. After about ten seconds she said, "Maybe I should do the talking. You just look pretty and conservative in your suit."

Mex could not begin to express his relief. "But I'm taking my gun."

"I wouldn't have it any other way."

He pulled back onto the road. He thought about what he knew about Cade and her connection to either suicide or depression—or both. About how Cade might feel the need to act now in the heat of passionate information rather than wait for a more studied, logical approach. "We have to agree that we're not going to take them now. It's going to require surveillance to know the best way to get Dia out of there—if that's where she is. We're just after intel. Are you with me? Neither of us can come close to risking this girl's life." Not to mention Sedona's life.

"What if I get the feeling that it's now or never?"

"Then we pull away and come up with a secondary plan based on what we're able to ascertain from the first contact."

"But Mex, I've done this dozens of times. Sometimes you only get one chance. I've learned the hard way that sometimes waiting for the best time to move in is the same thing as putting them in a bonus position."

"Let's do it this way. If there's an immediate threat to Dia's life, we act. If it's anything else, we pull back first to analyze the situation. Between the two of us, thinking without pressure, we should be able to develop a plan that incorporates all of our new intel.

CHAPTER THIRTY-SIX

Dia laughed at the face Pilar was making. She was so funny. Dia couldn't remember laughing like this since her mother died. She was sure she'd laughed with her mom. With her brother too. And with their friends. It had been a long time.

She missed VV. She should give him a call and let him know she was okay. That she'd found a new family who loved her and spent time with her. He'd probably try and find out where she was, who she was with. Try and talk her into coming home. Which is why she hadn't called him already. Well, that plus the fact she didn't have a phone.

The little stilt-home was beginning to fill up with guests. Pilar said they should all be here in a day or two and then they'd have the important ritual. Dia had tried to help Pilar prepare some of the items but Pilar had shooed her away and told her it wouldn't be appropriate. Appropriate? Maybe because she was still too young. She had a lot to learn about the ins and outs of Santeria.

Pilar stopped making funny faces. "Okay, *ma chère*."

Dia loved it when Pilar spoke French. It sounded so sophisticated.

"It's time for you and I to begin to prepare our mid-day meal. We have a fresh chicken, but you need to pluck the feathers."

"Pluck the feathers?"

"It isn't easy. Hector will help you."

Hector handed her a pair of pliers. "You'll need these."

"Pluck the feathers?" Dia repeated. She thought she might throw up.

"*Ma chère*, it is an act of Santeria. Both a thanks and a preparation for the future. Think of it as your own private ritual."

"Feathers? Connected feathers?"

"Hector, please. Take her to the yard." Pilar stood and walked to the kitchen.

The young man waited. "We need to begin now, while the water is still hot." He held something in his hand.

"What's that?" Dia stalled.

"A blow torch."

"For what?" In spite of herself, she was intrigued.

"To burn off the bits of feathers that don't come out."

Gross. "Hector, I don't want to do this."

"Pilar says you must. But I will help. Come."

She rose and followed him into the yard. "Do we use the pliers to pull out the feathers?"

Hector didn't respond.

A wooden pole she hadn't noticed before stood in the yard. It was about four feet high with a metal rod coming out of it horizontally at the top. A dead chicken hung upside down from the rod. There was a plastic garbage bag stretched out directly underneath the bird, and a large metal bucket sat nearby.

Dia slowed her pace, eyes riveted to the carcass. She was sure she saw it breathing. "Where's its head?"

"Over there." Hector pointed.

She stopped. Swallowed. She'd known that certain ceremonies required an animal sacrifice and chickens were pretty common. The one she'd heard about involved five small freshwater fish in five small gourds, peanuts and parrot feathers, and the sacrifice of five young chickens letting their blood drip into the gourds. Five days after the sacrifice, everything is taken to the river with five cents. She thought of it as the Rite of Fives, even though she hadn't seen it done. Not even once.

Now, here was this headless dead chicken hanging in front of her. A creepy chicken that she was supposed to touch.

Hector grabbed the chicken and dunked it in the bucket of hot water. A crazy thought that he was drowning the chicken flashed through her mind. Dunk and swish. Dunk and swish. With a fluid motion, Hector hitched one of the chicken's legs into a noose made of thin rope and looped it over the metal pole. The chicken hung there, headless and wet. And really gross.

Hector grabbed a handful of feathers and pulled, dropping them onto the plastic bag. "See? *Agua caliente* helps to loosen the feather making them easier to pull." He stepped to the side. "You try."

Dia didn't move. She watched the swaying headless body of the dead bird, its neck swinging loose.

"Dia." Hector raised his voice. "Dia."

She pulled her gaze away from the horror in front of her to look at the young man who had saved her from the alligator. Surely he would not have her do something like this unless it was necessary. Harmless.

"You try. Now."

Dia moved in closer and reached her hand out. She timed the back and forth motion and pinched a single feather from the body, immediately dropping it to the ground.

"There, see? Not so bad. But if you do it that way, we will never eat. You need to grab many at once and pull. Try not to rip the skin."

Dia turned and ran. Before she hit the screen door she looked back and saw Hector stripping the chicken with sureness. She thought it odd that he had one feather sticking out of the pocket of his shirt.

CHAPTER THIRTY-SEVEN

Mex and Cade found the house without any trouble and took a few minutes to scout the neighborhood. The pair was silent as Mex drove block after block.

Small, older houses. Most in need of some kind of repair but nothing actually crumbling. The landscaping however, varied. Some were pristine with flowering shrubs and trimmed lawns. Others were pigsties. Rusting parts from who-knows-what mingled with weeds and errant trash. Most homes looked like early spring in Colorado—a little neglected but with potential. Then Mex thought, Pearl River, Louisiana, probably didn't have much of a winter. The potential quotient took a dive.

Manicured and maintained properties were losing out to the hopelessness and neglect of those occupants who had simply ceased to care. Mex had seen neighborhoods like this all his life. Hell, he'd lived in them as a young boy. People tried for a year or two, but if their efforts weren't rewarded, they gave up, and grew to believe they weren't worth anything more than what they had. An empty neighborhood park reminded Mex that it was a school day.

"We lived in a neighborhood like this," Cade said, breaking into Mex's thoughts.

He wanted to ask questions but decided silence might gain him more.

"My sister fell in love in a neighborhood like this." Cade sounded almost wistful. "And then she found a belief system no one else in our family could understand."

"System?"

"A screwed up catchall word for something organized. A cult. Delphine's was voodoo."

Mex held his breath and felt his heart expand. "And yet?"

Cade looked out the window. "And yet voodoo was completely contradictory to everything we'd ever been taught." Cade shifted in her seat. "Stick around for a while and there will be plenty of people to tell you the story. Maybe you've heard it already?"

"I'd like to hear the story from you. It couldn't have been easy."

"We grew up poor. Dirt poor. I had an angel who appreciated my mind and became a mentor. Delphine, though she was every bit as smart, didn't."

"That made the difference?"

"I think so. I loved my big sister. I looked up to her for so long. What happened was almost unbelievable. Delphine got involved with some screwed up people who were into voodoo and Santeria. Before we knew it, she'd become a fanatic and wouldn't listen to anyone."

"You mean she wouldn't listen to you."

Mex heard a soft gasp.

"Sorry. Didn't mean to go all interrogative on you."

"No, that's okay. You're probably right. Maybe she didn't know how much I loved her."

Mex waited for Cade to continue.

"Anyway, she eventually moved to an old abandoned shack deep in the bayou near our home. There, she could lose herself in her spells and no one would be around to try and change her mind. I would go and check on her regularly, take her food to make sure she was eating properly. I wanted her to know she had family who loved her. She seemed confused and depressed most of the time I was with her. Especially toward the end.

"One day I learned about people who extracted loved ones from cults. Back then we called them deprogrammers. I found one and hired him. He said it would be comparatively easy since she wasn't living in a commune or under the influence of others 24/7."

Cade stopped talking and Mex glanced in her direction.

"I was too late. When we got out to the shack, we found my sister's body. She'd slit her wrists just like she'd slit all of the throats of sacrificial chickens and goats over the years. Delphine bled out and died, and she died all alone."

Mex wanted to touch her. Make contact. He didn't. He maneuvered the SUV into a parking space on the street about a block away from their destination. "Did she leave a note?"

"She did. Maybe one day I'll tell you what it said."

"I'm sorry." Mex thought about how impossible it was for anyone to escape loss. "You ready to do this?"

"I'm always ready to do this. Are you?"

"I'm good at fights, verbal and physical. I'm good with guns. I'm good at figuring people out. My instincts are top notch and I can appraise a situation fast. I'm even acceptable at undercover work where I need to be deceptive. I can lie with the best of them, as long as I'm pretending to be a bad guy. I'm not so good as a religious crusader who needs to conduct himself in a certain way when what I really want to do is muscle myself in the door."

"Then you need to stay quiet and let me do the talking. It appears I'm a better liar than you."

***

Cade took deep breaths as she and Mex walked up to the front door of the house next to their target. In through her nose, out through her mouth. She became calm and centered.

Rather than go straight up to the home they believed might house Dia's kidnapper and maybe Dia herself, they'd begin one house over in the event someone spotted them.

"I'm thinking of this as a practice house," Mex said.

"They probably practice, but that's not what you mean, is it?"

Mex fell silent. Good.

Cade reached out and pushed the doorbell. She didn't hear it ring and looked at Mex. He shook his head. She pulled open the screen and knocked on the door. Again.

She heard someone approach the door and hesitate. There wasn't a peephole, but there was a window that was mostly covered by some white lacy fabric. Cade resisted the urge to look directly into the window.

The door cracked open. "Yes?"

The woman was in her late-twenties, on the fast track to looking fifty, and obviously suspicious.

Cade heard a child crying somewhere inside the house. She reached for one of the brochures she'd gotten at the hotel, making sure the logo of the swamp tour company was hidden.

"Hello, ma'am. We'd like a moment of your precious time to talk about something important."

"I don't have time to talk to you about anything, important or not."

Mex stepped into view.

The woman's eyebrows crawled up to her scalp line when she saw him. "Well, I suppose a moment would be okay." She pulled the door open and stepped out onto the tiny stoop. The crying grew louder.

"I'm afraid this isn't a good time for you," Cade said. "Your child needs you. Would it be okay if we returned a little later?"

"Both of you?"

"Yes, of course."

The woman patted her hair and brushed some crumbs from her blouse. "Yeah, that would be okay."

Cade knew she was thinking about fixing herself up to make a better impression in an hour or so. Too bad she'd be all dressed up with no place to go. And no door to answer.

Mex smiled and nodded. "One question, ma'am."

"Yes?"

"I see you're wearing a cross. Are you a Christian?"

The woman's hand rose to touch her necklace. "I am."

"Are all of your neighbors? What I mean is, is there someone we should be sure and talk to?"

Just as her hand had risen involuntarily to touch the cross around her neck, her gaze darted to the house next door. "Um, I couldn't say for sure."

"Well, thank you, ma'am." Mex and Cade turned to leave.

"Today? You'll come back today?"

Mex gave her a little salute.

"Do you always have that effect on women?" Cade asked once they got to the street.

"Seems like I do, at least some of the time and with some women. Others, not so much."

Cade was impressed. Aware and honest. Most men would either not have a clue or feign ignorance. "Your question was a good one. We got the confirmation we needed about the house next door." She looked at him. "I'm gonna have to unpack my bullshit meter when I'm around you."

"Well, it wasn't something that would hold up in court."

"Good thing we're not going to court."

They turned up the sidewalk leading to the house owned by the relatives of Luis Alvarado. It looked like all of the other houses in the neighborhood—someone had made lackluster attempts at maintenance that resulted in nothing beautiful, but also nothing falling out butt-ugly. Cade figured in another five years, the houses would simply be five years worse for wear.

Mex spoke quietly. "Remember, unless we see an immediate threat to Dia's life, we check out what we can and pull away to plan. We're not even sure this is where she's being held. Hell, we're not even sure Alvarado has her."

Shit. Cade stopped in the middle of the sidewalk. "Give me a little credit, cowboy. I've been in this rodeo before. Worked it and won. You getting cold feet? Want to go back to the neighbor's house?"

"Just want to make sure you don't go all G.I. Jane on me."

"I'd much rather make love than war. You agree?"

"Sorry. Guess I do."

Cade moved to the front stoop and Mex followed. She hoped he was a little cowed but seriously doubted it. He wasn't the type of man who could be easily chastised. Mex Anderson was a strange mix of more things than just his name.

This time when she punched the doorbell they could hear it ring inside the small home. They waited.

Cade hoped they weren't too late. She'd been there before. She didn't know if she could handle a second loss so close to the young man who had committed suicide.

Please, Dia. Be safe. Be ready for rescue. Just be. Cade realized she'd thought of the little girl by her name.

CHAPTER THIRTY-EIGHT

Mex's training kicked in as they approached the front door. He wanted to kick some ass, grab the girl, get Sedona back, crawl home to bed—dream of a certain Cajun—and be finished with this business. But he knew none of that was possible. At least not now. If Dia was here, any impulsive move on his part could kill her. And if Dia died, his sister was as good as dead. Then he might as well be too.

He needed to treat this as reconnaissance. Fact gathering. No more. Still, he confirmed the weapon in his shoulder holster by pressing his arm closer to his side. There would be no more people sacrificed in his life if he could help it. He was ready to die to make sure that didn't happen

Mex pushed everything aside as Cade pushed the doorbell. The sound would easily carry through the house. He listened for footsteps. They waited five seconds. Ten.

Nothing.

Cade looked at him and he nodded. She pushed the bell again and knocked on the screen door.

The door swung open, an older woman standing rather defiantly in the doorway. "Yes? What do you want?"

"Hello. My name is Sarah, and my friend and I are hoping you have a couple of minutes to talk about spiritual things."

The woman's eyes narrowed. "Spiritual? What kind of spiritual?"

Mex stepped in. "Well, to be honest, before we even get to that, we're thirsty. Do you think we could get something to drink? We'd be grateful."

The woman looked at him and considered her response. "I guess. Wait here."

They could hear cupboard doors being opened. A faucet turned on. She came back with two glasses of water.

Mex drank deeply. "Thank you."

The woman nodded.

"My name is Ricardo." He waited.

"Rosa."

"Nice to meet you, Rosa." He handed back the empty glass. "Do you think we might come in for a quick moment?"

"I don't think that would be—"

"Please. My friend, Sarah, suddenly felt unwell as we walked up your sidewalk. Can you just let her sit for a minute? Then we'll be on our way."

The young woman shifted her eyes to Cade. "I suppose. But just for a minute. I have things to do."

Mex smiled at her. "As do we all. Thank you so much for your kindness." He put his hand on Cade's elbow and guided her into the house.

"Just don't talk any of your religious beliefs to me. I have my own and I don't have time to argue with you."

"I promise. Not a problem. We won't say a word to you unless you ask us a question. She just needs a place to sit for a minute, then we'll be on our way."

Mex and Cade found themselves in a tiny living room to the right of the entrance. They could clearly see into the dining room with a hallway that presumably led to bedrooms to the left. There was another room off the dining room.

He was pleased when he saw Cade swallow the rest of her water. She sat down and lifted the glass to their host. "Would you please?"

The woman took Cade's glass and walked the few steps through the dining room to what Mex assumed was the kitchen. While the woman was out of sight, he took careful note of everything he saw.

A typical living room and dining room told him nothing except that the family was ordinary. There were no signs of Santeria, no signs that the people who lived here were anything other than your regular neighbors. The only thing slightly out of place was a backpack on the dining room table. Could be any teenager's backpack. Justin Bieber? Okay, a pre-teen girl's backpack.

"Here." The woman handed Cade another glass of water.

Mex was almost amused when he saw Cade shake slightly when she took the glass. *Good show, woman.*

"Do you have children?" Mex did his best to make the question come out smooth.

"Oh, no. It's just me. I have a sister and nephew in N'awlins and two cousins, one in Slidell and one in Baton Rouge, but I live alone. I haven't seen any of them in six months or more."

Other than the obvious subterfuge, the simple amount of communication would have put Mex on high alert. Who would volunteer this much information to a total stranger?

Mex rose. "My partner is obviously unwell. Would you mind if we came back at another time to talk to you?"

"You can always try. I might not be here."

"That's okay. We kind of believe that whatever happens is God's will."

"Ah. Well, maybe you should just skip this house. We're good with what we believe."

Mex noticed her switch to plural. "Are you believers?"

"You could say that."

Cade handed the glass back to the woman. "Thank you. Would you mind if I used your bathroom?"

Rosa narrowed her eyes. "I guess not."

"Where, um…"

Mex watched the woman evaluate which visitor she trusted the least. Not surprisingly, he won. She would stay with him while Cade used the restroom.

"It's just down that hall, second door on the right."

They both watched Cade walk down the hall and Mex decided a little diversion was in order.

"How long have you lived here?"

"Thirty-two years."

"Thirty-two. I don't know anyone who's lived in one place that long. Did you ever think about moving?"

"Nope." The woman edged a little closer to the hallway, trying to get a view.

Mex needed to get her attention away from that hallway and Cade.

"Could I please ask you for another glass of water?"

Mex followed the reluctant woman into the kitchen. He looked out the windows to the backyard. There was a lot of space, but no other outbuildings. Mex wondered where they got their chickens to sacrifice.

"Wow. Did you ever have a garden?"

"A long time ago. Now it doesn't seem worth the time."

"I know what you mean."

Before Mex had to come up with another weak diversion, Cade appeared in the doorway.

She nodded to their hostess. "Thank you for your kindness, but I need to leave." She looked at Mex. "Will you take me home?"

***

Cade sidled next to Mex as they walked down the sidewalk. "Dia's not here."

"Did you see the backpack?"

"I'm not saying she was never here, but she isn't now."

"How do you know?"

"Other than the backpack, there is nothing, I repeat nothing, in that house to say there is an extra guest. Not even anything to say there's anyone staying here other than the woman we just met."

"So where's Dia?"

Cade shook her head.

Mex pulled out his phone. "We need to confirm that the backpack could belong to Dia."

Thanks to caller ID he didn't need to announce himself. "Does Dia have a backpack?"

Silence. "I think I remember seeing her with one."

Damn. "Vega, are you shitting me? You don't even know whether your daughter uses a backpack?" Mex wanted to knock some sense into this absent father.

"Yeah, yeah. I'm pretty sure she does. What's this all about?"

"Find out from someone who would know what it looks like and call me back."

Mex thrust his phone into a pocket, jaws clenched and eyes narrowed. His entire body stiffened and he wanted to hit something.

The pair climbed into the rental in silence. Mex had fired it up and pulled away from the curb before Cade spoke. "Why are you so angry?"

Mex sniffed and considered a smart retort. He backed off. Drug cartels. Cults. "Doesn't the very thought of Santeria drill you? I mean, your sister and all?"

He was gratified that she seemed to consider her answer. "I could easily let it consume me. Make me so angry that all I felt was anger. But if I let that happen, what good would I be? Who could I help?" She paused. "I consciously choose, every day, to honor my sister's memory. To make her death matter. To—through Delphine—make a difference and give someone else a chance."

Mex was about to tell her about his family when his phone rang. "Yeah."

"She has a backpack. It features a young singer. A Justin Bieber."

Vega pronounced the teen idol's name as "Hue-steen Bee-ay-bear", but Mex knew he had a match. With a sudden wash of compassion for the father he said, "I don't have her, but the backpack confirms a good lead. Thank you. I'll bring your daughter home, Vega. I just hope you'll appreciate her when that happens."

Mex clicked off his phone and scratched his chin. "We need to check the house again to make sure Dia isn't there. Maybe they move her during the day. If she isn't at the Alvarez house, where is she?"

"We know she must be close. We must be missing something—some connection. I cannot allow another young soul to be sacrificed to this insanity."

Sacrifice.

"I know about Delphine—your loss." Your pain, he thought. "You know about mine."

"Can you tell me how you've dealt with it? Are you ready to talk about that part?" Cade's voice sounded sad and soft and hopeful.

"It hasn't always been pretty, but I wouldn't have mentioned it at all if I wasn't ready to share it with you."

Mex spent the next thirty minutes telling Cade about his diagnosis of depression and the efforts to find the best medication to address his situation. He talked about the sad days and the angry days, and finally the support he received from the Depression Center at the college. "For the first time, I had a place to talk about the things that brought us together as a family in laughter and love, and the final thing that brought me to my knees in tears and guilt. The center saved my life, and I speak at their fundraisers whenever asked. We're trying to take the "D" word out of the closet the same way we did with cancer and the "C" word." She never interrupted him. Not once.

"And Vega? Why help him now?" Cade asked when he'd fallen silent. Spent.

"I wish I could tell you that first and foremost it's the girl but that wouldn't be true. Vega promised me information on who gave the order to murder my family."

"And then it's the girl?"

"Yeah. Then it's the girl."

On the way back to the hotel, Mex felt the cloak begin to fall over him. The dark cape smothered his feelings and blocked out the world. He both hated and welcomed it. Anger and decisiveness were replaced by hopelessness and apathy. Sharp and painful awareness became blurred into drugged feelings of depression. Somewhere in the back of his mind he knew it was a chemical trick of his brain, but he didn't care.

He was tired of this battle. Tired of doing what was expected. Tired of struggling every day. Tired of always feeling bad. He knew it was treatable. But even that idea left him tired.

He thought about the young girl with her entire life ahead of her. Kids made stupid choices every day. None of this was her fault. If he didn't help Dia, who would?

He thought of Sedona.

Even though his medication had worked in the past, lately it seemed less effective. He needed to get back to Aspen Falls and see his doctor. In the meantime, he'd fight these dark feelings. Do what needed to be done. There wasn't time for him make himself a priority.

The glaring fact was that Dia's backpack was in the home of Luis Alvarez's relative and Dia wasn't.

Where the hell was she? Could they get to her in time?

CHAPTER THIRTY-NINE

The Diviner settled into her chair at the dinner table. She hadn't been able to take her eyes off the young girl since they'd been introduced. On one level she understood what role the daughter of Vicente Vega was to play in the future of her client—her patron. On another level she wondered what she might do to protect this young soul. She guessed it wasn't up to her.

She shook those thoughts out of her head. They were both worthless and potentially detrimental. Her job was clear, and although she was loath to admit it, the outcome could very well seal her fate. The ritual she'd been preparing for was the biggest in her career.

Pilar looked in her direction. "I hope everything has been to your satisfaction."

Part of the Diviner wanted to rip Pilar's throat out and tell her to stand with her power. Don't acquiesce. Be the future of Santeria. The other part rather enjoyed the platitudes and subservience.

She was so close, so terribly close. She had to believe. Victory was only a couple of days away. Eternal glory. Riches beyond imagination.

Or maybe punishment. Even death. She would not put it past her client to try and free his fear through retribution. Her failure to ensure his success could very well mean her life. It had happened to others.

"It appears you have been exemplary, Pilar. What we both need to hope for is that all we have worked toward will result in a satisfactory outcome, and that those who look to us for answers will feel gratified. Hopefully, neither one of us have made any errors prior to this point." The Diviner hoped she'd made herself clear—and provided a potential scapegoat should one be needed.

Pilar paled. "Errors? No, no. I assure you, I have made no errors."

"We'll know soon."

Dia sat her napkin next to her plate and worked her jaw until her chin jutted. "Pilar doesn't make mistakes. She knows what she's doing. She's been teaching me."

"And," the Diviner said, "as a student you're able to detect perfection how?"

Dia slumped low in her chair, trying to hide her face behind her hair. She mumbled.

"What did you say, girl?"

"Nothing."

The Diviner wanted Dia to exhibit a high level of character mixed with healthy respect. That would increase the power of the ritual. She softened her tone. "Sit up. Speak to me. Tell me what's on that child's mind of yours."

"Pilar has always been there for me. She has always helped me. She is leading me in my Santeria studies. I trust her."

Pilar pushed back from the table. "I need to take a walk."

Dia stood. "I'll go with you."

"No, Dia. I need to be alone." Pilar looked at the concerned expression on the little girl's face. "Don't worry. I'm fine."

Dia sunk back in her chair.

The Diviner reached out and brushed the little girl's arm. "This is okay. It will give you and me a chance to get to know one another." She winked. "I don't bite, I promise."

"When will Luis and Hector be home?"

"They are picking up a few items for me in Pearl River and Slidell."

"What items?"

"This and that for our big ceremony."

Dia brightened. "When will that happen?"

"Soon. We are waiting for the client's arrival."

"Client? Someone you're reading for?"

The Diviner nodded. The girl knew more about Santeria than she'd considered at this point.

"Is the client important?"

"Very."

"But you must be even more important if the client is willing to come to you."

"Ah, child. It is simply that his request is very big. So big that everyone associated with making it happen becomes bigger."

"What does he want?"

"That is a private matter."

"Does Pilar know?"

"She does."

The Diviner watched Dia process the information, no doubt calculating a way to get Pilar to tell her.

"Do Luis and Hector know?"

"I'm not going to lie to you, little one. Luis and Hector know as well. But you must not ask them. If they share the confidence with you or anyone, they will put the outcome in peril. And that could impact their futures."

"It's that big?"

***

Sedona closed the book she was reading, her mind unable to concentrate on the words. VV may not be much of a reader, but he stocked a full library to impress visitors. Considering his business, she was a little surprised at his extensive crime fiction collection. The bad guys generally paid the price every time. Fictional justice when reality often missed the mark.

She rose and began to pace. Late afternoon sun spilled into the room. How much longer would she be held here? What if Teo failed to rescue Dia? Was there some way she could get word to Vicente? If she could, would he help her or kill her? She shared history with VV's father but she also knew that blood meant more than any kind of history.

Who kidnapped Dia? The answer came fast—someone who wanted to extort something from Vicente. It must not be money. Vicente Vega could pay and would pay whatever price the kidnappers demanded. It must be something else. What? He held a lot of power in the Senora-Ciento cartel. Could it be a coup?

The door to her room flew open.

VV entered with his usual flourish.

Sedona ground to a halt and waited for him to speak.

He looked tired, as if at the end of his rope. A piece of cracked glass ready to fall into fragments. Did he love his sister this much?

What did Teo look like right now?

"Your brother has yet to find my sister."

She remained silent.

"Dia is vulnerable. Do you understand? She is a baby in so many ways."

Sedona nodded but didn't speak.

Suddenly VV was on the floor at her feet. "Don't you understand? She's all I have that connects me to our mother." His voice crescendoed and then cracked. "Do you remember anything about us?"

She sank to the floor and held her arms out. VV immediately filled them.

Tears ran down her cheeks and mingled with those of the tough young cartel man.

She'd made so many mistakes.

The two sat for the next several minutes in silence. Connected. Sedona began to hope that VV would have second thoughts regarding her captivity.

The young man pulled away and pushed himself to his feet. He walked to the window where he took each forearm and wiped his face exactly as he had when he was a little boy.

With his back to her he said, "You know I can't let you go. Others know. It's more than just Dia now."

Cartel pride. Beat or be beaten. Any sign of weakness and you're as good as dead, even if you are Vicente Vega's son. Especially if you are Vicente Vega's son. Sedona had lived long enough in Monterrey to know the score. It hadn't taken long. More than one family had let its own blood flow—even been the cause.

"You and your sister have always been special to me."

"That makes little difference now."

"I don't suppose so." Sedona wiped her hands against her thighs. "I just wanted you to know."

VV's entire body seemed to shrink. Without another word he moved to the door and quietly left.

Sedona's heart sank.

It was up to her brother to make things right. And damn, she couldn't count on him. After all, his choices had gotten her family killed, and he just might get her killed now.

Damn you, Teo.

She drew into herself and squirreled into the corner of a sofa. The view out the window was spectacular, but Sedona barely noticed. This would not end well.

VV's housekeeper walked in with a tray. Another mojito and some tantalizing epicurean temptation to go with it.

Fine. Sedona motioned for the tray to be placed on the table near the balcony doors.

"Thank you."

The housekeeper put the tray where she wanted it, then moved to leave.

"Wait."

The staff member halted, froze in place for a second or two, then pivoted to face Sedona. "Yes, *señorita*?

"Do you know Vicente Vega?"

"Yes, I do."

"Would it by any chance be in your interest to let him know I'm here? Against my will? And that his son is involved?"

"I cannot say."

"But would you at least consider it?"

The housekeeper looked at her, eye to eye, for the first time since she'd been held captive. Then she was gone.

Damn it. Sedona tried to think of a way to escape. Unfortunately the armed guards who patrolled the grounds torpedoed each and every one of her ideas.

Please, Teo. Do this job. Save the girl, save Dia. Save me.

CHAPTER FORTY

Mex and Cade sat at her table at Boudreaux's, picking over a pile of crawfish, their conversation centered on the missing little girl. A missing girl whose backpack, he would bet his life, sat in a house in Pearl River, Louisiana.

"What are we not seeing?" Cade asked. "Do you think she's already dead?"

Mex pulled out his phone and punched a number. The idea that they were overlooking something made him realize they'd stayed too focused on Luis Alvarez.

"Hey Darius, it's me. How's your family?"

"We're solid. Nothing wrong with being cautious."

"Glad to hear it. You up for some peripheral involvement?"

"You know it."

Mex tweaked a brief smile. "I need you to find out the names of everyone in the Slidell and Peal River areas that may be associated with Luis Alvarez or his family. I'm not interested in neighbors and casual acquaintances. The ones I want would also be involved in Santeria or have ties to the La Familia cartel, preferably both. That means some extra digging and some extra favors called in. While you're at it, include Pilar Villanueva. You up for it?"

"Already online. I'll get back to you if I find something interesting."

Mex picked up his home brew and pointed the top of the bottle in Cade's direction, using it to punctuate his words. "If Dia is still alive, and I'm betting everything I have that she is, then she's somewhere close. She's being held at a location that has connections with the house in Pearl River."

"My sister's place was close to Pearl River. Deep in Honey Island Swamp. Nobody ever went there so it was perfect for her."

"I know there are a lot of swamps in this part of the country. I've never heard of Honey Island."

"You and most of the world. Honey Island is one of the least explored swamps in America. Legend has it that pirates used to stash their plunder there."

"Hell, if there was even a rumor of treasure, surely the place would have been overrun by fortune seekers."

"Well, there's another legend that sort of counters those who are after an easy score. Honey Island also has its own Bigfoot."

"Really? A monster? What's it called?"

"Well, around here we have a very special name for it."

"What?"

"The monster."

"You're kidding me. All of the imagination that has settled here and you call it the monster?"

"Between you and me, *mon cher*, the lack of a name ascribes a certain authenticity."

They continued to pick at the meal Boudreaux had prepared for them.

Mex stuck some meat in his mouth. "Tell me about your sister."

Cade closed her eyes and sighed. "She's never very far away from me. I loved her and worshipped her as my older sister. Why I didn't follow her into voodoo, and out to the swamp, I'll never know. Even with the teacher who believed in me, my sister's influence was strong."

"What was the draw of Santeria?"

"Delphine was beautiful both inside and out. But she didn't see it. She only saw herself as lacking. She had a hole that needed filling—an empty ache. When she discovered voodoo she saw it as the way to fill that ache. My sister, my beautiful, sweet and smart sister, was drawn in from the first time she was exposed to the religion.

"I always compared her to a crack addict. You know, the person who's addicted after the first hit? Delphine went to one lousy ceremony and that was the beginning of the end."

"Is suicide a part of Santeria?"

"Not that I've ever found."

Mex tried to find the right words, and couldn't come up with any. He decided to be blunt. "So why do you think she killed herself?"

Cade drained her home brew and signaled for another. "I'd been out to see her a week earlier. She told me then that she was tired. Something had discouraged her. I knew better than to ask her what. Her religious practices had long been banned territory for the two of us. I was equally certain that there was no love interest in her life. I would have known."

"So what then?"

"I will never know for sure, but what I believe is that a part of her had begun to seriously question the faith she'd put into the orishes and proverbs and sacrifices of this belief system she'd totally committed to. This thing that once felt like a calling had betrayed her in some way. Not lived up to her expectations."

"She would kill herself over that?"

"Because of *that*, she had alienated herself from everyone in her family except me. Because of *that* she had cut the trajectory of her life short and forced it in a new direction. Delphine may have believed there was no way back."

"Even to get back to you?"

A tear slid down Cade's cheek. "Even back to me."

***

Darius had arrived home about two o'clock in the morning to a stressed out wife and two cranky children who had undoubtedly been influenced by their mother's anxiety regardless of how she tried to hide it. It took a hot bath at three o'clock, with candles and a Maxwell CD, for Pamela to finally unwind. Because the kids were whining and fighting, somehow wired, he'd taken both of them to the other bathroom for a middle of the night bubble bath so Pammy could have some time to herself. Maybe if it worked for their mother, it would work for them.

Darius loved bath time with his children. It wouldn't be very long before they wouldn't want to bathe together, and they for sure wouldn't want either of their parents in attendance. He tried hard to etch these times in his memory, and this one would certainly be a highlight. Less than twenty minutes later, both of his angels were bathed and sound asleep.

After her bath, he and Pamela lay together in bed while he brought her up to date on everything. If someone had dragged his wife into this, she deserved to know everything he knew. Typically, her concern was for the little girl in imminent danger and—because her family was now safe—she was no longer as afraid for her own loved ones.

"It's because you're here, Darius. I know the threat is still out there, but you're home now. The bad guys can think you've backed off the search." She had taken his face in her hands at that point. "Please tell me you haven't backed off the search for Dia."

Darius had never loved Pamela more.

He'd spent the last several hours organizing his notes and pulling together an outline for his book. He'd give anything to be back with Mex right now. Anything—except his family.

After Mex's call, he got a few names from Deirdre of people connected to both Santeria and La Familia. None of the names were familiar. Then he'd contacted Martin Van Buren to see what he could come up with on the property rolls. He was gonna owe these two contacts big time. Van Buren he could deal with. Deirdre, on the other hand, might be a problem.

Darius pushed his readers on top of his head, then rubbed his temples. The computer screen cast a glow in the darkened room.

Pamela walked up behind him and began to massage his shoulders. "You were an investigative journalist for a long time before we met, weren't you?"

Darius arched his neck, loving the deep touch his wife applied. "Yeah."

"If I remember right, some of those, especially at the end after you'd become well known, required an alias. Do I remember right?"

Darius scrunched his face. "Yeah."

"So now you came home to protect us and call off the bad guys. You've done both. The bad guys know you're here and no longer with Mex."

"Yeah..."

"So what I'm thinking is that you get back to Louisiana using another alias. You help your friend find that child."

"But—"

"I've thought about this. If you use an alias, take my laptop and leave yours with me, I can go online every now and then and get on Facebook or something else to make them think, if they're watching, that you're home. We'll be safe and you can help Mex. You can help that little girl."

"Am I hearing hormones or Pamela?"

His wife smiled her sweet smile. "Probably both. But I didn't marry a dummy and I'm expecting you to jump on this offer."

Darius felt the tingle he'd always trusted as a journalist. "Yeah?"

"The drama has passed. They know you're home, and if we play it right, they won't know you've left. If I can play a small role in saving a life that's what I want to do."

"What about the danger to you?"

"That's where the subterfuge comes in, Mr. Journalist." Pamela stopped the massage and moved around to where he could see her.

She wore a determined look on her face. "Look. We're safe. We can relocate to other locations if we need to. That sweet thing isn't safe and she has no options. No place to relocate even if she knew she needed to, which based on her situation, I'm guessing she doesn't.

"Mex is good. He's smart. He has the best chance of making this turn out right, but he has a better chance if you're there to back him up."

Darius rose to wrap her in his arms. "I love you, P.J."

"Yeah, well... I'm also counting on your book sales to put our three kids through college." She pulled away a bit. "I'm also counting on not finding another headless creature in our mailbox. If you stay under the wire, and I pretend to be you from here... we'll be good. Right?"

"You are an amazing woman. How did I get so lucky?"

"Just tell me we'll be good."

CHAPTER FORTY-ONE

Mex pushed his coffee cup away with one hand while holding his phone to his ear with the other. He dropped his voice and glanced at Cade, moving so his back was to her. "Are you sure about this, Darius? What about the threats to your family? Is Pamela okay with you leaving? Coming here?"

A minute later he hung up and looked at Cade again. "Darius is coming back. He was just boarding his flight."

"So I gathered. I sure hope he can sleep well on planes. We could use another pair of boots on the ground."

Mex shook his head. "They *think* they have everything under control. He and his wife *think* they have a plan to make sure they continue to fly under the radar." He closed his eyes. "And if they don't? I mean, how important is it for him to be here? Is it worth it for him to risk his family?"

Cade swallowed. "His decision, not yours."

"Look, I'm thinking we can handle this. Darius can run our intel side. He doesn't need to be here."

"You're right. But Darius also wants to get the story first hand. He doesn't strike me as the kind of guy to sit behind a computer to get the details. He likes to get the *feel*."

"At what price?"

"Don't make me defend him. He knows what could happen. This is his call."

"I don't think we need him here. He might be distracted." Mex held his phone, ready to make the call to tell Darius Johnson to get off the plane and go home to his family.

Cade reached out and grabbed his hand. "Wait. Why are you so dead set against more help when we have to move in?"

"I'm not against help, at least the right kind of help."

"What then?"

"I have enough guilt." He laid the phone down on the table. "Hell, Cade, I have four lifetimes worth of guilt. I'm depressed, I'm medicated, and I'm operating in unfamiliar territory. The right kind of help doesn't have a family. A pregnant wife."

Her voice was barely above a whisper. "You don't think we're going to find Dia, do you? You think we're going to die."

Mex didn't say anything.

"You do, don't you? You think we're going to die."

"People die."

"What kind of answer is that?"

"The only one that would be true."

"Then we need to talk a little bit about how I operate. I couldn't do this every day of my life if I thought I would fail. Yeah, I've lost some people, but mostly I haven't. Yeah, I've been in danger but because I plan well, that danger is seriously mitigated."

"We need to check the home where we saw Dia's backpack. We need to clear it. We need to know for sure they didn't just move her out during the day."

"I agree." Cade pulled a notepad out. "If we can wait for Darius to get here, our odds for not getting killed go up. Are you willing to work with me here?"

"Only if Darius buys into the plan."

"I wouldn't have it any other way."

Cade made a rough sketch of the home. "We know there's the main entrance from the street. I saw a back door when I went to the bathroom. Because the garage is in the back of the house on the alley, it's unlikely there's a side entrance but we can't count on that for sure."

Mex nodded, intrigued with her thought process. Well, not so much intrigued really as hopeful.

"The problem with a full-on approach is that if Dia isn't there we've alerted them to our presence if even one person is in the home. So the entrances are more of an FYI thing. Agreed?"

Mex nodded. He got the feeling Cade was winging it. But he also got the feeling that Cade's 'winging it' would lead to a solid plan.

"So we need to do one of two things. We either need to wait until we actually see Dia enter the house, which is unlikely, or we need to have a way to contain Rosa Santos so she doesn't sound the alarm and we can do an in-depth search."

"How do we do that? How do we contain Santos?"

Cade took out her own phone and hit a button. "Hey. I need a favor."

Mex, instantly aware that he was bothered by her intimate tone, wanted to know more. Who was she calling? What was their history? And she'd just hit one button. Speed-dial. He wasn't happy about that.

He heard Cade ask whoever was on the other end of the line if he—Mex knew it was a he—could find anything on Rosa Santos. She gave the address. "I need the info quick. Like ten minutes ago."

Four seconds later she laughed, that deep full laugh Mex had initially been drawn to. "Call me."

***

Cade looked at Mex. If he weren't already stretched to the limit she'd make some kind of joke about the call she'd just made. As it was, Mex looked like he was about to bag everything—especially her.

She ran a hand through her hair. "I have a friend in the St. Tammany Parish sheriff's department who owes me. He's going to do a search to see if Rosa Santos might need to be called in to the department to take care of something. Even if he doesn't come up with something on her, her name is common enough that she might just have to come in to prove she isn't the one they're looking for. Either way, that'll give us a chance to check out the house with no one home."

Mex sat silent.

"Well? Good plan?"

"It might work."

"Thanks for your encouragement."

"What do you want from me, Cade? I'm struggling right now just to stay human, let alone be a cheerleader. This is hitting closer to home than I'd counted on."

"Look, Mex. We're only talking about a couple of more days. Three at the most. And maybe even less if my friend comes through. We're gonna get this little girl and she'd damn well better take her life and make it into something."

Silence.

"Damn it. I need to know you think this is doable. That you aren't walking into any step we take with a doomsday attitude. I'm here for you; I've got your back. But I need to know you're ready to get mine and that you won't just give up or walk away."

More silence. The darkness, Mex thought, is pushing me down but Dia's urgency is pushing me forward. If I'm going to succumb, I'll succumb after we've completed our mission. He spoke. "I know what's important. I'll be there. I've got your back. " He paused. "It's doable. We can make this happen."

Cade looked at the man sitting in front of her. He knew he did not inspire her confidence right now. "What time does Darius's flight arrive?"

Mex looked at his watch. "It's about a three hour flight. Have your sheriff friend get Rosa Santos's attention before he leaves his shift. I'll pick Darius up, we'll catch some shuteye, and we'll meet you at the house. You'll need to confirm that she leaves."

"You're suddenly sounding down with this."

"There's no other way to be. Make sure you carry some protection with you."

"I didn't know you cared, *mon cher*, but you should probably know I always pack. That whole line of work thing."

CHAPTER FORTY-TWO

Mex turned off the SUV's headlights a block before he pulled up behind a pickup truck and shut the motor off. The houses they saw were dark, the occupants away, asleep, or passed out. He and Darius waited in silence while Cade got out and moved into the backseat.

"Has she left?"

"Not yet. I called my friend at the sheriff's department. He was just going off his shift." She leaned forward, handed Mex a gun he'd asked her to bring, and tapped Darius on the shoulder. "Welcome back, Darius. Glad to have your help."

"Thanks."

"Does your friend know we're breaking in to someone's home?" Mex asked.

"He knows what I do, and he knows that sometimes that means I have to bend the rules to save lives."

"Bend the rules?"

"It's not like we're going to steal anything."

Darius twisted in his seat. "Why is it okay with him for you to break the law?"

"About eight years ago I got his brother out of a cult situation."

"Santeria?"

"Nope. A group called Christ Enlightenment."

"Christian?"

"They think so, although I seriously doubt if any Christian church operates even close to the way those guys do."

Mex nodded toward the house. "Look, a cab just pulled up."

They watched as the woman Mex and Cade had spoken with earlier walked slowly out of the house and got into the cab. A minute later it pulled away from the curb.

"No one else in the house?" Mex asked.

"No one I've been able to see."

"You ready?" Mex asked Darius.

"Let's do this."

Mex and Darius got out of the SUV first and walked around to the back of the house. Cade would follow a minute later and approach the front door. A tiny house like this one, they'd hear her ring the doorbell. After three rings, Mex would break in the back door.

He and Darius both had their weapons drawn as they rounded the corner, keeping the guns pointed to the ground as they moved rapidly to get in position. Mex hoped there wasn't a dog. There hadn't been any sign of one earlier but they hadn't checked the backyard.

Pressed against the exterior of the house, on either side of the door, they listened for the doorbell. Mex and Darius heard it at the same time and looked at each other.

One down.

No other sound came from inside the house. The doorbell pealed again and Mex could almost feel how empty the place was. *Two.* Unless Dia was drugged, he didn't think she was here.

A third double tone and Mex was at the back door. It was a cheap and simple lock. They were inside in less than a minute.

He pointed to the front of the house. "Let Cade in."

If Mex had hoped to see two plates on the table he would have been disappointed. The kitchen was tiny but neat. He opened the refrigerator. It didn't look like there was enough food in there to feed one person let alone two. He pulled out all of the drawers and checked their contents. Nothing.

"Mex, I've got the backpack," Cade called from down the hall.

He hurried through the dining room, where Darius was looking into the cupboards of a sideboard, to what looked like a spare bedroom.

"It's Dia's, no doubt about it." Cade held up an iPod with Dia's name written on it. "Santos must have moved it after we left."

Cade dumped the contents out onto the bed. Nothing that wouldn't be in the typical teenage girl's backpack collection of things they considered important. Except for the cowrie shells.

"Why would she have these?"

"They're used in Santeria ceremonies and rituals. She must have been practicing."

"Okay. Her backpack isn't going to tell us where she is. There's got to be something in this house that can tell us where she's being held."

Cade pointed out the door. "There's a small desk in the next room. Probably our best bet."

"You look through that, I'll check the master bedroom."

Darius called from the dining room. "I found some photos. Could be something here."

Mex hurried to the dining room and looked at the photos. A young man and woman were in most of them.

Darius pointed to a woman in one of the pictures. "That's Pilar Villanueva. I recognize her from my online research."

"So that must be Luis Alvarez." Mex turned the pictures over looking for a date or a location. There was nothing to identify either.

"Did you bring your camera?" Mex asked.

"Yeah." Darius took the photos and laid them on the dining room table. He pulled out his camera. "Gotcha. We need to see if we can match the backgrounds to locations."

Mex nodded. It would take far too long to do it that way. Dia might be long dead. But it was all he had to go on and he wanted to encourage his friend. Maybe keep him busy and out of the way. And unharmed.

He walked back to the master bedroom and searched it carefully. There were some more photos of Luis and Pilar but that was all he found. Both the small master bathroom and the main bathroom yielded no results.

Cade walked up to Mex with an envelope in her hand. It was addressed to Luis Alvarez in Florida. There wasn't a return address. Mex opened the envelope and looked at the signature at the bottom. There was only the initial "P" but there was little doubt as he skimmed the letter it was from Pilar to Luis.

"Look at the postmark."

"This means that Pilar spent time in Pearl River while her boyfriend was in Florida."

"At least long enough to post it."

"I'm thinking there might be more to it than just passing through. Maybe she lived in this house for a while."

"Or maybe she has some other ties to this place. I mean, why would she live here?"

"Good questions. You check your sources and Darius will check his. If the nanny has another tie to this place, we'll know."

Mex wanted to call VV. Make sure Sedona was okay. Let him know they were getting close. He wanted to call Vicente. Tell him the same thing. Make sure the cartel boss didn't send off any vibes that he hadn't made good on his promise to provide the name of the man directly responsible for having his family gunned down.

To his surprise Mex was more interested in appeasing VV than VV's father, who had hired him in the first place. The bloodlust Mex felt against the instigator of the horrific murders of his family members did not stack up against getting his sister home and safe.

He looked at his watch. They'd been in the house almost an hour. The sheriff's department was ten minutes away. "We need to get out of here."

"Get the photos?" Mex asked Darius as they moved through to the back of the house.

"I think so. I'm not sure what to do with them but I'll figure something out."

"Good. Let's go."

The three froze as they heard a key in the front door.

Shit. Mex motioned both of them to get out the back door. He didn't need to remind them to move fast. And quiet.

Mex screamed words in his head. Please don't let her be thirsty or have a sudden need to check out her back yard. Please let her need to go to the bathroom. Please let the three of them get out of here without being caught. Please let this all happen so Dia can stay safe. So Sedona can live. *Please.*

Cade and Darius made it out the back door, Mex hard on their heels. He eased the door to the frame and prayed that it slipped rather than snapped into the closed position.

Less than a minute later they were all in the SUV.

Mex looked around at his fellow criminals. He was thinking about the fact that they still didn't have Dia. "Was this worth it?"

Darius spoke first. "We can eliminate this house as a holding point. Because of the photos we have other places to check out we didn't know about before. So yeah, we made some progress."

Cade waited until Mex looked her in the eye. "We learned that we can operate as a team. If every other piece of information we got tonight was shit, we learned that. And *that* is gonna carry us forward. Do you agree?"

Darius nodded and Mex continued to look at Cade. He would only let them go so far. He would not risk their lives when it came time to get the girl.

Cade settled behind the wheel of her truck and leaned out the window. "We also learned that Pilar Villanueva might have some as yet unknown connection to the area other than Luis." Cade paused. "That connection could be significant."

CHAPTER FORTY-THREE

Dia's arms were sore. They'd been cleaning the stilt house for hours getting ready for the last of the company. Some important man who everyone called The Client. He was supposed to arrive tonight.

The plan was for a big celebration dinner, and then tomorrow night they'd have the ritual everyone had been talking about. And she was going to get to attend with the grownups.

"Dia!" Pilar called from the kitchen.

She plodded to the doorway. "Please, Pilar. No more scrubbing. Everything has been cleaned twice."

Pilar laughed. "And it looks grand. Now, off with you to get cleaned up. Wear whatever is your nicest and then come help me with the dinner. We're going to have a huge feast."

Later, Dia was setting the long table. Six places. Even though the dishes didn't match, she thought they looked pretty together. Hector brought extra candles from the store for their dinner.

They were really going to celebrate tonight.

Pilar came and put an arm around her. Dia snuggled in for the hug.

"Tonight I want you to sit next to our special guest."

"Really? Me?"

"Part of the reason he's coming here is to meet you."

"Why?"

"We've told him how special you are."

"But why, I mean... I don't..." Dia pulled away from the embrace, suddenly wanting to be home. With VV. She could hear Mamá calling her name, and Mamá was home. She had no idea what she'd have to say tonight to such a special guest. The Client would expect her to be able to talk about things and know things and her tummy was beginning to feel sick.

"Don't worry, Dia. Just be yourself. You're charming and intelligent and I know you'll do fine."

Dia's shoulders sloped as she walked away. "If I don't throw up."

Pilar gripped Dia by the arm and spun her around to face her one-time nanny. "You will do this. You will not embarrass us or place us in any kind of bad light. Do you understand me?"

She swallowed and tried not to cry. She wanted Pilar to be proud of her, not ashamed. And she wanted Pilar to think of her as a friend and not a little girl she had to take care of. "I... yes. I understand."

"Quit your shaking then. I wouldn't ask you to do this if I didn't think you were ready." Pilar held her at arm's length and stared hard into her eyes. "You are ready, aren't you?"

Dia sniffed and straightened her shoulders. "I'm ready."

CHAPTER FORTY-FOUR

Mex and Darius were at Boudreaux's waiting impatiently for Cade. The plan was to make a plan.

Where the hell was she?

Darius had edited out the faces of the photographs he'd copied and sent them to his local contacts, Martin Van Buren and Deirdre Benoit. Maybe by some miracle they would recognize the background in at least one of the pictures. He'd told them both it was urgent. Possibly life or death. He hadn't heard back from either one.

This had always been the hardest part of law enforcement for Mex. The waiting. He was ready. He'd been trained for action. For making things happen and reacting when they did. But for now... wait.

Darius's phone rang. He looked at Mex. "Van Buren."

"Hey, Martin. What do you have for me?"

Darius made a note and Mex craned to see what he'd written. *Honey Island Shooting Range.*

"Anything else?"

He made another note. "Okay. Thanks, Martin. You've given us a direction. I'll be in touch."

Darius looked at Mex. "Van Buren recognized a couple of the background shots. He said it looks like Honey Island Swamp might be one of the locations where those photos were taken. It's just outside of Slidell and Pearl River. Might or might not be important."

"Get on that damn phone of yours and find out everything you can about Honey Island Swamp."

Before he could get online, Darius's phone rang again. He didn't want to take the call but he checked the caller ID anyway. "Whoa." This time he put it on speaker so Mex could hear.

"*Mon cher*. I have some interesting information for you."

"Deirdre, you're on speaker. My partner, Mex Anderson, is here with me."

"Ah... so I should not get too intimate. I understand."

Darius looked at Mex, shook his head and rolled his eyes. "What have you found?"

"You must understand that even the tightest organization can spring a tiny leak. And I cannot name names."

"We understand."

If this woman doesn't get to the point, Mex couldn't be held responsible for what he might say.

"Word is an important figure is coming to town for a significant Santeria ceremony."

Mex felt his body both fire and freeze at that statement. Cade's information was confirmed. *Dia. Sedona.*

Darius pushed. "What kind of important figure?"

"Only the head of one of the biggest drug cartels in Mexico." Deirdre paused for what Mex thought of as dramatic effect. "It must be something big or he wouldn't be involved. If this is true, it's a major event. Something he's willing to risk his life for."

"Risk his life?" Mex asked.

"Word gets out that you're in a certain place then your enemies have a place to put an attack together. It doesn't matter how much security you think you have. There will always be leaks. There will always be people looking to take advantage."

Mex couldn't stand it any longer. "What's the name of the drug cartel?"

Suddenly Deirdre turned quiet. Almost shy. "*Mon cher,* I never divulge the names of certain people I know. You must know that. What is not in their best interest is definitely not in mine."

"I'm not asking for any individual's name. Just the name of the damned cartel."

Deirdre's voice took on an edge. "You do not know me, Mr. Anderson, and my death wouldn't even register with you. Know that I am risking my life to make this call."

Darius gave Mex a look that said, *back off.* "I understand."

The hardness left and the sultry tone was back. "Boudreaux's makes a particularly good Cajun martini. One of these days, I'm gonna make you buy me one."

"How did you—"

"It's a tiny world, *mon cher*, and with the number of people I know, it's even smaller."

The call ended.

Mex ordered two more home brews. He studied Darius. "You sure there's nothing going on between you two?"

"Deirdre comes on a little strong, but she knows I'm married."

Mex arched his eyebrows. "Since when does that mean anything to women like Deirdre?"

"How do you know what she's like?"

"Tell me I'm wrong."

Darius laughed. "Okay, you're not wrong. It's kind of flattering though, and she's been a good source over the years."

"For what kind of stories?"

"Got me again. I did a series a few years ago detailing high-level escort services in major cities throughout the country. Deirdre provided both my New Orleans and Atlanta information."

"I know how you like to experience every part of your stories..."

"Not like that."

"Fine. We'll continue this conversation later. In the meantime, I'm pretty sure it's safe to assume the name of the cartel is the same one Luis is involved with."

"La Familia."

"La Familia is in competition with Senora-Ciento, Vicente Vega's cartel."

A rush of air came their way as Cade LeBlanc flew into the restaurant. With one hand over her head she signaled for a drink as she whisked toward them. In her other hand she held some paper that she slapped down on the table.

"You'll never believe what I've found."

CHAPTER FORTY-FIVE

Cade stood in front of him and Mex could barely breathe. Her eyes were bright with excitement and energy and Mex immediately felt ten degrees better.

"You'll never guess what I found out." She didn't wait for Mex to respond, even if he could have found his voice. And Darius seemed amused by something. "Our Luis Alvarez is not the only actor in our play with family ties to the slow and sticky."

Darius, full-out grinning now, asked, "Slow and sticky?"

Cade laughed. "Kind of a pet name for a swamp. You know, the water? Slow and sticky."

Mex cleared his throat. "And?"

"And, the extended family of Pilar Villanueva also has holdings in St. Tammany Parish."

"Let's go then. What are we waiting for?"

"Hold on, cowboy. It gets a little tricky now."

"Tricky?"

"There's not an exact address, just some general landmarks that were written down decades ago. It's that old. And with special visitors along the lines of Katrina, those landmarks are probably long gone. We'll need to spend some time with someone familiar enough with Honey Island Swamp to at least get us in the general direction."

"How big can it be?"

Cade cocked her head and pumped an eyebrow up. "Does 70,000 acres make you think you can pinpoint anything? I've got a lead on two old-timers who might be willing to help. Just waiting for callbacks."

"Why no address? I mean surely the state collects property taxes."

"They probably do, but there's a chance no one really knows the property is there. And it might be a boat launch for all I know. I'm willing to bet it's a family homestead that's well hidden from prying eyes, which would make it perfect for Santeria worship."

Cade warmed to her subject. "There are things that have been hidden in there for hundreds of years." A smile played on her lips. "All kinds of things."

Darius perked up. Mex figured his friend knew a good story when he heard one. "What kinds of things?"

"Pirates, for one. As late as 1850, pirate ships that pillaged the Gulf and the Caribbean waters found refuge in Honey Island. An unusual pirate from Scotland was known as the King of Honey Island. His real name was McCullough and he had a New Orleans mansion. But on Honey Island, he used the name Pierre Rameau. After McCullough, another gang terrorized wealthy plantation owners throughout Louisiana, Mississippi, and Alabama. The Copeland gang brought the stolen gold and jewelry to their Honey Island headquarters and buried it. Legend has it it's still buried somewhere in those 70,000 acres."

Cade paused. "Then there's the monster."

Amused, Mex watched Darius pay rapt attention to Cade's story about the strange creature said to roam the slow and sticky. He struggled with the need to wait for more information from the local historians and his strange response to Cade's sudden appearance, seeing her all glowing and out of breath. He didn't much like either. He liked control.

She was on a second home brew when her phone rang. She checked the Caller ID and said, "This could be one of our sources."

While she moved away to talk privately, Darius scooted his chair next to Mex. "Can you believe it? Pirates *and* monsters? This is just too good to be true."

"Before you get too excited, we still need to focus on Dia. You can go looking for buried treasure and monsters after we have that little girl safe."

Darius immediately looked offended. "Right. Of course I'd completely forgotten about Dia. I'm a shallow feather-brain without an ounce of compassion or willingness to take risks."

"Sorry."

"Should be." Darius shifted in his chair, chin up. "I still think the pirate and monster thing is pretty cool. Some good swerve to the book I'm gonna write about our successful rescue of a young girl."

"I may have forgotten to mention this, but change my name, will you?"

"Sure thing. I was going to ask you anyway. Your name is kind of wimpy. I was thinking something along the lines of Mando or Tank. Either of those work for you?"

"My name is wimpy? Are you telling me that Egbert isn't? Or for that matter, Darius?"

"Story's not about me, my wimply named friend. I'm just a tag-along. And if ever you use Egbert against me, I will truly have some counter ammunition."

Cade slid back into the conversation. "We're on for first thing tomorrow morning. La Pines is the place he wants to meet at six-thirty."

Darius spoke first. "Not anything we can do now. I suggest we get some sleep. Meet up tomorrow morning at our hotel and head out from there."

Cade looked at Mex. "Agreed. We should head off to sleep on our own, then reconnect in the morning."

Mex simply nodded and moved to the exit.

On the way back to their hotel, Mex caught an earful from Darius. "You are some kind of idiot. That fantastic looking woman is hot for you and all you can do is tuck your tail and head back to the hotel. Aren't you even interested? Even short term?"

"Nope."

"Are you crazy?"

"Yep."

Darius was silent for a moment. "You're looking for something more, aren't you?"

Mex sighed. "Maybe."

CHAPTER FORTY-SIX

La Pines Cafe, pronounced L-A Pines by the locals, was, as advertised, right next to the Slidell water tower. At six-thirty in the morning, the parking lot of the restaurant was already packed. Mex waited for two pickup trucks to pull out before he pulled in. The place was jumpin'.

Cade led Mex and Darius toward the door. "Mr. Allain told me the café opens at six, but he likes to give the guys who need to get to work a chance to eat and get going. He should be at a table against the back wall."

The trio entered and scanned the busy diner. Mex had enjoyed some of the best meals of his life at dives like this one. It reminded him of Juan's Place back in Aspen Falls, except there weren't any booths, only tables. And it was light and not dark. And it was a breakfast joint, not a bar. And it was packed. Okay, it reminded him of Juan's because of the locals who were obviously hanging out at "their" place.

An old man wearing a red plaid shirt, gray hair tumbling over the collar, sat at a four-top up against the wall straight ahead of them. When he made eye contact with Mex, he nodded. Mex pointed the way to both Cade and Darius.

The old guy moved to stand at Cade's approach but she waved him down. She made introductions and they settled in. A few minutes later, fresh coffee in front of everyone, the waitress was ready to take their order.

Paul Allain, menu in hand, asked, "You buyin'?"

Mex nodded.

He pointed gnarled fingers at the page he held. "Then I'd like me the Number Five with both the ribeye *and* the pork chops, *merci beaucoup*."

Mex smiled. "You're welcome."

Mama Jim, presumably the chef-owner, had a pretty complete menu that was about as far from Weight Watchers as you could get. The Number Five was the most expensive with three eggs, a *choice* of the ribeye or two pork chops, grits, hashbrowns or home fries, and either a biscuit or toast. Darius placed his order for one of Mama Jim's Awful Waffles and a side of hot sausage.

Mex waited for Cade to decide.

The usually decisive woman seemed torn. "So many things that remind me of my *mamere's* home when I was little. My grandmother could fry up everything with the best of them." Finally, she went with a short stack of pancakes, an egg and a side of smoked sausage.

Mex ordered the Philly Cheesesteak Omelet with toast. If any of them could move after this breakfast he would be surprised.

While they waited for their food, Cade explained what they were looking for. "It's an old home, Mr. Allain, out in the Honey. Belonged to the same family for generations until they sold it about twenty years ago."

"What's the old family name?"

"We don't know."

"Well, the new one then."

"Villanueva."

Allain squinted his eyes then shook his head. "Nope. Not Cajun. Not familiar."

Darius sat his coffee cup down. "Wait." He dug through some notes he'd brought in with him. "Our girl's full name is

Estrada Velasquez Villanueva. At least some of her family were from Cuba."

"Cubans? Got a few of those over the years. Hold on, let me think."

The waitress came by and refilled the cups with more strong Louisiana coffee. Paul Allain rapped his swollen knuckles on the table in a soft rhythmic pattern and seemed to disappear in thought.

"*Sacré Bleu!*" Allain reached into a pocket of his shirt and pulled out an iPhone. Mex wondered how the arthritic old fellow was going to work the small keys with his large digits.

He held the phone in front of him. "Call *Henri.*"

Mex did an internal eye roll. Man, he needed to get caught up.

Allain held up a finger asking for silence, the finger actually pointing more toward the wall than straight up. Some soft and quick words that Mex assumed were a mix of French and Cajun and English poured from Paul Allain's mouth while the three of them sat in respectful silence. Mex kept stealing glances at Cade to see if she might be following the one side of the conversation they could hear. If she was—if she could—she didn't let on.

The man completed the call and slipped the phone back into his pocket. Without the modern gadget in his hands, there was no longer visual conflict for the casual observer.

"Do you have images from about twenty years ago? Only need the north part of the swamp."

Darius hauled out some copies he'd made and riffled through them. "Here. These are twenty-two years ago. North end." He spread the papers out on the table just as the waitress came up with a tray loaded with their food.

"*Coo-Wee*! That's the best looking food I've ever laid my eyes on. The *frissons* are runnin' up my arms."

Mex gestured for Darius to put the papers away and looked to Cade for translation.

"Goosebumps. *Frissons* are goosebumps."

"And *Coo-Wee*?"

"Just what it sounds like. It's a way of telling someone to look at something amazing."

Allain reached for his napkin. "I was worried I wasn't gonna be able to help. Now that I know I can, I can eat this food with the enjoyment it was meant to have. We'll go over the swamp details after we're done full."

Mex stilled his impatience. Nothing to do for the delay, and there was every chance they'd have a solid direction to take.

If they weren't too late.

CHAPTER FORTY-SEVEN

Cade had actually listened carefully to Paul Allain's side of the conversation. He'd focused on Cajun words, followed by French and only the occasional English word filtered in. Like she wouldn't understand.

The good news was that she understood it all. *Hello?* Her name was Acadia LeBlanc and she lived in New Orleans. Like she wouldn't get it? Still, she tried to keep an ignorant face while she heard the soft tones on their end of the phone call.

Between Paul Allain and the friend he was talking to, Henri, they knew exactly where the house in Honey Island Swamp was located, at least where it was located twenty years ago. But there were a couple of questions: first, how to find it now after decades of storms, including Katrina; and second, did either one of them really want to get involved with the powerful Santeria group known to operate from the area. The cult's connection with La Familia could mean all kinds of bad endings for anyone stepping in from whatever fringe.

After the call Cade was able to breathe. Paul Allain seemed to be willing to do the right thing. When he was both ready to eat his breakfast and take a look at old photos to identify landmark locations, she knew they were dealing with an honorable man.

The foursome dug into the heaps of food in front of them. Cade wanted to put her house up for sale and move into the restaurant. She felt as if she'd come home.

Twenty minutes later, miraculously emptied plates swept away, they focused on something other than good food.

Paul Allain pushed his empty coffee cup toward the side of the table. "Before we continue this little exercise, can you at least tell me why it's all so get out important?"

Cade started to answer, but Mex beat her to it. "This is all my doing, Mr. Allain. I need to find this house because I believe a young girl is in danger. The reasons I'm here are complicated, and like you, this isn't something I'd normally find myself involved in.

"I recognize that the risk you've taken by simply breaking bread with us this morning, let alone sharing any concrete information, is enormous. There is evil at work from all sides. If you choose to back away now I can't stop you, but I can't stop myself from being upfront. I believe you're the kind of human being who is invested in courage, your own and that of others. The kind of endurance required to fight enormous odds.

"Without your bravery today, we probably won't be able to locate the child in time."

"You're purty good with people, ain't ya?"

Mex met the old man's eyes. "Some people, some days."

"Well I must be one of them people and this must be one of them days." Allain looked at Darius. "Spread those photos and maps back out here, young fella. Let's get to work."

The restaurant wasn't as packed as it was earlier, but Cade had the impression that it wouldn't matter. Paul Allain had his table here for as long as he wanted his table.

"Henri remembered a Cuban family who lived in the Honey when he wasn't much bigger than a *zirondelle*."

Cade touched the old man's hand. "Please, either translate for my friends quickly, or refrain from using the words of our people. We have too much ground to cover."

She turned to Mex and Darius. "A *zirondelle* is a dragonfly. So we can infer that Henri was just a little kid."

Darius grinned. "A little bugger."

Cade watched as Mex's neck and jaw clenched in unison. He squeezed out some words. "Do the names fit? The timeline?"

Allain shrugged his shoulders. "It's what we have. My gut says this is all good."

Cade had run on less. "Good. Let's put it together."

***

Two hours later, they'd pinpointed two homestead possibilities. Cade felt the odds falling in their favor. With a couple of big caveats. One was that most Santeria groups just wanted to practice their brand of religion. They weren't prone to violence or counter-measures unless they felt like they were on the receiving end of negative attention. Then things had been known to get ugly. The people involved in this particular group knew Mex and company were after them. They'd be on alert.

More worrisome was the cartel connection. This was easily the biggest threat. Cartel members didn't think twice about killing anyone they didn't like. The kill du jour. Might be because you were the competition, might be because you had the wrong color of eyes. Kill scores had stopped being counted years ago. Who they killed didn't matter. What mattered was that *they* were still walking around.

Allain rubbed his temples. "You've checked out topographical maps, current landmarks and access routes. You've made a plan."

Cade noticed that Paul Allain's Cajun lingo was gone. She wondered about his background.

"What happens if you're wrong? What's your backup?"

Mex swallowed the last of his coffee and set the empty cup down with a smack. "There is no backup."

***

They were back at the hotel in New Orleans. The detritus of hours of consideration and debate and anxious snacking littered the room. Cade picked up an empty lemonade can and threw it in the trash. Anxiety battled fatigue.

Mex rolled his shoulders. He wanted to move now but he knew better. "We need to pick one. We can't afford to split up and we can't afford to be wrong. Any whiff of our presence and we could lose them for good." He looked at Cade and Darius. "Which location do you think is the most likely?"

Cade pointed a finger at a place on the map. "This one."

"Why?"

"According to what Darius pulled up from St. Tammany Parish records, it's been recently updated. No telling what condition the other property is in."

"Darius? What's your opinion?"

"Cade makes sense, but respectfully, I'm not ready to give up on the other and commit our resources because a house has a new bathroom."

"Okay," Mex pointed to their other option, a little farther north. "What I like about this one is that it's even more remote, if that's possible. A better place to hide and keep your ceremonial tendencies private."

Cade nodded. "I agree, but is a spoiled little rich girl willingly going to stay someplace rustic?"

Mex popped half a handful of almonds in his mouth. "First, from our interviews in Monterrey, Dia was ready to strike out on her own regardless of surroundings. All she wanted was to get away from her father. And second, the willing part might have been over within hours of their leaving Monterrey."

Cade stood and paced to the window. "I disagree. Based on my experience, it's in the best interest of her 'captors' to keep her feeling like part of the team. She'll remain happily engaged in all the events surrounding her until the very last minute."

Darius sat his stack of papers on the table and reached for his drink. "You're right about Dia wanting to get away from Papa. The princess might be spoiled but she felt like a prisoner. My bet is she was more than happy to go rustic if she was with people who she thought appreciated her and would not try to control her."

Cade felt the sun on her face as she looked out the hotel room window, but what she saw was a one-room shack in the bowels of the swamp. She felt rather than saw the pulsating movement of water just beyond her vision, moss hanging long and low from the trees filtering sunlight. Ahead of her, the long wooden walk, boards both bleached by the sun and slippery from the swamp, reached to the empty silence that filled the air. Inside the doors of the cabin, deep blue in the shadows, was the body of her sister. She'd known it even before she experienced it.

She turned into the room and worked to hide the picture in her mind. *Push the feeling of loss from your chest, Cade.* This wasn't the time. Mex was right. The most remote stilt house was the one they wanted. If Dia was being held here, it would be in the home buried the deepest in Honey Island Swamp. If she was already there, it was only a matter of time before they lost her.

Lost her to what?

Usually Cade dealt with loss in terms of abandonment. People who left behind their families, their lives, to live in a fabricated and delusional world, making a choice to follow the false god of the moment. Cade had scored an astounding success rate, but whenever she lost someone, she suffered heartbreaking devastation. Failure. Her sister all over again.

With the young missing girl, Cade knew the loss would not be a choice on Dia's part. The child's loss would mean her life. Final. If they didn't get there in time, her religious beliefs and choices wouldn't matter. Because the daughter of Vicente Vega would be dead.

"You've convinced me," she said to Mex. "We go to the remote house." And pray that's where she is, Cade thought.

The trio sat late into the night talking strategy. The following night they'd make their play.

More than one life depended on them being right.

And successful in their rescue.

CHAPTER FORTY-EIGHT

Loud noises caused Sedona to prop herself up onto her elbows in bed. The word 'keening' came into her head. *Keening? Really?*

She didn't remember falling asleep, but she'd been doing that more and more often lately. Stress? Boredom? Drugs? Hard to say. What she knew now was that people were shouting and... keening. What was going on?

Her captors had secured her ankles to the bed frame with just enough room to sit up with her wrist ties. She was a good six inches short from being able to reach her ankle restraints. They'd done this before.

The shouting continued for a few seconds more, then silence. The keening... had someone died? Was it Dia? If Dia was dead so was she. But maybe it was something else. Was the house on fire? Would they forget her?

"What's going on?" Sedona shouted. "Hello? Someone come to me!"

No one came. Sedona continued to scream. Maybe someone outside would hear her. Come to her rescue. Carry her out of this hellhole.

After a while she fell silent. Matching the soundless house. She closed her eyes, laid back down and willed herself to another place. She imagined her family in Mexico, going about an ordinary day doing the things that needed done, from household chores to hide-and-seek. Sedona saw them all, breathing and living and moving, as if she'd just seen them that morning.

But it had been six years.

Tears streamed from her eyes, puddled into her ears and finally fell onto the bed. Her family. Her devastated brother. Maybe her own death.

The circle was closing.

The silence pulled her out of her own thoughts. What was happening? She concentrated to hear any sound within the house. Nothing. She was alone.

Sedona tried to comfort herself. She'd been alone before. This was no different. Right?

The shouting and wailing she'd heard earlier could be for any number of reasons. VV's staff probably all had families. Things happened to families. She knew this better than almost anyone. Someone had suffered a loss and was expressing pain. Didn't mean it impacted her.

Clearly it wasn't a fire. Or a crime where law enforcement had been called.

Silence filled her ears.

A whimper escaped, surprising her. She restrained her emotions and waited. It would do no good to be found weak.

What had happened? Where had everyone gone? She knew, beyond any doubt, that she was alone in VV's Monterrey home.

In all the hours and days since she'd been abducted, Sedona had never been entirely by herself. There'd always been someone to monitor her. Someone to feed her. Someone to wait while she showered or peed.

Someone.

Goosebumps crawled up her legs, crawled up her arms. Warnings. Something had happened. Something bad. She struggled against the bindings knowing it wouldn't do any good.

Sedona had no choice but to sit on her bed and hold her bladder. She watched the light fade and the scents of Monterrey shift from day into night. From heat and exhaust to the fancy chorizo and *milanesa nuevo* chefs developed to entice diners into their restaurants.

Oh God, she wanted to be out there. On the street. Discovering the neighborhood. Well really, *rediscovering* the neighborhood.

Sedona had been truly alive only once in her life—on the streets of Monterrey—where the electricity of the city flowed through her. She'd been full of passion. Belonging. Full of promise.

The last several years felt like a penance. A punishment for every bad decision she'd ever made. Payback for the joy she'd experienced in Monterrey. She didn't think she had any tears left, but a drop fell onto her lap and disappeared.

Time passed. How much time she couldn't say but the light was fading in her room. She heard the key in the lock.

The housekeeper hurried into the room.

"Thank goodness! I need to use the bathroom right away."

Then she saw the knife.

CHAPTER FORTY-NINE

Sedona's eyes never left the blade. The hair on the back of her neck lifted and she bit back a scream. She focused on not peeing and not screaming and not showing fear.

The housekeeper moved toward her and spun around once with the knife in her hands. Then she sat it down on the dresser. "I brought a knife in case I was unable to quickly untie you." The woman bent toward Sedona's bonds and went to work.

"What has happened?" Sedona's pulse was racing. If the danger wasn't from the housekeeper, it was from someone else.

"You must leave quickly. Get away from this house. Mr. VV is dead."

The final tie undone, Sedona raced to the bathroom.

VV dead? Dead? The little boy she'd watched for so many hours was gone. Murdered? The housekeeper hadn't said but knowing his line of work it wouldn't surprise her.

She flushed the toilet and washed her face and hands.

"How did he die?" Sedona asked as she walked back into the room. She was alone.

And the door stood open.

Senses heightened, Sedona stood in the doorway and listened. Only the silence of the empty house met her. She stepped into the hall, listening and watching for any movement. Sedona kept her back against the wall as she moved to the staircase and slipped down the steps as quietly and quickly as she could.

The front door was closed. Was this where she'd be found out and returned to her room?

A flash of movement shot cold air through her body, her heartbeat pounding in her ears. She tightened her body to the wall and waited, not daring to breathe, trying to silence the incredible volume of her heart. Her fingers moved along the wall behind her as if they contained some weird form of radar. An ability to sense another presence through vibrations.

Nothing. Maybe.

Sedona exhaled slowly and edged to the corner of the wall where she'd seen the motion. She couldn't bring herself to stick her head around the corner enough to see. *Damn.* Where was her courage?

A moment later she saw a reflection in a glass cabinet in the entryway and immediately relaxed. Sheers billowed with the breeze coming through the windows. She almost laughed out loud. There was her threat. The big bad window coverings.

Almost giddy with relief, Sedona reached for the doorknob.

It turned under her hand.

While her heart had been belting out of her chest a minute ago she swore it now stopped cold. Her immediate other thought, however inappropriate, was relief she'd emptied her bladder.

Could she back away and hide somewhere? Her feet were planted. No amount of brain screams in her remaining seconds of life would change anything.

Her eyes widened as the door pushed open. She prepared herself to be shot. To finally end this intense event in her life. It would be over. No more fear. No more guilt.

It was impossible to tell who was more shocked. She, waiting for the bullet that never came, or Vicente Vega who'd unlocked the door to his dead son's home only to find a woman from his past.

She reached for the door to steady herself but her hand slipped. Before she fell to the floor, she felt Vicente's strong arms grab her and stop her fall.

***

When Sedona once again became aware of her surroundings, she was lying on a sofa. Soft light filtered into the room. Two accent lamps shed golden light onto highly polished tables. The tiered ceiling added volume to the cozy space.

She tested for restraints. There were none. Not willing to believe she was completely out of danger, Sedona shifted to get a better look at her surroundings.

"You are awake."

Sedona froze. Vicente Vega.

"You were only out for a couple of minutes. How do you feel?"

She nodded, unable to find her voice.

"Good. I've brought a member of my staff and have asked for some tea. It might take a few minutes though because he is unfamiliar with my son's kitchen."

Tea? All she wanted was to get out of here. To catch the first flight back to Aspen Falls. She forced herself to a sitting position and fought a wave of dizziness. When it passed she felt better. More in control.

Sedona began to rise. "I need to leave."

"Please. Not yet. I have some questions."

Sedona understood that the *please* was merely Vega's polite way of saying she wasn't going anywhere until he told her she could. She settled back onto the sofa and waited.

"Why are you here? Why are you in my son's home?"

***

The next morning Dia woke up early. The sun pushed through a hazy sky heating up the already hot day. Even though the stilt house was filled to the gills with people it was strangely quiet. Must be the muggy weight of the air.

She pulled on her shorts and her favorite sleeveless t-shirt and went in search of something to eat. She didn't want much but the reason she'd woken up was a growling stomach.

The quiet felt weird. *Where is everyone?* Dia opened the refrigerator and drew out some milk, then went to find some cereal. She was grabbing a bowl out of the cupboard when Pilar walked in.

"Good morning, Dia. I'd be happy to make you breakfast. Would you like pancakes?"

Dia smiled. Pilar knew pancakes were her favorite. "It's too hot for pancakes, but thanks. Hey, where is everybody?"

"Luis and Hector have taken our guests on a tour of the swamp."

"Darn! I want to go." Dia pouted.

"You wouldn't want to go on this trip. It's more business than pleasure. They were looking for some special things you would find boring."

"Maybe they'll see the monster. Wouldn't that be cool? Did they take a camera?"

Pilar shook her head. "I told you, it's more like a trip to the grocery store than an amusement park."

"How long are the guests going to be here?" Dia didn't much care for either of them, especially the man.

"Not long."

Pilar pulled some flour and sugar down from the cupboard onto the counter.

"What are you making?"

"Sweet bread."

Dia remembered Pilar making that for her when they were still in her father's house in Monterrey. It was wonderful.

Pilar took some eggs out of the refrigerator. "While I put this together, I want you to go and take a long, wonderful bath. I've put out some of my special scents for you. I think you'll love them. Then, after I've baked the bread, you and I are going shopping. You need a special dress for tonight."

The bath didn't excite her as much as the idea of the two of them shopping together. She didn't care about the new dress. Well, not much. But the idea of hanging out with Pilar like girlfriends or sisters made her happier than she'd felt in a long time.

"What's tonight?"

"If Luis can find what is required we will have that special ceremony you've been waiting for."

Dia was excited. But she'd been thinking about her brother. "Pilar, could I use your phone?"

Pilar's back stiffened. "What for?"

"I just kinda want to call VV. Let him know I'm fine. I sort of miss him."

"Tomorrow, Dia. You can call your brother tomorrow. I promise."

Excited about shopping with Pilar, the sweet bread, the ceremony, and the idea of talking to VV tomorrow, Dia pranced off to the bathroom where she sampled the different scents Pilar had left for her to choose from.

She couldn't remember being this happy since her mamá died.

While she was soaking in the tub, she heard Hector and everyone get back. From the sound of things, they'd been successful in finding whatever it was they were looking for.

Tonight was going to be special.

CHAPTER FIFTY

Mex, Darius and Cade met up for lunch at the sports bar in the hotel. Mex missed the casual homegrown feel of La Pines Cafe, but the food was good here and they had more privacy. They didn't stand out in a hotel filled with strangers.

Today was the day. He felt it in his bones. If they didn't rescue Dia tonight, alive and well, he feared they'd lose this battle. And he'd lose Sedona. He'd called Vicente Vega earlier to let him know what was going on. His message had gone to voicemail.

Mex noticed everyone was paying attention to the television. A weather reporter stood in front of a map of the gulf coast showing a storm and its potential paths.

"Please tell me this is the anniversary of Katrina," Mex said to the others. Darius and Cade turned in their seats to see what Mex was talking about.

Oh no. None of them had been paying any attention to the news. How long had this weather threat been happening? All three of them moved closer to the television just as the program broke for commercials.

"Commercials," Darius said. "Can't be too serious if they're still running commercials. Right?"

Cade waded into the group that had been watching. "What's going on?"

A man wearing pressed jeans and a designer shirt looked her over before answering. "Tropical Storm Claudette is now a hurricane. Landfall is expected sometime in the next eight to twenty-four hours."

"Landfall? Here?"

"Yeah. Hotel says we're safe. At least for now." A woman with blazing white teeth and a wedding ring set that dripped diamonds up to her knuckle appeared at his side. Her smile was huge but her eyes said, "Keep away, Bitch."

Cade almost laughed, but felt too sorry for her to make a desperate situation worse. The poor woman was in an impossible relationship that had probably been doomed from the beginning.

The three friends regrouped at their table. Darius had his laptop out and was Googling weather information.

Mex didn't like the idea of riding out a hurricane anywhere but especially not in a swamp. "Do we need to do anything different because of the storm? Do we need to head out there now?"

This time Cade did laugh. "Most of our weather is stuff we can work around. You guys just hear about the big ones that drive us to our knees, or worse. That doesn't happen with every bit of wind we get."

Darius looked up from his computer. "This one is gaining strength and could be a big one, according to the National Hurricane Center."

"They have to say that. Standard cover your ass stuff." Cade signaled their waiter. "Another beer, boys?"

Mex and Darius both shifted in their chairs. "Are you sure?" Mex asked.

"Look, we'll take some good rain gear and tactical flashlights, and we'll stay in touch with the best local weather guy I know."

"Don't know that I like someone else having a clue what we're doing," Mex said.

"You know him," Cade said. "Besides, we don't need to tell him what we're doing."

"Who are you talking about?"

"Boudreaux. He knows his 'canes. If he tells us we gotta move to shelter, we'll move to shelter. If he doesn't, we're good."

"What if he can't?"

"Then none of us will need to worry about tomorrow."

***

Vicente Vega listened to Sedona's story. As she spoke, the heaviness and cold feeling he'd had since learning of his son's death left, replaced by muscle tension and heat that flowed like lava through his veins. *How dare VV?* How dare his son go behind his back and take this brazen action? He'd exposed them all to attention they didn't need.

Sedona seemed to sense his anger. "So you'll let me call my brother—let him know I'm okay?"

That's when Vega considered the reason why VV had orchestrated the abduction of a woman with ties to their past and with ties to their current situation.

He suddenly felt stronger. His son, his flesh and blood, while not exactly defying him, had taken action that would risk his father's wrath. VV was well aware that legend had it that Vega could issue a death warrant with one twitch of an eye, but he'd stepped up to protect his sister. Vicente Vega couldn't remember when he'd felt more proud.

Carlos Garcia, VV's longest lasting bodyguard, had betrayed his son. Twenty-thousand dollars was all it took. Garcia would be found by tomorrow and his death would not be so swift.

His gut clenched. Dia was all he had left—if she was still alive. VV had applied extra pressure to Mex Anderson by taking Sedona as collateral. Maybe not the way Vicente would have operated, but all in all, not a bad move.

"I don't think so, Sedona. We will contact your brother, but not at this moment." He stood and walked toward the door. "Are you hungry? I know of an elegant French restaurant not far from here. Well, actually, it's in New Orleans."

***

Dia wore her new dress. It was white and lacy with blue, pink, and yellow ribbons sliding through the lace at intervals and forming bows. The underneath part was also white. She felt special when she wore it. Plus, it twirled when she spun and even moved when she walked. She loved this dress. Though her father had paid for nice dresses before, he'd never actually helped her pick one out like Pilar had. She'd even bought Dia a new pair of shoes. Tonight's ceremony was going to be great.

Hector, Luis, and the guests had all returned. Everyone seemed happy so Dia figured they'd found the plant stuff they needed. Since no one mentioned a monster, she knew she hadn't missed out on anything special.

She'd actually taken a second bath when they got home from shopping. The muggy air made her feel dirty all over again and another bath seemed like the right thing to do. Now, in her new dress, she felt like a princess.

Soon she'd be able to talk with VV. Dia had a hard time deciding what she looked forward to the most... talking with her brother tomorrow or attending the special ceremony tonight. She decided to take one thing at a time. Tonight would be wonderful. Tomorrow would be even better.

Dia walked through the stilt house and onto the back deck. Everyone was talking in what sounded to her like scary whispers. She thought something must be going on. When they all suddenly fell silent, she knew for sure something was up.

She knew better than to interrupt an adult conversation, so she stood there waiting for something to happen.

The Diviner was the first to speak. "Dia, you look lovely. Won't you join us?"

She sent a grateful look to the woman and moved toward the table where they were all seated. "Thank you."

Luis was his usual silent self. She pretty much knew they'd never be friends. Fine with her. He reminded her a little too much of her father.

But Hector made room for her. She squeezed in next to him.

The Client spoke. "We were just talking about alternative sites for our ceremony tonight."

Dia didn't feel like she should actually say anything so she just looked at the man and nodded.

"A storm is coming and it could get quite bad, but this ceremony is imperative to me."

A storm? "What kind of storm?"

Pilar reached for her hand. "A hurricane might or might not make landfall near us. Even if it doesn't, we're in for some strong winds and rain."

Dia felt a pang of disappointment. "What about the ceremony? Can we have it now?"

The Diviner straightened her shoulders. "We need to begin the ritual at the right moment. Now is much too soon. I cannot be responsible for the results if we don't adhere strictly to the timeline I've been given."

Pilar squeezed her hand. "We have an option. It's not optimal because we'd much rather be in our private open space, but it could work."

Dia remained silent. Her stomach knotted.

The Client slapped the table. "We're moving to the alternate location. We need the ceremony to happen. We also need to be safe. My decision is final."

Dia wanted to trust the Client because he reminded her a little of her father. He seemed strong and decisive. But she also thought he might be very cruel. She thought he didn't really care about any of them, including her.

She pumped up her courage. "Alternate location?" What she really didn't want to do was get in the car again for hours and hours.

The Client didn't look at her. Neither did the Diviner. Finally Pilar spoke. "The storm could very likely wipe out this house even though it's managed to survive all of the storms that have come before. We have a place that's safer. It's been recently built and meets the hurricane codes."

"Hurricane? Like Katrina?" Suddenly her father's home in Monterrey sounded like a good place to wake up tomorrow. Even if he were there.

"Probably not like Katrina," Pilar said. "People like to embellish. Especially news people."

Dia believed her. But she still had a question. "Where is the safe place?"

The man guest started to say something but the Diviner waved him silent.

"Do you trust me?" Pilar asked.

"You know I do." Dia hated that her voice sounded so tiny and young.

"Do you want, with all your heart, to attend the ceremony we have planned for tonight?"

Dia cleared her throat. "Of course. I've been looking forward to this since you first told me about it."

"Then you need to trust me that we will be moving to a safe place where we can hold the ceremony, even in a hurricane. Do you trust me?"

She thought about all the times Pilar had comforted her when her father had berated her for being a girl—or worse—ignored her. Other than Pilar, no one had hugged her since her mother died. Only Pilar...

"Yes. I trust you."

THE SACRIFICE

CHAPTER FIFTY-ONE

The skies were dark with threats of what was to come. Menacing winds bounced from every surface they touched. Mex understood the emotion of the weather better than most. It matched his internal battle.

Right after lunch, Mex and Darius headed off to search for the house in Honey Island Swamp while Cade made a court appearance on another case. It took the two of them almost an hour to find the property once they were in the slow and sticky, but they did. The GPS in the Navigator was useless for finding anything in this area. They parked about a half-mile past the turnoff and hiked back.

They found a vantage point that obscured them from both the road and the house and settled in. Within minutes, they'd observed five adults, three men and two women, at the tiny stilt house. There was no sign of a girl, but Mex knew in his gut she was there. All the pieces fit.

He figured out which one was Pilar and that made it easy to spot Luis. They were the only couple. The other woman was older and dressed in priestess garb. The youngest man seemed set apart from the others, almost like he didn't belong.

Then Mex saw the older man in the sunlight. He sucked in a breath and pulled out his field binoculars. No doubt about it. It was Benito Chavez, head of the La Familia cartel. Whatever was going to happen would happen soon. He couldn't imagine

Chavez spending much time without the luxuries he'd become used to. The lack of bodyguards underscored the tight wraps the cartel head was operating under.

Mex and Darius then paced off the property, assessing the best access points to get in without being noticed. Their options were limited but not beyond the realm of possibility.

Especially if there was a hurricane in the neighborhood. Mex shuddered. What he wouldn't give for a good old Colorado blizzard.

He called Vicente to give him an update. Better he should interrupt him than the other way around. Again, like his last call, his message went to voicemail. That was fine with him. The less contact with Vicente Vega the better. Mex left the new information, then called VV and did the same.

Now back at the hotel, Mex waited for Darius to finish one more phone call with Pamela, and for Cade to show up. He refocused on the task at hand and tamped down his anxiety. He did his best to separate his internal demons from the true dangers they faced. The whole operation was proceeding more on a wing and a prayer than the way he liked to operate. Especially when both his sister's and a young girl's life were at stake.

He wasn't feeling good about any of this. Worse, he didn't know if he was being rational or if the depression crap was feeding into his data.

A sudden blast of wind pounded the hotel window. His chest tightened. Where the hell was Cade?

A knock on the door brought him to his feet. *Damn time.* He pulled the door open and Cade walked in, on a phone call of her own.

The tightness in his chest intensified. He reminded himself that Cade and Darius were here to help. They had the same goal and yet he was getting the bigger payoff all the way around. After this was over, he'd make sure they were both well compensated from the Vega cash deposit.

After this was over... His jaw clenched and his hands formed tight fists. He had to be successful. That was the only way this could end. He couldn't lose Sedona.

Mex turned and walked back into the room. Counted to ten. Slow. He cleared his throat.

Darius mumbled something to Pamela and clicked off his phone. Cade was slower to react. She squinted in his direction and waited.

"Thanks for being here with me. I'm sorry if I've been short tempered and hope you can forgive me. I'm a little on edge. I appreciate that you both have personal lives, but we have a job to do. We're at the end now and need to be ready to act."

Cade took a breath. Two. Then she sat her purse down on the coffee table and turned her back to end her call.

When she turned back to Mex her face was set. Her hands dug into her hips, knuckles white. "It sounds like you're questioning my professionalism. That you're concerned I might be distracted with my *personal* life. Is that what you're suggesting?"

Before he could respond, Cade continued. "I'm a little on edge too, Mr. Anderson. Don't you ever—*ever*— question my focus or professionalism again. Don't you ever—*ever*—be so wild-ass needy that you make assumptions and mess up something I'm involved in. Am I clear?"

Mex heard his own heavy, rapid breathing. His stomach tightened. He concentrated on his breaths. In and out. In and out. Slower now, in and then out. In and then out. The tightness in his chest subsided and the darkness lifted, if only a little. "I'm sorry. That was uncalled for. No excuses."

Cade didn't take her eyes off him. "Are you able to be with us on this? Or would we be better off if you stayed here?" She stood right in front of him. "I need to know."

Mex nodded. Swallowed. "I'm good."

He watched as she seemed to come to a decision. "Fine." She turned back into the room. "That phone call was from

Boudreaux. He's pretty sure Claudette is gonna make landfall near New Orleans. He also thinks we have a few hours before it happens."

"How many hours?" Darius seemed willing to give up his online research in favor of a local who knew his way around these things.

"At the least? Two or three. At the most? Four."

***

Dia was placing a few of her favorite things in her replacement backpack when Hector walked in. He never said much but it seemed to Dia that he'd been even quieter lately—sadder than usual too.

"You okay, Hector?"

"Yeah. Just want to know if you need anything." His tone was soft, like you'd use in a hospital room. Was Hector sick? She hoped not. He'd been so kind to her. The thought occurred to her that VV would like him.

She shook her head. "I'm excited about tonight. Are you?"

"I, um... you..."

Pilar hurried in to the room. "Hector, go see if Luis needs any help." She watched as the young man left the room, then put an arm around Dia. "Are you about ready? We need to leave before the storm makes it impossible for us to travel."

"I'm ready."

"Good. I need your help. We need to move as many things as possible to the tops of the counters and up high on the shelves."

"How come?"

"Flooding." Dia followed Pilar into the main living area, surprised at how everything looked in the shuttered window dimness. Pilar handed Dia a stack of plastic bags. "Use these until they run out."

Luis and Hector began hauling in the furniture from the deck. As usual, they ignored Dia.

"Where are our guests?" Dia asked.

"They've gone to prepare the new location for our ceremony tonight."

"Where's the new location?"

Pilar stopped and turned to look at her. "Are you familiar with crypts?"

Dia's stomach fluttered and she heard a roaring in her ears. She squinted at Pilar. "You mean a place where they put dead people?"

"Well, yes. Except there are no dead people in this one. It's brand new and is designed to hold up against hurricanes. It's the best place for us, and it's pretty big. We'll be close together but not on top of each other."

"Is it yours? You have a crypt?"

"It belongs to my cousin's family. The same people who own this stilt house."

"Has there ever been a dead body in it?"

"No, Dia. I told you, it's new."

"How long will we have to be there? Inside? Will we have to sleep there?"

Pilar's jaw tightened. "You're asking way too many questions. We have work to do. And I don't think you want to be stuck alone in this house when the hurricane hits and the water rises."

CHAPTER FIFTY-TWO

Mex rubbed his head. He was tired. He worried that he'd be unable to pull this off, even with the help of Darius and Cade. "We know there are at least five adults involved. We need the element of surprise or we'll never be able to separate Dia from them."

"Can we get any help from the locals?" Darius asked.

Cade inspected her Glock for the second time since she'd arrived. "Not without probable cause. And even if we did have time to convince them, with Claudette here any time they have their hands full. The new system in place post-Katrina is pretty intense. They're doing advance preparation and pre-positioning now with tons of other agencies."

Mex focused. "The storm will help us. We'll park where I parked earlier and walk in. We'll get them. They won't be expecting anyone with a hurricane on the way. Get your weather gear. Let's get on the road."

Ten minutes later the three rescuers were in the rented SUV and on the highway to Slidell and Honey Island Swamp. Traffic was crazy backed up going the other way. Mex hoped they didn't run into any roadblocks headed their direction.

Silent, they made their way quickly to the stilt house. Mex had been in this situation many times before. People focused on their own private protocols before going into a dangerous situation. He couldn't know exactly where others went with their thoughts in times like these but he suspected they were much like his.

He pictured the house, its doors and windows, their approach. He considered the occupants and played out different possible scenarios in his mind, mentally rehearsing the responses he would make that were by now automatic. Still, by thinking about these things he stayed focused.

Slidell came and went, rain sheeting the windshield and completely obliterating objects in the rearview mirror. Mex was forced to slow his speed, thankful no cars were headed in their direction. His concentration now was on keeping the Navigator from heading off the road into who the hell knew what.

When they arrived at Pearl River the community was like a ghost town. Windows were either boarded up or shuttered and the electricity was off. Mex was glad he and Darius had been here earlier because they never would have been able to find their way now.

***

Pearl River reminded Cade of so many places in her childhood. Wonderful days spent chasing bull frogs and naming anhingas, big birds *Maman* called water turkeys. The hurricanes they'd ridden out in her family's storm shelter. Her family...

Her thoughts moved to the little shack Delphine had made her home—her place to practice spells and rituals. Cade had watched her sister's luminous eyes grow more vacant as the weeks and months went by. Cade didn't know how to help her. All she could do was bring her groceries, clean the place up and try to convince Delphine she had people who loved her. Make sure Delphine knew she had options.

I wasn't able to help her, Cade thought. She'd sworn the day she found her sister she'd figure out a way to help others. Deprogramming had been her lifeline. *Her* cult. *Her* ritual.

Dia would need her and she was ready. Cade couldn't, wouldn't consider the possibility they might lose the child.

***

Darius closed his eyes and wondered what he'd gotten himself in to. He'd never been one to avoid conflict in the past but neither had he sought it out. He called people who did that confrontation junkies, fools and idiots. And worse. Yet here he was, heading out into a gulf-style, major hurricane for a house in some strange swamp where people practiced a religion that involved human sacrifices.

And for what? A friggin' story. Okay, more than that. A book.

And yeah, there was something more. He was doing this for a man he considered one of his best friends. His wife had understood that before he did. When he and Pamela talked about his returning to New Orleans, she told him she could give a rat's ass about his book. It was the fact that his friend needed him that made her believe she and the kids would be safe until his return.

CHAPTER FIFTY-THREE

Mex didn't bother pulling off the road to park. He figured there probably wouldn't be much traffic tonight. "Okay, there's no use in trying to get a lock on the subjects in the dark. Darius, you and Cade take the front entrance. I'm at the back." He checked his weapon and his extra magazines, hoping he wouldn't need them.

Cade handed out rain gear. "We'll give you thirty seconds to make it around to the back. Then Darius and I will storm the front."

They'd talked about all of this earlier, but Mex knew it would help calm everyone's nerves to go through it one last time. Darius and Cade bantered back and forth another moment, then paused. "We good?" Mex asked.

The other two answered in unison, "We're good."

They pulled on their rain gear and moved out. A combination of weather and mission urged them to move quickly down the access road to the stilt house.

Mex pushed gallons of water from his face as it fell and for a moment he flashed on the drought in Colorado and other western states. If this was God's sense of humor, he wasn't amused.

Darius and Cade were making their approach to the front entrance while he hustled around to the back, working hard to control his accelerated breathing and trying to keep a kind of mental countdown so they'd enter the house as one unit. He slipped twice and noticed the water was rapidly rising.

They were here. They were ready. They had the element of surprise.

He rounded the back of the darkened house. The electricity was off all over the area so the darkness didn't surprise him. Still, he peered through shuttered windows looking for any sign of light—candle or lantern. He didn't see anything.

In Colorado, he knew that most of their wildlife would take shelter in a blizzard. He could only hope that the same premise held true for a hurricane in Louisiana. He did not have the energy to deal with alligators and bad guys at the same time.

He made it to the steps leading to the raised deck. Ascending quickly because the noise was lost in the sound of the rain and wind, he faced the back door expecting it to open at any minute. When it didn't he figured his team was pushing through in the front of the house and he didn't want them facing any danger without him.

Mex drew back and raised his right leg. With one fierce kick at the latch the door swung open and he was in the kitchen, searching it closely for any hidden danger. He could hear Darius and Cade in the front of the house doing the same thing.

It didn't take long to figure out they were the only ones there.

Shit.

"Darius, I hope to hell you brought your laptop and that we have some friggin' connection out here."

"What do you need me to do?" Darius was already moving back out the door. "It's in the Navigator."

"Let's go," Mex said. "There's nothing here."

Mex made a point to touch Cade on her shoulder. "We're good. We'll get there. Don't give up on me now."

Back in the SUV, Mex told Darius what he wanted. "We need to know if there is any property near here under the same ownership. And we need to know it now."

Darius opened his laptop and they waited while he booted it up. "Sorry, Mex. There's no internet signal I can tap into."

Mex wanted to hit something. "What I want are real estate records. Didn't you search for those earlier? Get something from Van Buren? Did you save any of them?"

Darius's fingers flew over the keys. "I did. But I don't know if I have what you —"

"Anything. What else do you have?" Mex pushed up in his seat.

"The same family who owns the stilt house recently commissioned a crypt at Harrison Cemetery in Slidell. It was completed three months ago." Darius looked up to see what Mex had to say.

"A crypt? A fucking crypt?"

Cade, engaged for the first time since they'd arrived back at the SUV, looked at them both. "It's perfect, assuming it's a fairly big one. New crypts must be built to be hurricane resistant. If it can fit the necessary people into it, they have a combination shelter and ceremonial space."

Mex dialed Vega and bent near the GPS keyboard. "What's the address?" Mex almost shouted the question.

As Darius gave the address on Daney Street, Mex left it on Vega's voicemail. If something happened to them, at least Vega would know where to look.

It took him three tries to input the information into the GPS due to the intermittent, scattered signal from the satellite, but he got it entered. He trusted that the signal would hold well enough. This had to be easier to find than some bit of swamp.

At least he hoped so.

***

Dia didn't think too much of this whole crypt thing. First of all there wasn't a bathroom. She didn't need one now, but later? And she could figure that the smells were gonna get tight. A whole lot tighter than gym class. She didn't like that idea any more than she liked not having a bathroom.

They'd walked in about ten minutes ago and as far as she could tell, the two important guests hadn't done squat to make the space livable through the hurricane. Instead they'd only worked on setting up ceremonial stuff in the far corner of the space. Dia kept looking around for any sign of a dead body. Any of that and she was out of here, hurricane or no hurricane.

She decided to think of the crypt as a really big doll house. There was room to play but she wouldn't want to live in a doll house.

"We should begin the ceremony now," the Diviner said. "I can prepare the initial offerings to the *orisha* so we can commence."

In spite of her feelings about the drawbacks of the crypt as their shelter, Dia was intrigued. She sat cross-legged in the corner where the Diviner had set down her supplies. "Can I watch?"

The woman glanced in her direction. "Fine. But don't ask any questions."

Dia wondered how she was supposed to learn anything without asking questions but decided she didn't trust the answers this woman might give her anyway. She thought maybe she'd like to go sit by Pilar instead.

CHAPTER FIFTY-FOUR

Mex followed the GPS directions. Heaven help them if the graveyard rivaled the size of the ones in New Orleans. They might never find the crypt.

Assuming that's where they'd gone.

Damn. This whole thing was falling apart, as was much of the area around them. The rain, to his surprise, had intensified, and the winds were driving it sideways.

Cade pointed. "There! Turn there!"

Mex pulled into Harrison Cemetery. The deed for the crypt was relatively new so he drove toward the back. "Look for vehicles. If they're here, there's at least one car that will be parked close."

They spotted the crypt at the same time. A big one. Probably the biggest in the whole damn place.

Unconcerned about anyone hearing their arrival through the storm, Mex pulled the SUV up close to the structure in a way that prevented the parked passenger car a quick escape.

Darius pushed forward on his seat. "How do we do this? All of us at once, or do we split up?"

This was one scenario they hadn't discussed. Mex looked at them both. "I think we split up. I'll go in first. Pretend to be someone caught in the storm, looking for shelter. If there's going to be a response, it'll happen fast. You count off ten seconds then follow."

Cade shook her head. "We're more likely to be successful if the three of us go in well armed and in charge."

Mex started to mount an argument when headlights threw the interior of the SUV into shades of silver. All three would-be rescuers stopped speaking and watched the car approach.

Torrents of rain made it impossible to see who was in the car and Mex pulled his weapon onto the seat beside him. Cade and Darius did the same. The noise level inside the SUV was outrageous between the lashing wind and driving rain.

They waited while the beams from the now stopped vehicle, directly in front of their SUV, picked them out and made them perfect targets. Any sign of a door or window opening and all hell would break loose.

They waited.

Damn. They needed to get inside that crypt, not dance around with whoever this was.

The car's headlights went dark, taking away the immediate danger. Mex, Cade and Darius instinctively shifted their positions just in case.

The interior light came on. Mex could make out two figures. Slowly both the driver and passenger doors opened, and two people came to stand in front of the car, bent into the wind, clearly making themselves targets.

Mex found the switch, turned the headlights on, and watched as the newcomers were bathed in light.

What the hell?

Mex couldn't believe what he was seeing. He blinked. This didn't make any sense at all. It couldn't be.

Even as he struggled to understand, his hands were on the door handle and he was outside and rushing toward the woman, tears lost to the rain.

"Sedona!"

His sister fell into his arms. She was thinner but alive. He walked her back to the SUV. The man she was with followed.

Darius stood at the side, his door open for the pair. Within a short time, four very wet people were gasping, two of them crying.

Cade turned to Darius and said, "Open my duffle, Darius. There are some towels on top."

Darius did a double-take. "You packed towels?"

"I figured they might come in handy."

She then got Mex's attention, her expression demanding an explanation.

"Cade LeBlanc, meet my sister, Sedona." Mex kept his arm protectively around the sister he thought he might have lost. He brought her even closer as he spoke.

Cade's eyes opened wide and she looked between brother and sister. "I see the resemblance."

Mex clenched and unclenched his hands. His muscles quivered. He needed something to hit. Preferably the man sitting in the third row of the SUV. "And *that* is Vicente fucking Vega whose family has used me and mine one more time."

"This is what's been underneath the surface, isn't it Mex? What's been bothering you?" Darius asked.

Mex nodded.

Vicente Vega crossed his arms and shook his head. "You don't know what you're talking about, Anderson."

Mex twisted in his seat, rising on his knees. "You son-of-a-bitch! How dare you—"

"I bring you your sister and this is the thanks I get? Who's the real son-of-a-bitch here?"

"How do I know you didn't instruct your asshole son to take my sister and threaten her life? If it weren't for your daughter I'd dump you out right here and leave you to the ghosts. I saw the family films, Vega. You don't deserve Dia."

Cade put her fingers to her mouth and whistled. "Speaking of Dia, you boys can take this outside later. Right now we need to get in that crypt and save a little girl." She looked pointedly at Vicente Vega. "*Your* little girl."

Cade took control. "You two remain here." She looked at Vega and Sedona. "It's a small space and things could get complicated. You being here complicates everything more and jeopardizes a good outcome. Do you get me?"

Vicente Vega gave a quick nod, but his face had gone from olive to ruddy. His nostrils flared.

Mex couldn't stop. "Why the hell I agreed to find the daughter of the man whose cartel was responsible for the annihilation of my family I will never know. Your family has screwed with mine for the last time, Vega."

Cade grabbed his arm. "Mex. We need to go now. We'll do it your way. You go and Darius and I will follow in ten seconds."

Mex put his hand on the door handle. "You don't understand family, Vega. Yours is fucked and so are you."

Vicente Vega exploded. "Family? Understand family? You have never understood Sedona. If you're looking for someone to blame beyond yourself for the deaths of your *family*, you don't need to look any farther than the backseat. Look at your fucking sister."

Cade almost pushed him out the door. "Now!"

CHAPTER FIFTY-FIVE

Focus. He'd deal with Vega and Sedona later. Right now a little girl was in danger. *Focus, Mex. Fucking focus.* He thought about the young girl whose entire life was ahead of her. It didn't matter who her father was.

He barely felt the rain, but the wind took his breath away. This was a bad storm and it was growing stronger. He bent into it and forged his way to the door of the crypt. He reached a hand up and pounded hard. Pounded hard again. A third time.

Mex couldn't hear a thing, but the car parked outside evidenced occupants. *Shit.* What if it was just an offering of some kind and they'd wasted all this time not considering other options.

There weren't any other options.

About to pound again, the door creaked open. Mex could see a surly face.

"Hey, saw your car. Was hoping there might be someone here. Can I come in?"

"This is not a good time."

"Please. I need to get out of this storm so I can have some quiet to make a phone call."

Mex shoved his way in, and seriously hoped Darius and Cade wouldn't take the full ten seconds. He looked around. They'd opened the door for a reason. "Were you expecting someone?" He needed to be ready.

"Another family member, but probably not in this storm." A woman dressed in island clothing spoke. "But they could be here at any time. You should make your phone call and leave."

His entrance had caused several candles to blow out, but there must have been hundreds. He quickly noted the adults and stored the information, but he really wanted to see Dia. When he didn't locate her right away, his heart began to pound. Were they wrong? Was this just some kind of weird orgy?

Finally, one of the men moved to the side and he saw her. She looked so lost and lonely. Her hands were bound. *Shit.* It was about to happen. They'd readied her for sacrifice. Only she looked so calm. Why wasn't she screaming her bloody guts out?

Because she thought this was just a special initiation ceremony.

Mex moved to his right where he gauged a more direct line to Dia. If he needed to move quickly, he would not have to power through one of the adults from this angle. But it was a small space. Things—obstacles—could shift quickly.

He heard more raps on the door. Good. He could use some friends.

The man Mex recognized as Chavez, head of the La Familia cartel, moved forward, blocking the door. "Don't answer it. What the hell kind of coincidence would it be for more people to approach a fucking crypt in the middle of a hurricane?"

Mex shrugged. "I'm sorry. That's probably my wife and a friend. They're kind of freaked because of the storm."

Dia spoke up. "And they probably don't like being in a cemetery with a bunch of dead bodies."

Mex smiled at her. "Probably not."

One of the young men opened the crypt door. Before Cade or Darius could say anything, Mex went into his role. "Hey, honey. I told you to wait. Ever since we got married you quit listening to me."

Cade flashed a look around the room. "Yeah, that's because you have so little to say." She slipped deeper into the tiny space.

Mex moved closer to Dia, blocking her deeper into the corner. He turned into the room and, as if choreographed, he, Darius and Cade all drew their weapons. With his gun pointed solidly toward Chavez, the cartel leader, Mex reached behind him to the young girl. "We're going to leave now. You've missed your sacrifice, but at least you won't be sacrificing your own lives. I don't care whether or not you've broken any laws." He grabbed Dia. "We're done here."

He forced her to his back gripping her with one hand and made his way carefully to the door.

"Stop! You can't take me!" Dia struggled away from him.

He twisted toward her. "Don't you understand what was about to happen?"

Cade stepped forward, cupped her hands around Dia's face, and whispered something in her ear. Mex saw Dia's face change. She gave a weak nod and meekly allowed Cade to escort her toward the entrance.

Mex nodded to Darius. "Go."

He looked around, knowing that if they really wanted to kill him they could. He was backed into a far corner. "So, we're done here?"

A move toward the exit drew an answering move and the head of the La Familia cartel produced a weapon. It looked like a 9mm Glock. In his peripheral vision, Mex saw one of the other men and both women each draw a gun.

This wasn't going to end well.

Mex took a rolling dive just as Chavez got a shot off. Cade shoved Dia out the door, then she and Darius both spun around, weapons firing.

When the dust had settled, literally, in the small space, Mex, Cade and Darius were still breathing in various positions of crouching. Dead or bleeding out were four of the five other adults. The young man, the one who had opened the door initially and whom Mex decided wasn't Luis, shoved his gun aside. "This was wrong from the beginning. She's only a little girl."

Mex kicked the gun farther out of reach. "You made some bad choices."

Sad brown eyes met Mex's hard stare. "Don't we all?"

CHAPTER FIFTY-SIX

After all of the police reports were complete, Cade walked to the doorway that separated the adults from where Dia waited. Vicente Vega stiffened in his chair and opened his mouth but Cade froze him with a glare that said "Fuck you." He fell back, a hand rubbing his forehead.

Dia was curled into the corner of a sofa while a uniformed cop sat in a chair tilted against the wall. Cade looked at the girl and pushed her own breaking heart aside. She plopped herself into the opposite corner of the sofa, legs tucked under her.

"Hi, Dia. I thought I'd introduce myself. My name is Cade."

Dia fixed a narrowed stare in Cade's direction before visibly dismissing her.

"Do you understand what was happening tonight? What almost happened to you?"

Dia's eyes drilled Cade. "You killed my friends."

"Why did your friends bind your hands?"

Silence.

Cade was ready to go all night, all week if necessary. Dia Vega Arroyo would not become another Delphine LeBlanc.

***

It was good to be home. Aspen Falls had never been so perfect—the exact place Mex was supposed to be.

The awareness of Sedona's role in the horrific deaths of his family—her family—haunted Mex. Her affair with Vega shocked him. Her desire for wealth at any cost shocked him even more. And then her hatred of him for paying her way all of these years almost broke him.

Sedona met Vega when she and a girlfriend took a week off from school and went to Monterrey. With Vicente, she felt like a queen—a fairy tale come true. She left her meager life in Agua Prieta behind her. It didn't matter that Vicente was married. It was understood that a powerful cartel boss would have a mistress.

Designer clothes, lavish parties… and drugs. She loved them all. Almost a second mother to the Vega children, part of her loved them as her own. Months went by and she thought the fine life would never end.

It didn't take long for the drugs to take over. When they did, Vicente Vega wanted nothing more to do with her. She was willing to do anything to get that life back.

Anything.

For her next fix, and the promise of a flight back to Monterrey, Sedona agreed to make sure their entire family was in one place at one time. She even called in the false B&E report to take Mex across town. It wasn't easy to get everyone on the little farm at once, but she'd done it. Afterward, she tried to convince herself she thought the cartel underling who had promised her the drugs and her return to Vicente only intended to frighten her family. To convince Mex to accept a very favorable business proposition.

Mex felt angry for a long time after learning about the role Sedona had played in the deaths of his family. He didn't know if they'd ever be able to come back together. Still, she was his family. People make mistakes. Horrible mistakes. He was working hard to forgive her. It would take a while. In the meantime, he would continue to support her.

Then there was Cade LeBlanc. Damn, that woman was a hotbed of potential. And attitude to avoid at all cost. He hadn't quite decided what to do about her.

But they'd scheduled some time for her to leave her beloved Louisiana and share some Colorado wonder.

He'd asked her later what it was she'd whispered to Dia in the crypt that had such an immediate effect on her. Cade had laughed. "All I told her was that she belonged with the living, not the dead." He didn't ask her the details about the four days she spent with Dia before reuniting her with her father—who had left the cemetery in his rental car before anyone knew he was gone—and the hours the three of them had spent together back in Monterrey. Although their future wasn't up to Mex, he hoped it would be one filled with communication and mutual respect. He doubted whether they would ever have much of a relationship, but Cade seemed to think Dia would be able to hold her own. Having the phone number of the woman in her corner would hopefully provide Dia the kind of support she needed.

Hurricane Claudette was a mean one, but nothing compared to Katrina. By the time they'd made it back to the hotel, it had moved on. Cade called her friend in the sheriff's department and everything was expedited in the only way Louisiana could expedite things.

Darius was busy working the last few weeks into the grist of his book. True crime or novel, he hadn't yet decided.

Darius had also gone to the safe deposit box. He'd offered to retrieve the sealed envelope and bring it to Mex. It didn't take Mex long to make a decision. He told Darius to destroy it. Whatever details or names it held, Mex knew the murders of his family wouldn't have happened without Sedona's help. Darius said he'd hang on to it just in case, but wouldn't open it.

Mex sat at his booth in Juan's and felt peaceful for the first time in weeks. A couple in the front of the bar began arguing.

Mex smiled.

He was home.

The Sacrifice

Acknowledgements

I've read a lot lately that acknowledgments pages in novels is no longer de rigueur. So, to those who agree, skip this page. It's okay. My feelings won't be hurt.

But the truth is, putting a book together that's worthy of your time takes a village, and acknowledging the people in this village makes me feel good. Please indulge me with a few warm fuzzies.

Early encouragement came from Marianne Franklin, the Executive Director and organizing force behind her husband, Les, and the Shaka Franklin Foundation. Both as a friend and someone who wants to get the message out about depression and suicide, she gave the nod toward my attempts to show that depression can be managed. If there are errors in my depiction, they are mine and not Marianne's.

My thanks extend to author Lala Corriere, who not only loves and supports me because she has to as my sister, but also provides great feedback as an early reader. Author Polly Iyer fell into my life with all of the ribbon and glitz a gift can have. She was more than an early reader for me, she was an early editor. I'm in her debt.

Patty G. Henderson outdid herself with this cover. If you hadn't noticed, the badge on the cover bears the words, "Agua Prieta" which is the tiny town in Mexico where Mex was in law enforcement. It's all about the details. Not only is Patty a talented and intuitive cover designer, she's an author as well. She's also become a friend.

This book was edited by an enormously talented woman. Much like Polly Iyer, Peggy Hageman fell into my life as a gift when I was flailing and desperately searching. Peggy pushed and pulled and tugged and questioned and expressed her opinion almost to the point of distraction. If this book hangs together, it's because of Peggy's attention to detail and nuance. If you take issue with anything, it's probably something I chose to ignore.

Two good friends played with me to come up with a book that wouldn't make readers gag. Kel Darnell (with whom I also had a blast brainstorming in the early planning stages) and Kathleen Hickey—who in the past have each demonstrated the beautiful detail orientation one needs in a copyeditor—offered their time and talents to the village. I promise, Kel, to never jump the publishing gun again without first getting your input.

An amazing pinch-hitter, when I really was afraid my book was going to be forced to be birthed without the benefit of a good proofread, was Bill Myers. He has editing skills beyond what I was looking for, but oh, my. He heeded my plea and made this book that much stronger.

The support from my husband, George, is so steady and perfect I sometimes take it for granted. Thank you for loving me.

And then there are my readers who keep me sitting on clouds, trying not to giggle. My goal is to never disappoint you. Your faith that I can come up with a few hours of entertainment one more time keeps me going. I know it's cliché, but it's true: you are the wind beneath my wings.

About the Author

A Colorado native, Peg Brantley is a member of Rocky Mountain Fiction Writers and Sisters In Crime. She and her husband make their home southeast of Denver, sharing it with the occasional pair of mallard ducks and their babies, snapping turtles, peacocks, assorted other birds, foxes and deer named Cedric.

You can learn more about Peg at:
http://www.pegbrantley.com or meet up with her on

Facebook at:
http://www.facebook.com/pegbrantleyauthorpage

From Peg: I absolutely adore hearing from readers. You make my day when you take the time to contact me, and I make every effort to respond. When you leave a review on Amazon, Barnes & Noble, Goodreads, or some other place readers like to gather, you help a reader decide whether or not to give me a try. I treasure every one of your words.

Made in the USA
Charleston, SC
21 October 2015